Praise for *The Tu*

CW00550200

"World Fantasy Award winner Co
monsters . . . Plenty of charm!" —

"There's so much to adore about the *The Twice-Drowned Saint* . . . [a] sublime short novel."
—Ian Mond, *Locus*

"Many have spoken about how angels can be both terrifying yet beautiful, but few have successfully captured the idea well—until *The Twice-Drowned Saint*, at least. A sumptuous, saw-toothed read, it is a jewel box of a novel, glittering with a thousand details and a bright longing we're all familiar with, this want for a place better than we're in now."
—Cassandra Khaw, Bram Stoker, Shirley Jackson and World Fantasy award-nominated author of *Nothing but Blackened Teeth*

"With *The Twice-Drowned Saint*, C. S. E. Cooney once again crafts dazzling feats of imagination grounded in human frailties and plunges her audience inside head-first. Her boldly unique characters live in a fever dream of balletic, graceful description that will make you gasp, even as they find their own escape through the seemingly-mundane world of movies. Like nothing else you've ever read, or will ever read."
—Randee Dawn, author of *Tune in Tomorrow*

"Fabulous Gelethel is a city of godless angels who intoxicate themselves on human death, but within its icy walls a hidden saint and a dissident angel are hatching a plan. This story left me wrecked and rebuilt: it's a truly glorious tale of family bonds, forgiveness, sacrifice, courage . . . and how gods are born. Written with Cooney's signature soaring prose, humor, and imagination, this tale shines a light on cruelties both fantastical and familiar. It honors sorrow and embraces joy—I will treasure it always."
—Francesca Forrest, author of *The Inconvenient God*

"The way Cooney does world building, she makes the world absolutely gigantic, and then she focuses the lens onto these intimate moments in people's lives . . . My clumsy words don't do justice to *The Twice Drowned Saint*. Just read it. It is a sunrise, where all things are beautiful and possible, and it is blood on the ground surrounded by those who lap it up, hungering for more. This is one of the best pieces of fiction I've read this year."
—*Little Red Reviewer*

Praise for C. S. E. Cooney
World Fantasy Award winner

"C. S. E. Cooney's prose is like a cake baked by the fairies—beautifully layered, rich and precise, so delicious that it should be devoured with a silver fork."
—Theodora Goss, World Fantasy and Mythopoeic Award-winning author of *The Collected Enchantments*

"C. S. E. Cooney is one of the most moving, daring, and plainly beautiful voices to come out of recent fantasy. She's a powerhouse with a wink in her eye and a song in each pocket."
—Catherynne M. Valente, *New York Times*–bestselling author of *Space Opera*

"C. S. E. Cooney's imagination is wild and varied, her stories bawdy, horrific, comic, and moving—frequently all at the same time. Her characters are wickedly appealing, and her language—O! her language. Lush, playful, poetic, but never obscure or stilted, it makes her magic more magic, her comedy more comic, and her tragic moments almost unbearable."
—Delia Sherman, author of *The Freedom Maze*

"Stunningly delicious! Cruel, beautiful and irresistible are C.S.E. Cooney's characters and prose."
—Ellen Kushner, author of *Swordspoint*

"C. S. E. Cooney is a master piper, playing songs within songs. Her stories are wild, theatrical, full of music and murder and magic."
—James Enge, author of *Blood of Ambrose*

"Newcomers will find Cooney's glittering narrative skills and vivid worldbuilding addictive, her diverse characters intriguing, and her message of justice and freedom stirring."
—*Publishers Weekly*

"Few people create worlds as lavish and sensual as those that spring from Cooney's effervescent imagination. Her writing isn't so much inspirational, but inspiration itself: gentry-magic spun into pages and paragraphs of glittering, fizzing, jaw-dropping beauty."
—Cassandra Khaw, author of *Breakable Things*

THE
TWICE-
DROWNED
SAINT

Also by C. S. E. Cooney

Novels
SAINT DEATH'S DAUGHTER

Novellas
DESDEMONA AND THE DEEP

Short Fiction Collections
BONE SWANS: STORIES
DARK BREAKERS
JACK O' THE HILLS
THE WITCH IN THE ALMOND TREE AND OTHER STORIES

Poetry Collections
HOW TO FLIRT IN FAERIELAND AND OTHER WILD RHYMES

THE TWICE-DROWNED SAINT

C.S.E. COONEY

◆ ◆ ◆

Mythic Delirium
BOOKS

mythicdelirium.com

The Twice-Drowned Saint

Cover art and design and interior illustrations © 2023 by Lasse Paldanius, lassepaldanius.com.

FIRST EDITION
February 7, 2023

Trade Paperback ISBN: 978-1-7326440-9-0
E-book ISBN: 978-0-692-60323-9

Published by Mythic Delirium Books
Roanoke, Virginia
mythicdelirium.com

Library of Congress Control Number: 2022950439

Our gratitude goes out to the following who because of their generosity are from now on designated as supporters of Mythic Delirium Books: Saira Ali, Cora Anderson, Anonymous, Patricia M. Cryan, Steve Dempsey, Oz Drummond, Patrick Dugan, Matthew Farrer, C. R. Fowler, Mary J. Lewis, Paul T. Muse, Jr., Shyam Nunley, Finny Pendragon, Kenneth Schneyer, and Delia Sherman.

In Memory of Gene and Rosemary Wolfe

With thanks to Magill Foote

CONTENTS

THE TWICE-DROWNED SAINT

Being a Tale of Fabulous
Gelethel, the Invisible
Wonders Who Rule There,
and the Apostates Who
Try to Escape Its Walls

ANALEPSIS: PORTRAIT OF A CHILD SAINT

THERE WERE TWO THINGS EVERY GELTHIC CITIZEN KNEW.
One: only saints could see the angels who ruled us.

Two: Alizar the Eleven-Eyed, Seventh Angel of Gelethel, had no saint. He hadn't had one for a long time.

Now I will tell you what the angel Alizar looks like. I can do that—because I was the saint no one else in Gelethel knew about. I was the Seventh Angel's best kept secret.

And he was mine.

◆   ◆   ◆

THE ANGEL ALIZAR SOMETIMES LOOKED LIKE A HUMAN-SHAPED paper lantern, or a sudden release of soap bubbles, or a cloud. He glowed on the inside as if he'd swallowed a hive of horny fireflies, and on the outside, he looked as if a toddler with a glue gun had gone wild with the craft buckets containing outrageous feathers, and twining golden vines, and trumpet-like flowers, and thin, prismatic insect wings.

Alizar also had the ability to spontaneously produce eyeballs whenever and wherever he fancied, though I'd never seen him sport more than eleven at a time, hence his name.

When he was in his human/lantern shape, two of his eyes were pretty much where you'd expect them—affixed to the center of his head—only his eyes were elongated ovals, perfectly symmetrical, of a deep, unending, twilight blue. No pupils or sclera or anything; Alizar the Eleven-Eyed couldn't be bothered with minutiae. Higher up on the center of his forehead, he had one all-black eye, glossy as a wolf spider's. Another eyeball resided where his nose should have been: yellow and slit across the center like a goat's. Three smaller eyes, green like those of a robber fly, beaded the lower part of his face like a mouth. He had no mouth otherwise. A torque of three round red eyes opened like cabochon carnelians right above his collarbones, if he had collarbones, which he didn't. One great golden eye blinked sleepily from the curve of his breast, bright amidst a nest of pale down.

He loved to be admired. He was very vain and always preening—but good-naturedly, willing to see beauty in everyone else around him, too. His problem was, of course, that only a handful of saints could see him, and they were all wrapped up in their own angels.

I was supposed to be the one who devoted my whole attention to him—only I'd refused his offer when I was eight years old, and that was three decades ago.

As my saint, you could have everything you ever wanted, he'd sung to me that day, in that way angels have of singing (which was a little like having your head held underwater and your feet set on fire, while being tickled) (and also a little like being licked by a giant oyster tongue, only on the inside of your body). I shook my head.

"Gross," I'd said, very softly, so no one else in the Celestial Corridor could hear me.

Alizar pulled back a bit on his singing, and the overwhelming urge to pee and giggle and vomit left me.

He said coaxingly: *If you confess your vision of me to the Heraldic Voice, they will know you have tested true. We can have you crowned, gowned, and cloistered before lunchtime. You shall live your life emmewed with thirteen others of your kind: one saint per angel, appointed till death does us part. You'll be given every luxury: a closet stuffed with fabulous clothes, all the jewels of the treasury, the finest foods, a host of servants, the best education, and unlimited access to the Hagiological Archives of Gelethel. All you'd have to do in return is never leave the walls of the Celestial Cenoby. Ever.*

"No thanks," I'd muttered under my breath. "I'm going to grow up and be like my bad uncles. Or maybe like one of the Zilch, and ride around the desert on a viperbike. Or maybe, like, I'll run away and be a movie star or aeroplane pilot or something."

Oh, you like movies, do you? Alizar seemed very interested, which made me more interested.

"Oh, sure!" I said, and then we got to talking for a while about our favorite films, and the whole conversation ended quite amicably, with both of us agreeing to look the other way and pretend that this whole thing had never happened. Only it had. Irrevocably.

Mind you, Ish, you're still my saint—whether anybody knows about it or not, Alizar warned me. *That's not something I have any control over. It just happens.*

"Just don't tell anyone. I don't want to be stuffed in a cell to pray all the time."

I won't tell if you won't. Alizar batted all eleven of his eyes at me, even going so far as to grow extra eyelashes for greater effect.

And anyway, he mused with typical angelic obliqueness, *it might be better, after all, if no one knows about you—for now.*

Interior:
The
Celestial
Corridor

I N FABULOUS GELETHEL, WE CITIZENS OF THE ANGELIC CITY operated on a fortnightly calendar: fourteen being the perfect number. Each day was a feast day named after one of the fourteen angels. Each feast day had its own bespoke rituals and miracles.

And then there was the fifteenth day.

Officially, it didn't exist. But everyone observed it anyway. Gelthic citizens reserved fifteenth days for our most distasteful chores—in memory of Nirwen the Forsaker, the Fifteenth Angel. She'd abandoned Gelethel about a century ago, ascending the impenetrable blue serac that surrounded and protected our city, and shaking our dust from her feet.

This royally pissed off the other angels, who proclaimed Nirwen's memory disgraced forever. They scorched her face out of every wall mural, scratched it off every bust and statue. All references to Nirwen the Artificer (as she'd once been known) in the Hagiological Archives received a black slash through it.

Not that Nirwen cared. As far as we knew, she'd picked up and left the day her last saint died, and she'd never looked back.

Petition days in the Celestial Corridor were always on the fifteenth day.

My earliest memories of petition days were of pilgrims coming from outside Gelethel to beg the boon of citizenship from the angels. The Holy Host would lower a long bridge from the ramparts of the serac, and then a small group of pilgrims—chosen by lottery in Cherubtown—would ascend and enter Gelethel.

It used to be, they'd bring gifts with them. Something precious and particular. Something that meant a great deal to the pilgrim personally, which they would then offer to the angels in hopes of winning their favor. That was how my dad gained his citizenship—as well as Quicksilver Cinema, Gelethel's only movie palace, which he ran for many years.

I'd practically grown up in the Quick, and now I owned it. I'd also grown up with a soft spot for pilgrims, because, well . . . *Dad*. That was not true for most citizens of Gelethel.

These days, petitions were less about gifts and more about sacrifice. They'd become sort of a spectator sport for Gelthic citizens—with pilgrims acting as unwitting gladiators and angels playing the dual roles of monsters and referees.

Dad had stopped attending petition days years ago, when the war in the Bellisaar Theatre had grown so bad that Cherubtown, once a small shrine outside the serac for pilgrims seeking congress with the angels, swelled into a refugee camp with a population double the size of Gelethel.

They came to be safe. Everyone knew that the Angelic City, protected by its fourteen Invisible Wonders, was the only haven left in this part of the world. Dispossessed families came by the thousands wanting in.

Impregnable Gelethel! Immaculate, untouchable. Where the war could not hurt them anymore.

They came with very little to offer, these new pilgrims. Some offered nothing but themselves, in exchange for citizenship for their children. Some offered the lives of their aged parents, or superfluous orphans, or an enemy they'd made in Cherubtown.

And the angels, who rarely refused a sacrifice, were hooked.

It was like nothing they'd ever tasted before, the death offering of a human being. Oh, the jolt of it! The juice! The effervescent intoxication! No longer could the Invisible Wonders who ruled Gelethel rest content with a steady snack of life-long worship from their long-lived worshippers. And why should they, when they could just mainline pilgrims instead?

So bright, so foul. Such meat to feed on.

Thus, every fifteenth day, we let the bridge down. We invited the pilgrims, in groups of fourteen, into Gelethel. Seven of these were hand-picked by the self-designated sheriffs of Cherubtown—officials on the take from our Holy Host, willing to do us favors in exchange for goods passed to them over the serac. Those chosen seven were quietly given to know that the angels were happy to hear their petition for citizenship, but would require a sacrifice—of the human variety. Cherubtown's sheriffs left it up to the pilgrims to choose whom they would bring over, usually by force. The unlucky seven never saw what hit them.

Alizar the Eleven-Eyed, alone among the fourteen angels, did not partake of the sacrifices. He attended petition days, but recused himself of the feast. Some of his colleagues looked at him askance, some scoffed, but in the end, they allowed him this eccentricity; after all, it meant more for them.

Every time I asked him why he refused his sup, Alizar gave me a different answer:

I do not want to be beholden to strangers. Or, *I'm saving myself for my true love.* Or, *Some habits reward one with diminishing returns.*

The Seventh Angel may have been gentle and vain, may have liked pretty, silly things—but he was not a liar, and he was not stupid. His reasons for abstention, vague though they may have seemed to me, made sense to him—and, I have to admit, it was a relief to be spared sharing the feast. Bad enough for me to catch the ricochet when the other angels fed. But if I had to experience it directly, through him? I wouldn't have remained his secret saint for long.

I knew this much: angelic politics were vicious. Alizar had been out of favor with the other thirteen angels ever since Nirwen the Forsaker left Gelethel. The two of them had been the fastest of friends. Her disgrace had also been his, and Alizar bore it proudly, holding himself aloof and lonely. A few of his former allies among the angels tried coaxing him back to the fold from time to time. Others, like Zerat and Rathanana, thought him weak.

Alizar longed for Nirwen—but he took comfort in me. I, in turn, had Alizar and my family and that was it. It wasn't that saints couldn't make friends. It was just, as I got older, I found our secret too burdensome for intimacy. Alizar saw how it weighed on me, kept me isolated, disinclined to engage with my peers. To make up for it, he did his utmost to be all things to me: friend, confidante, beloved. He rarely asked me for favors.

Except, that morning, he had.

Like Dad, I tried to stay away from petition days whenever possible. But today, the Seventh Angel let me know—even before my eyes came unstuck from sleep—that my presence in the Celestial Corridor was requested.

Something is about to happen, he'd told me in his inimitable way, humming behind my eyelids and in the pits of my teeth.

Something is coming from beyond the serac, he said. *Something I was promised a long time ago. And, Ish*—he'd added outrageously—*I am going to need an extra pair of eyes.*

◆ ◆ ◆

"**Y**OU," SAID THE HERALDIC VOICE, POINTING AT A PILGRIM.

"Herald," replied a young man who was standing right next to me.

"Step forward and state your petition," said the Heraldic Voice.

They were resplendently dressed in voluminous purple silk, with wide sleeves that covered their hands, and filigreed cuffs adorning the tips of their ears, proclaiming their position as official interpreter for the angels. Set against the backdrop of the Celestial Corridor, which was vast enough to engulf several city blocks and white enough to write on, they looked properly imposing.

While not themself a saint, the Heraldic Voice, through long exposure to the divine and rigorous study, could take all of those pressure-cooker, biting-on-foil, blood-on-the-boil, icicles-in-your-organs sensations that were the sound of angels singing, and translate it into words for the laity. It was a thankless job—which was why the saints did not do it. It may also have been the reason that the Heraldic Voice's face was so stern and set. They were like the Celestial Corridor: as hard, as dazzling—as if they, too, were composed entirely of bricks of compressed salt.

The Heraldic Voice stood at a podium at the foot of the Hundred Stair Tier, around which the fourteen pilgrims from Cherubtown had been corralled. The rest of the Celestial Corridor was crammed full of Gelthic spectators, there for the best entertainment Gelethel had to offer. The Invisible Wonders watched over the proceedings from fourteen empty thrones at the top of the stairs. Between them and us stood rank upon rank of the Holy Host.

I was among the bystanders—as close to the pilgrims as I could get. After all, Alizar had told me to keep my eyes open.

The boy upon whom the Heraldic Voice had called now shuffled forward a few steps, dragging with him what appeared to be a sack of rags and ropes. He stood hunched, head bowed, as if it would take too much effort to straighten up. None of us in the Celestial Corridor were allowed to sit. Sitting was for angels, who didn't need to.

Typical pilgrim fare, this one. Fresh from Cherubtown (which was to say "fetid"), where conditions were rife with drought, starvation, lawlessness, crime, and disease. A stunted gangle, more marionette than flesh. Short on chin, long on nose, snappable at wrists and ankles, desiccated as a desert corpse. His eyes were pitfalls. He had a brow on him like a pile of rock at the point of collapse: the brow of a powerful but perhaps not very thoughtful man, a brow he had yet to grow into. His skin and hair might once have been a handsome bronze; now he seemed to be flaking all over into a friable rust. He smelled oddly sweet beneath his stale sweat, a little like fruit, a little like yeast, though from the look of him I couldn't imagine he'd been anywhere near food like that for fortnights on end.

"Herald," the boy rasped into the waiting silence. "I am Alizar Luzarius."

I shivered inwardly at his forename and took a cautious step closer to him. Was he the one the Seventh Angel was anticipating? The promised "something" from beyond the serac? His name couldn't be a coincidence—could it?

"I have come," continued the boy in his flat whisper, "to offer sacrifice to the Invisible Wonders who rule Gelethel and to petition them for citizenship."

He had the words exactly right, by rote—but he'd mispronounced Gelethel. A point against him. You can always tell a foreigner by the way he pronounces the name of the Angelic City. He softens the "g" almost to a "zh". His first syllable holds the accent, making his "zhgel" rhyme with the third syllable's "thel." Natives of Gelethel know that the "g" is hard, that the accent is on the second syllable "leth," and that in "thel" the vowel is swallowed.

Dad, who wasn't a native, says it makes more sense the way natives say it; the Angelic City, he says, deserves no poetry.

Between the boy and the angels stood a thousand shining warriors of the Holy Host. They stood, ten to a stair, a hundred stairs to the vertex, shields locked, spears sharp, white eyes shining and mouths smiling like benevolence itself. From the polished bronze and boiled leather of their armor to the jaunty tips of their plumes, the Holy Host was the dedicated force of Gelethel, trained up at the Empyrean Academy from adolescence to adulthood, and committed—body and soul—to the objectives of the angels.

The boy's tarpit-on-fire gaze lingered lovingly on their ranks before lifting and peering beyond them.

He could not, of course, see the angels. But he could see the fourteen vacant thrones, each carved and bejeweled with the various aspects of the angel who sat upon it. His face shone with a ferocious light—ah! An ascetic. Having grown up with Mom, I knew the signs.

We had our cynics in Gelethel: Dad, my bad uncles, and myself among them. But there were others—devout and pious types—who, after years of careful observation, might be rewarded for a lifetime of worshipful attention by fragments of angelic discernment. The lightning flash of an eye; the scintilla of a pinion; one wet ruby heart beating mid-air, two separate hands skewering it on long silver fingernails; a rotund belly like a great fissiparous pearl swollen to the splitting place; a capillary-popping pressure on the ears and eyeballs that meant the angels singing.

It was the most anyone but the saints ever perceived of the angels. Some people spent their whole lives pining for a single glimpse. Some hated the saints for being so blessed. Others worshipped the saints as second only to angels, even petitioning them as intermediaries for their deepest concerns. I didn't know which this kid might be: saint-hater or saint-prater. I only knew that he wasn't a saint.

The sack at his feet, on the other hand . . .

A buzz in the back of my skull alerted me to the Seventh Angel's interest in that sack. So while the Heraldic Voice was asking the boy all the usual questions ("Tell the Invisible Wonders of *Gelethel*," stressing the correct pronunciation, "why they should choose *you* for their citizen, Pilgrim Luzarius?"), I sidled in for a closer look.

It was a person. A girl.

She'd begun to stir, then to writhe, when the boy first dragged her forward—probably just waking up from the clout or drug that he had used to knock her cold. A pointy chin emerged from the sacking. A compellingly large nose, wide mouth.

I pegged her for the boy's sister, maybe cousin. Of the same too-skeletal, too-sunburnt, too-seldom-washed pilgrim type, she nevertheless seemed more lively than her upright counterpart. Even lying there, trussed and gagged, she bore a greater resemblance to a stack of dynamite than a lamb for slaughter. Her hair was short but heavy, nearly black at the roots, glinting red at the tips. It curled around her head like a nest of vipers. Her skin was starved-to-rusting dark, but her eyes were light. If lucid were a color, that would be the color of her eyes.

Her gaze was fixed, unerringly, upon the Seventh Throne. She was a saint.

What's more, she was *his* saint. Alizar's. Like me.

"Shit," I said aloud.

The Heraldic Voice tripped on their tongue and turned a bespectacled and accusatory scowl upon me. "I beg your pardon?"

"Sorry," I whispered, offering no further excuse for the Heraldic Voice—and therefore the angels—to examine me too narrowly.

As I sweated in my coveralls, the Heraldic Voice went on to grill the boy: "Pilgrim Luzarius, you claim that your father was a citizen of Gelethel."

I turned from the girl—the saint—to look at the boy. I'd somehow missed that part. But hey, you can't catch everything when you're in the middle of a *divine revelation*. Right, Alizar?

"My . . . my father was born in Gelethel," the boy stammered his reply. "He t-told me I was named for the Seventh Angel himself, that citizenship was, is, my birthright . . ."

The Heraldic Voice interrupted him. "This morning, you arrived with the other pilgrims from Cherubtown—from outside the Gelthic serac—did you not?"

The boy nodded.

"Those who come from outside the Gelthic serac have no rights in Gelethel. *Citizens* of Gelethel never venture beyond the serac, for they know that to do so means their citizenship shall be revoked, and they shall be named traitor unto the angels who succored them—"

Here the boy interrupted him: "My father was no traitor! He was born a citizen of Gelethel—he said so! He was named for the Seventh Angel, and I am named for him too. He told me I was entitled—"

"He told you lies," snapped the Heraldic Voice. "You are entitled to nothing but what all pilgrims who come to the Celestial Corridor are offered: a chance to humbly beg the boon of offering sacrifice unto the angels, who may, if pleased, decide to grant you leave to stay in fabulous Gelethel."

Their inflection promised nothing, hinted at grave doubt. I watched the boy struggling to decide whether or not to argue. Or perhaps he was just gathering his strength.

And then I stopped watching him, because an eyeball popped open on the back of my hand, right under my knuckles.

It looked up at me imploringly. My mouth filled with the taste of ghost pepper and ozone. My ears began to ring.

Oh, bells.

Fucking angel bells.

Furtively, I cast a glance up at the Seventh Throne. It was hard to miss, decorated as it was with eleven jewels cut into the shapes of eyes. But those gleaming gems were obscured to my vision today; I had eyes only for the Seventh *Angel*—who'd apparently gone totally lathernutted.

A green-gold glow beaconed out from his paper-lantern skin. Each little insect wing and bird-like bit of him was fluttering with adoration and distress as he divided his attention between preening for the new girl—who was staring at him, open-mouthed—and pleading with *me*. One of the cabochon eyes that grew in a collar about Alizar's throat was missing. Because it was on my hand.

Nirwen sent her, Ish! Alizar told me excitedly. *Nirwen sent her here to me! She's the sign I've been waiting for! We must help her!* A pause. *Don't let the other angels see you do it, though.*

"Fine," I breathed—not so much speaking as grinding the chewy gong of Alizar's entreaty between my teeth. Unobtrusively as possible, I scooted closer to the girl, reaching for the penknife in my pocket. Carefully, I palmed it, unfolded it, used it to cut a hole in my canvas pocket, and then let it drop down the length of my leg.

It slid soundlessly off the side of my boot and onto the floor, spinning to a stop near the girl's right ear. Distracted by the movement, the girl turned her head and met my gaze. Her limpid, cunning eyes narrowed. Her gaze went right to my hand and the glossy red eyeball protruding from the back of it. It rolled at her in bright excitement, then blinked gratefully up at me, then disappeared.

A moment later, on the Seventh Throne, the Seventh Angel pulsed vividly, all eleven of his eyes restored to him.

Meanwhile, the *other* Alizar—Alizar Luzarius—had decided to escalate his argument with the Heraldic Voice after all.

"When I am a citizen," he rasped, "I mean to serve as warrior in the Holy Host." The real Gelthic citizens let out a corridor-wide gasp at his audacity. "My father was a soldier. Like him, I am strong and able," he continued, mendacious but determined, "and I will train at the Empyrean Academy, and become the pride of the Holy Host . . ."

Thoroughly nettled now, the Heraldic Voice said witheringly, "Your father may have been a soldier, but he was never one of the Holy Host. Nor can you be, Pilgrim Luzarius—even if the angels grant you citizenship. You were not born in Gelethel."

"Give me a sword," the boy returned implacably. "I will use it to defend the angels—and Gelethel. I will prove myself to the Host. I will—"

I lost the thread of his boast as I looked down at the girl again. Her eyes raptor-bright, her face furious, she had rearranged her body to mask her hands, which were working my penknife for all it was worth. She had lots of knots to deal with—the boy had been nothing if not thorough—but my penknife was a gift from the Seventh Angel himself, manifested for me on my thirty-seventh birthday; I was pretty sure it could cut through ropes or even chains like so many silken threads.

"—and then the Host will name me their captain, and follow me into battle!" the boy finished in a blaze of triumphal delusion.

The crowd laughed; the boy was amusing. But the Heraldic Voice was finished arguing. Adjusting a piece of parchment on the podium, they asked merely, "And what is your sacrifice to be, pilgrim?"

Alizar Luzarius bent down, grabbed the trussed-up girl by her ropes, and hauled her to her feet. "I offer my half-sister, Betony Luzarius, as sacrifice to the angels!"

The angels reacted immediately, with pleasure and approval.

I knew it at once, but it took the Heraldic Voice a few seconds longer. When they finally got the message, they gave an involuntary start, and hissed. Their fingers twitched. They threw back their head, every tendon in their neck straining as they listened to thirteen voices singing rapture and rhapsody and euphoric acceptance of the sacrifice. Probably to the Heraldic Voice it sounded like being on the receiving end of thirteen static shocks in close succession.

It was worse for me, being a saint. I could hear the angels with absolute clarity, at full volume, with all the bells and whistles layered in. But I'd been learning to control my expression for decades. Right now, I was doing a damned fine impression of a cow waiting placidly in a squeeze chute.

I'd never seen Dad look so sick with disappointment as he did the day he watched my face as I watched my first human sacrifice. When he saw no change whatsoever in it. But what could I do? It was either go cow-faced or tell all. I couldn't risk letting go, not even a little. Couldn't surrender, even for a moment, to the sensation of angels sucking up death offerings. To do so would have sent me into total transverberation. I'd've been pierced through with invisible arrows and lifted aloft by the sound of their singing: all those angels, all experiencing such orgiastic ecstasy. No, I couldn't let anyone see me crack, not even Dad. I had to be icy as the Gelthic serac. I'd promised Alizar. Like he'd promised me.

But, this being her first time, it was even worse for Betony.

Good for her that no one, human or angel, expected a full-grown woman—or older teenager, anyway, and a pilgrim from Cherubtown at that—to suddenly turn saint. Anybody looking at her might mistake her trembling for fear, perhaps devotion.

But I knew what those short, sharp convulsions meant. I saw her toes curl, her feet leave the floor—just half an inch, just for a few seconds. This was not the angels in full voice. No one, after all, had been sacrificed yet. Their singing was merely anticipatory.

But Betony heard it all. *And understood it perfectly.*

At the top of the Hundred Stair Tier, thirteen angels leaned eagerly forward in their thrones, urging the Heraldic Voice to move things along. I tried not to look at any one of them directly but kept my eyes vague, receptive at the periphery. Even so, even after all this time, the angels left a deep impression, like a bright scar on my brain.

In order of their feast days, they were: Shuushaari of the Sea, crowned in kelp and bladderwrack, her body an ooze of radular ribbons, like a thousand starveling oysters without their shells; Tanzanu the Hawk-Headed, whose human-ish shape was just that— an assemblage of hawks' heads; Olthar of Excesses, also called the Angel of Iniquity, who was three big shining bellies, each piled on top of the other like giant pearls, each on the point of splitting open; Rathanana of Beasts, all matted fur and bloody fang, snarling maw, curving claw; Murra Who Whispers; Wurra Who Roars; Zerat Like the Lightning; Childlike Hirrahune, solemn and sad; Thathia Whose Arms Are Eels; Kalikani and Kirtirin, the Enemy Twins; Impossible Beriu and Imperishable Dinyatha, who had only one heart between them.

As they sang, red mouth-slits began to gape open on previously smooth expanses of angelic skin or hide or chiton. New, raw, wet lips, parting like cruel paper-cuts, appeared on shoulders, backs, arms, palms, throats, beaks, tentacles, tails.

All of the angels were singing, and all of them sang: "Yes!"

All of them but one.

Alizar the Eleven-Eyed, as usual, sat apart from the sacrifices, and sang nothing. He sat very still, looking anxious and troubled. Strange, to watch a creature who was mostly eyes and incandescence cogitate so desperately.

He was coming to some momentous decision; I could tell by the way he kept smoothing down the curling blue feathers on his arms, tugging and twining the trailing plumes around his pinkie talons, then letting them spring back in release. Thin coils of gold pushed out of his pores and wound up his limbs like morning glories, occasionally lifting bell-like blooms as if following the path of the sun. They all yearned toward the girl, Betony.

But when it came, Alizar's resolve was absolute. He shook his head sharply, saying something to the other angels that pierced their song like a wire going right through my right nostril.

An emphatic *No!*—angelically-speaking.

The Heraldic Voice shook their head, trying to interpret this new message. At my feet, Betony went into micro-convulsions again, her *left* nostril beginning to bleed.

Her half-brother noticed nothing of this, too busy watching the Heraldic Voice's fraught face for any sign of the angelic approval.

"Well, Herald?" asked the boy eagerly. "Will they accept her? Am I to be a citizen of Gelethel?"

"It is unclear," said the Heraldic Voice. "There is some . . . division. That is, I think . . ."

Outraged at the Seventh Angel's interference, the other angels overrode his song, upping their decibel level and drowning him out. I slowed my breathing as my molars tried to dig their way deeper into my gums.

As this went on, the Heraldic Voice gradually lost their lost expression. The angels were very explicit. They communicated the strength of their desire, their wholehearted approval, and their eagerness to *get the hell on with it.*

"Yes, your sacrifice has been deemed acceptable by the angels of Gelethel, Pilgrim Luzarius," the Heraldic Voice told the boy, almost kindly. "Leave it at the bottom of the stairs. We will present you your citizenship papers when the sacrifice is complete."

Radiant with gratitude, the boy complied. His grip tightened on his half-sister's ropes, trying to drag her forward as the Heraldic Voice commanded.

But Betony abruptly jerked away from him, the ropes falling at her feet. Up flashed her hand, slicing the gag from her mouth. Then she leapt forward and jammed the point of her penknife—my penknife—beneath the boy's chin.

"Lizard-dick!" she bellowed. She had a deep voice, a smoker's voice. "Beetle-licker! Should've left you in the desert. Let the Zilch eat you. You'd make better barbecue than a brother. Just like your fucking dad."

"Don't you talk, don't you *dare* talk about my father!" The boy's monotone cracked down the middle; he looked ready to burst into tears. "You—you're a bad girl, Betony. A burden. A liar. Loose and wanton. You'll, you'll do anything for scraps."

A stunned pause. Betony stared at him. Then her long mouth tightened, her bony fist whitened around the knife.

"Scraps I shared with *you!*"

"I would have rather starved," the boy retorted.

Throat-cutting words if I ever heard them. Betony stepped closer, knife still raised to his throat. A tiny thread of blood ran like a worm down the boy's skin.

"You are offal," he whispered, the frail sandpaper of his voice fraying. "Kill me, I die a martyr. But you are offal, and offal is for sacrifice."

At a gesture from the Heraldic Voice, two warriors of the Holy Host marched off the Hundred Stair Tier to flank the girl. Bronze gauntlets clapped heavily on her bare shoulders, on the flesh above her elbows, but Betony ignored them, her gaze burning into the boy's face.

"You aren't my brother anymore!" she spat. But she didn't strike him down. She withdrew instead, slumping into the fists that gripped her as if suddenly spent.

Despite her skin-and-bone appearance, her dead weight must have made her unexpectedly heavy to the Hosts; their biceps bulged to keep her upright. The penknife, I noticed, was gone. Disappeared, between one blink and the next—I'd bet, up her sleeve. I hadn't seen sleight-of-hand like that since my bad Uncle Raz, "the Razman," pulled a contraband Super 8 camera out of his hat for my thirtieth birthday. The high-end, newfangled kind that also recorded sound.

"Take her to the sacrificing pool," the Heraldic Voice commanded.

I followed where they dragged her. I, and her half-brother, and the other pilgrims, and everyone else in the Celestial Corridor who wanted a front-row view of her death.

The sacrificing pool was at the other end of the Hundred Stair Tier: a deep, round tank made of gold-tinted glass, redolent of warm brine and eucalyptus oil. It had been cleaned and refilled to brimming for petition day. Water sloshed over the sides onto the floor around it, which, unlike the rest of the corridor, was paved in red brick, not white. New flooring had to be put in a few years ago after surplus water from the pool damaged the original salt-based tiles beyond repair. A golden staircase with wide steps and delicate rails led to the top of the pool, where a shallow lip, like a gilded pout, allowed a Host to kneel as they held the sacrifice under.

At the sight of the sacrificing pool, Betony remained limp. Oddly limp, I thought, for a girl with a hidden knife and a strong grasp on reality. She didn't struggle (and at this point in the proceedings, most sacrifices usually did, even the very old or infirm), remaining completely flaccid when one of the two Hosts slung Betony over her massive shoulder and began carrying her up the golden stairs.

The other Host stood guard at the bottom, spear planted before him, the white shine of his eyes warning all of us who stood too close to come no nearer.

The warriors of the Holy Host were called "hosts" because they were sworn receptacles of the Invisible Wonders who ruled us. At need, the angels could fill them with their influences, their attributes, and puppet them around Gelethel like angelically-endowed meat-sticks. In our poems and literature, the Hosts were referred to as "chalices of the angels," sometimes "chariots to the angels." But my bad uncles said that the Hosts were more like "cheesecloths for the angels." My bad uncles said that my *good* uncles, themselves all high-ranking Hosts on the Hundred Stair Tier, spent so much time in the Celestial Corridor that they'd become practically porous. Ripe for possession. Ready garments for any angel to put on.

The Host standing guard at the bottom of the sacrificing pool was but lightly possessed at the moment. No particular angelic attribute had manifested on his person, as it would have done if an angel were paying the Host more than passing attention. But if I squinted and looked sideways, I could see a sort of shimmering tether in the air, connecting him to the angel Beriu.

The Host who was carrying Betony, however, was rapidly filling up with angels. Three this time, I thought.

All warriors of the Holy Host were strapping. They had to be; it took a lot of muscle mass to host an angel, and then to recover from possession afterward. This warrior, already a tall woman, was growing taller with every step. Angelic influence flowed into her, augmented her.

The angels take turns on petition days, sharing sacrifices between them. Seven deaths between thirteen angels. But not all deaths are equal. Some pilgrim sacrifices come to them practically mummified already, so catatonic with despair and trauma that it is as if the animating spirits have already fled their bodies. To the angels, these lives, given up so lethargically to them, hardly seem a morsel.

But today, in this girl Betony, they foresaw a feast. Three angels had elected to feed on her death—and the most rapacious of the Invisible Wonders, too: Zerat, Rathanana, and Thathia. Her soul, they'd decided, was large and lively enough to satisfy.

So eager were they for Betony's oncoming death that they began engorging their Host too quickly. Not only was she swelling in size, but angelic attributes from all three angels began popping out all over her skin like boils—blue sparks, foul smoke, a slick of aspic, a roiling patch of fur. The rapid intensity of her transformation startled the Host, slowed her down as she mounted the steps, made her movements stiff and clumsy.

So when, at the top of the golden stairs, Betony blazed into action, the Host did not react quickly enough. She staggered, simultaneously flailing for balance while trying to pull the penknife out of her neck.

Freed from that sinewy grip, Betony went from limp to monkey-limbed in a shaved second. She twisted herself down from the Host's shoulder, dropping to the slippery lip of the sacrificing pool with the hardened agility of a street fighter. From there, she immediately barreled into the Host's knees, tripping her up.

The Host flew backwards. She landed hard, cracked her head on the side of the pool. And then she rolled off the edge, fell five feet to the floor, and hit the bricks with a moist thud.

Three angels screamed at once, fleeing that broken body like rats from a plague ship.

They could have healed her—she was one of their own!—but I hadn't seen the angels heal anyone for years now. Their excuse, according to Alizar, was that what with the fortnightly influx of pilgrims swelling the population of Gelethel, it was impractical to continue healing our sick or miraculously extending our lives the way they'd done since time immemorial. What if the citizens of the Angelic City should bear fruit and multiply to the point where the serac could no longer contain them?

Still, the Host was their responsibility. And the angels were not above bending their own rules from time to time, so long as they all sang an agreement. So we waited, we citizens of Gelethel, breathless, expectant. All our eyes had tracked the Host as she fell. But when she did not again stir—when the angels did not surprise us with mercy—we turned away and looked for the next moving object.

This should have been Betony, atop the sacrificing pool. Only she was no longer there. Or anywhere else to be seen.

I smiled to myself, hard and dry as the salt pan, a smile I'd learned from my bad uncles. Betony had done it—what no other sacrifice had managed before. She'd killed a Host and escaped her fate. A true saint. This, her first miracle. She was gone.

Not yet! Alizar groaned, and my salt-hard smile melted, brine-splashed. *She hasn't made it to the doors!*

That was when, from behind the clear gold walls of the sacrificing pool, I heard a familiar deep boom call out: "Tiers one through five: activate!"

The Hosts stationed on the first five levels of the Hundred Stair Tier descended in perfect lockstep. White eyes shining, fifty warriors marched off their steps and into the crowd of pilgrims and Gelthic laity gathered in the Celestial Corridor. We heaved, adjusting. Alizar Luzarius, probationary citizen, reeled drunkenly, lurching into me as he tried to see what was going on. I automatically reached out to steady him. He didn't even know I was there. He was moaning:

"I gave her a chance. One last chance to do something good. To be righteous. But she is ruinous. She *always* corrupts *everything.*"

My hand tightened on his elbow. "*You* brought her here," I growled. "What do you think they'll do to *you?*"

Bewildered at such venom from a total stranger, Luzarius glanced my way—first at my hand on his bony arm, then at my face. So close to him now, I saw that he was much younger than I'd thought—too young for peach fuzz, undersized for his age.

Withered child of a war-ripped desert, this boy had nothing—had *never* had anything—except his faith in the angels. I doubted he could've overpowered Betony and dragged her this far had it not been for some stronger will puppeting him over the serac. From hints the Seventh Angel had let fall, Luzarius was the angel Nirwen's tool—and he didn't even know it.

I released him like noon-baked scrap metal, and turned away, standing on my tiptoes to scan the teeming corridor. Nothing but confusion. The Hosts on the floor were conducting a systematic search, and the Gelthic citizens were eager to help.

"Run, Betony," I breathed, so sub-vocally that only the Seventh Angel, eavesdropping on the inside of my throat, could hear me. "Run, Saint Betony. *Run.*"

And then the angel Alizar lent me his sight, and I glimpsed her.

She'd made it to the far doors at the end of the Celestial Corridor. Each door was hewn from chunks of salmon-pink salt crystal as large as the Hundred Stair Tier was tall. Each door was as wide as three banquet tables set side by side and carved in reliefs of the original fifteen angels, along with their aspects and attributes.

The face of the Fifteenth Angel had long ago been gouged out. Because of that, Nirwen was the easiest angel to recognize at a glance: a featureless giantess with a tool in each hand, surrounded by a knotwork nimbus of her Lesser Servants, lab-created creatures whom she'd taken with her over the serac when she'd abandoned Gelethel.

Betony made it to the doors, but not past them.

I may have lost sight of her for a moment—so had the rest of the laity—but Alizar and the other angels had not. The Seventh Angel knew it, and despaired. Once the angels had marked her for sacrifice, Betony was theirs. Alizar the Eleven-Eyed's claim on her as his saint meant nothing to them; they'd drowned out his protest before he could fully voice it. And now they would drown *her*, with even greater glee and giddiness and appetite than before.

Because Betony had run.

And angels liked when sacrifices ran.

◆ ◆ ◆

WHAT IS THE SOUND OF THIRTEEN ANGELS SLAVERING AS THEY sing? It is the sound of scalding solfatara and bitter saliva. It is the hard trill of a dentist drill going right down to the root. It is the sound of children throwing live frogs into their campfire, then throwing back the ones who leaped out, but not before smashing them dead with a rock.

The angels reached out, and claimed what was theirs.

◆ ◆ ◆

Today it was my good Uncle Razoleth, oldest of the Q'Aleth boys, who caught Betony.

I'd thought I'd heard his voice earlier, bellowing out the order to activate the five tiers, but I hadn't seen him, jostled as I was by the crowd. Now there was no unseeing him.

The angels Thathia, Zerat, and Rathanana, fleeing the slain Host who'd fallen at the foot of the sacrificing pool, had scarpered across the room to inhabit their most trusted and senior warrior: Razoleth, Captain of the Hundred Stair Tier.

All my uncles—good and bad alike—were tall. But Razoleth, oldest of Mom's younger brothers, was tallest. His bronze helmet sported a comb of fourteen spikes from forehead to nape, the first spike topped with a round nob proclaiming his rank. Captains of the Hundred Stair Tier always got the biggest nobs because, and here I quote my bad uncles, "they were the biggest nobs." Now, trebly swollen with angelic intent, Razoleth expanded as he walked, increasing in size until he was twice the height and girth of anyone in the room, massive and slab-like.

Unlike the dead Host, who was currently being cleared away from the corridor floor, Razoleth grew more graceful with each incursion of angels. He moved more easily, more swiftly; he wore his angels well—even when the attributes of the three angels, pouring into him at speed, began to warp him out of all recognition.

First, the kidney-pink leather of his breastplate glowed like flayed flesh. And then it *became* flayed flesh. The angel Rathanana of Beasts was draping him all about in freshly skinned animal hides, tacky and membranous, still dripping blood.

My uncle did not have to roar like the angel Wurra to make room for his progress through the Celestial Corridor. Not with the angel Zerat inside him. No, pilgrims and citizens sparked away from him on contact—for he crackled with Zerat's lightning as he paced forward, his dark brown eyes swamped in blue electrical fire, the smell of singed hair filling the air like burning feathers.

Razoleth had become a mass of muscles, a rockslide tearing across the room towards Betony—all except for his arms. These were lengthening and slimming down to a filament-thinness. From his shoulders to his fingertips his dark skin was ghosting to gray-white, glistening with mucus. His elbows and forearms were fringed with delicate fins. Where his hands had been a moment ago were now two bulbous heads. His fingers fused into needle-fine jaws curving away from each other, lined in hooklike teeth.

Now he had the angel Thathia's arms. The angel Thathia's reach.

And the angel Thathia reached—the other angels with her—through my uncle's body, for Betony.

They snagged her snarled hair in Thathia's eel-mouths. The shock of Zerat's lightning bolt blew the rags off Betony's feet, set her tatters afire. Rathanana's cloak of raw flesh peeled itself away from Razoleth's broad chest, flew off of him, and flung itself around Betony's bucking body, rolling her up like a carpet.

Caught.

Without a pause, Razoleth bent down, picked up the bundle and carried it back to the Hundred Stair Tier, to the sacrificing pool.

As my uncle passed me, he looked down and gave a short nod. My good uncles were not as loquacious as my bad ones, but they still held me dear: the only daughter of their only sister. I couldn't bear to meet his eyes, and he was too tall this way besides, so I dipped my head. Best, with the good uncles, to show a subordinate face.

By now, Betony had recovered enough to squirm an arm free of Rathanana's foul cloak. It was all I could see of her: one bare arm patterned in branching red ferns—a new red tree blooming out from the seed of her lightning strike—one desperate hand, fingers stretched as far as they could reach. Muffled by the stinking skins that wrapped her, she screamed, "Alizar! Alizar!"

Beside me, the half-brother who bore that name trembled. He shook his head, covered his ears. But it was not to him she cried out.

I glared up at Alizar—the other Alizar—he whom Betony had known and loved the instant she had beheld him. Alizar the Eleven-Eyed, to whom she had been sent, all unbeknownst to her, by the Fifteenth Angel—a gift from across the serac. Alizar, the Seventh Angel, who had made Betony his saint. His second saint. Something none of the other angels had.

"Do something!" I hissed at him aloud—though he could have read my thoughts just as well. No one else heard me; all attention in the Celestial Corridor was fastened on Razoleth, who, with Betony in his arms, was mounting the golden steps to the sacrificing pool.

High above us, the angel Alizar shifted on his throne, his inner glow increasing until it overspilled his skin in an agitated nimbus.

What can I do, Ish? Oh, Ish, what must I do?

During the New War, when the Koss Var Air Force tried to bomb Gelethel the way it had bombed our neighboring city-states Sanis Al and Rok Moris, the airborne ordinance would make a certain sound when it dropped within two hundred meters of our city. It was the sound of a glass mountain shattering. The bombs never made it into the city; they would simply atomize. A smear of light would streak across our skies, and Gelethel would tremble within the cold blue diamond of its surrounding serac. The serac itself would whistle and tinkle, like wind chimes made of ice. And then the Angelic City would fall silent, unhurt and untouched. Nonplussed but undaunted, the KVAF tried again and again to bomb us into memory—hoping to one day surprise a way past our defenses. They never succeeded.

That glass-shattering sound was just a memory. But it was what I heard when Uncle Razoleth dumped Betony into the sacrificing pool. It was the sound of Alizar's heart breaking. Or mine. Not much difference between us these days.

Inside the pool's deep glass bowl, raw animal skins unfurled from Betony's body like a ball of flowering tea. They drifted away from her, floating in clouds of their own blood, helped by Betony, who was thrashing herself free of the last of them. Bobbing to the surface, she splashed her way to the pool's edge, surprisingly nimble in the water for such a sand cat.

But Uncle Razoleth was kneeling on the lip of the pool, waiting for her. His hands-turned-jaws grabbed Betony by the hair and thrust her back down.

Betony gasped hugely and in vain before the water closed around her. I moved closer to the sacrificing pool, helpless, reaching out.

Her eyes met mine through the gold-glazed glass between us.

So did the large pale eyes of Thathia's eels, the eels that were now my uncle's arms. Were the angels suspicious? Was Thathia herself watching me, and through me, Alizar?

I couldn't be sure—and anyway, Uncle Razoleth was merely possessed of angels, not an angel himself. I was allowed to see him fully, just like everyone else, and if his fingers wanted to have a staring contest with me as they drowned this girl, well, there was nothing I could do about that. Better to stare into those eyes than watch Betony refuse and refuse and and refuse and then, finally, take that fatal, watery breath.

I tasted brine all the way down my esophagus.

Thathia, Zerat, and Rathanana shrieked in three-part discord as they fed on her death. Their jubilation, their rapture, and the intense, disorienting bliss they communicated through song blacked out the rest of the Celestial Corridor to my sight, just for a moment—until the angel Alizar, high above me on the Hundred Stair Tier, flamed up hugely like a pillar of fire.

Then flickered out. Like a snuffed candle. Like the light in Betony's eyes.

I gasped, gut-punched.

Alizar's thirteen colleagues twisted in their seats to look for him. But he was no longer there. The Seventh Throne was as empty to their angelic senses as it was to the Gelthic laity. They stirred, uneasily. My molars started up the root-canal ache of their singing. They were calling for him, demanding he return. But they could not reach him, and it frightened them.

I swallowed a yelp as Alizar flashed into existence *right in front of me.*

Opposite Uncle Razoleth, who could not see him, he landed on the rim of the golden pool. On toes like golden claws he perched, clinging like a bird, glowing down into the pool intently, frowning with all his eyes.

And then a new voice sliced through the enamel-stripping song in my mouth. It flooded my tongue with copper and gentian, like biting down on a toothy bit of aloe vera.

Alizar the Eleven-Eyed was speaking from two red mouth-slits that had appeared like slashes down either side of his face. He spoke softly, his words a prayer—a prayer not unknown to the other thirteen, who reacted variously: some crackling with rage, or cackling with terrified laughter, some sweating crystal clusters of resentful orpiment, others exuding miasmal perfumes of admiration.

It was the prayer of an angel declaring his saint for the first time in a generation.

Of course, no angel had claimed a dead person for their saint before; there wasn't a song for that. But now that the sacrifice was complete and Betony dead, Alizar could do with the body as he pleased; that was canon.

The angels watched him, fascinated. A few protested, others silenced them. The angels Zerat, Rathanana, and Thathia were practically formless with repletion, oblivious to events. These were Alizar's greatest critics, the only ones who might have stopped him—but they could not be bothered to move.

The waters in the sacrificing pool began to boil. Host Razoleth snatched his hand from Betony's hair—it was a human hand again, bereft of angels. Blisters immediately formed on his skin. He was abruptly off-balance, half the size he'd been just a moment before, stripped of the armor Rathanana had turned into animal skins.

Like all Hosts after a dispossession, my good uncle was urgently sapped from holding so much heat and light for so long. He swooned—and this time, his comrades of the Holy Host were there to catch him as he fell. They lifted him onto a stretcher, and bore him out of the Celestial Corridor—not without a few curious glances behind them at the foaming sacrificing pool, where Betony's body, released from Razoleth's drowning grip, was rising to the surface.

Eucalyptus-scented brine boiled and foamed around the corpse. After so many sacrifices, I knew that men mostly drowned face-down, and women face-up. This was not always true, but it was true today.

The angel Alizar made a quick, crooking gesture with his finger. No one saw this but myself and the angels. Everyone else simply tracked Betony's body as it skidded across the water toward him. Alizar flicked his finger again—one long golden talon entwined with trailing plumes and bell-like blossoms—and the body floated right out of the sacrificing pool.

It hovered above the surface, water sluicing from its hair and the torn remnants of its clothes onto the floor. A small wave ran over my toes, soaking my sandals. Corpse water. Martyr water. Dozens of

Gelthic citizens rushed in with kerchiefs and cloths to soak it up, to hoard as holy relics or to sell. Scavengers.

Other than me, only the dead girl's half-brother didn't fall to his knees and scrabble in the wet. He had raised his face blearily to the body buoyed up only by air, and I did not know what his expression meant. Regret, perhaps, at a loathsome necessity. Some fear. Some relief. Mostly regret.

He stretched his hand toward the body, as if wanting to snatch it down from its levitation, eager perhaps to honor it in death. But his half-sister's body was too high for him to reach, and out of his purview besides. He couldn't stop whatever was happening now, any more than the angel Alizar or I could have stopped Betony from drowning in the first place.

The Seventh Angel made a complicated gesture with his talon. Betony's floating corpse spun around until it hung just before him, its face level with his. A third mouth-slit appeared below the three green eyes on his chin, curving upward in a red bow, like a smile.

Live!

And then, aloud, for everyone in the Celestial Corridor to hear—and shining so brightly that everyone could also *see*, just for a moment, the fire and feathers and flowers and eyes torqued into the shape of a man—the Seventh Angel sang:

"LIVE!"

A jet of water shot from Betony's mouth and nose, voiding her lungs.

For the second time that day, three of the fourteen angels screamed in outraged agony. Their sacrifice was coming unsacrificed, the feast falling away from them. Bliss blinked out; they were left sullen and starving as a saint was resurrected before their eyes—and there was nothing they could do to get her back.

At my side, the boy Luzarius groaned and bent double, as though felled by cramps. He groaned again when the Seventh Angel reached out his golden talon next and touched the un-drowned girl on her water-beaded brow.

All eleven of Alizar's eyes slid from their fixed marks on the lustrous parchment of his skin, and sank into him. This left his aspect weirdly naked: a collection of rainbow plumage, fronds, blooms, and green-gold flickers of light. A second later, those eleven eyeballs all popped up again upon Betony's brow, forming a perfect circle around it.

The next moment, everyone in the Celestial Corridor gasped. This, *this* they could see!

Now it was not Alizar's *eyes* that adorned her brow, but *jewels*—eleven jewels, set at perfect intervals into a braid of shining platinum. There were two star sapphires, a black pearl, three square-cut tourmalines, a chunk of polished tiger iron, three faceted red beryls, and a yellow diamond. The scorched shreds of Betony's clothes melted away into a shimmering, and the shimmering resolved into gleaming garments: silver satin, silver lace, thread of silver embroidery, and more twinkling silver sequins than had been worn by all the dancers who had ever appeared onstage at the Sexy Seraph Cabaret on burlesque night put together.

Turning to the Heraldic Voice, the angel Alizar said something in a stentorian tone.

The Heraldic Voice understood the order immediately. Cracks appeared in the lenses of their pince-nez. Two capillaries popped in their left eye. Their right nostril began to bleed. But they nodded at once, and gestured for a nearby warrior of the Holy Host, who stepped forward and saluted.

"Take her to the Seventh Anchorhold in the Celestial Cenoby," the Heraldic Voice told the Host. "Show her all reverence due a saint of Gelethel."

"Yes, Herald," the Host replied. She mounted the steps and approached the saint, arms held before her in worshipful salutation. "Come, my saint. I will bear you home."

The Seventh Angel (eyeball-less now, but more for show and shock than because he couldn't manifest more of them) smiled approvingly at the Host with all of his mouth-slits. But his flirtations were, as usual, wasted on her; she could not see him. Nevertheless, Alizar sent his saint wafting toward her with little puffs of the tiny insect wings that glittered and chittered all over him. Betony floated into the Host's waiting arms.

At this, the boy Luzarius squawked, "A saint!"

He slopped through the mess on the floor to fall at the feet of the Heraldic Voice. "Herald, my sis—Betony—she, she *cannot* be a saint. She is smirched. She doesn't even believe in, in the angels. She worships the false god of Cherubtown . . . she is *unworthy*!"

The Heraldic Voice paused, uncertain of procedure. The angels were reacting variously, some affronted at the very idea of a god so close as Cherubtown, some still howling with disappointment over the lost sacrifice, and many, many of them casting furtive, fearful glimpses at the Seventh Angel, Alizar, who had just done what none of them could do, who had *resurrected* a pilgrim girl to be his saint.

Resurrection was not an angelic talent. Resurrection was for the godhead, and the angels of Gelethel had eaten their god long ago.

The angel Alizar said quietly, for my ears only, *I am spent, Ish. I must conceal myself awhile and gather strength. I will come to you anon.*

"Don't let the others find you," I told him in the quietness of my mind.

I could only imagine what they would do to him, weakened as he was, and after such shocking behavior.

And how.

And he vanished, agitating the other angels all over again.

"You, young person," the Heraldic Voice was coldly informing the boy Luzarius, "are in a precarious situation. We must consult the Hagiological Archives for precedent. Meanwhile, your citizenship shall be held in abeyance until such time as this matter is resolved. Until then, you shall be kept prisoner in our saltcellars."

With that, they nodded toward the Hundred Stair Tier. A detachment of the Holy Host stepped down at once to drag the wailing boy away.

ANGLE ON ONABROSZIA

"**H**I, DAD! YOU HOME?**"**
Opening the front door, I stuck my head into the faded yellow great room. Of course Dad was home. Where else would he be? Someone had to sit with Mom around the clock, and what with me running the Quick, my bad uncles working nights, and my good uncles working days, none of us were around to help much.

We each managed to take a few shifts every fortnight to free Dad up for sleeping or shopping or tidying the house. If Dad allowed us to, we would've all bartered dune-loads of benzies for cleaning crews or nurses for hire, but it upset Mom to no end to have strangers about. We tried it once, and she grew so agitated that Dad said it just wasn't worth it. That gentle tone of his. There's this awful, heartbreaking moment in the classic sav-nav film *Winds of Vicissitude,* when the protagonist (a sentient vessel known as the psi-ship *Vicissitude*), after being pirate-struck, looted, and left listing in the waters, decides to go down with dignity. Dad had sounded like that.

No answer from the house. I called out again, "Hello!?"

After a few seconds, I heard a muffled response from way in the back, so I headed deeper in. Not much to the place. After the great room, there was a hallway with three small bedrooms on the right, and a bathroom, linen closet, and kitchen to the left. At the back of the house was the master suite, maybe a handkerchief larger than the other bedrooms, with a sliding door that led to the back patio, and a half-bath big enough for an accordion to take a crap in (if the bellows were all the way compressed).

By the time Mom retired from Q'Aleth Hauling Industries—Gelethel's solid waste collection and management company, which she'd started herself at age eighteen—she could've afforded to live in a palace the size of the Celestial Corridor. Instead, the "Garbage Queen of Gelethel" had kept the long, low, L-shaped rambler where she had grown up and raised her younger brothers. There, she had maintained her public facade as the devout only daughter of Umrir and Zaripha Q'Aleth, impoverished Gelthic layabouts who'd lived low and died lazy. Mom's modest choices only made her more respected throughout Gelethel as the angels-sanctified business woman who upheld her friends, terrified her foes, and ruled over her family like an idol of the outer serac.

Only her immediate family knew about her secret life. And none of us would ever tell. Especially not now.

There was no one in any of the small bedrooms. Dad slept in the tiniest one these days. Mom was in the master suite, which was at present empty. But the sliding glass door stood open, the screen door letting in a bread-baking blast of heat.

"Hey!" I called out. "You two out back?"

"Yeah, Ishi! Back here!"

That sounded like an uncle. Dad would've just come inside to talk to me. He'd never raised his voice since I could remember.

I stepped out onto the back patio where Mom sat most days. Dad would drag her chair beneath a stand of verdy trees to take advantage of their shade, and had set up his own desk under an umbrella on the far end of the patio. There, on the typewriter he'd brought with him across the serac, Dad wrote his screenplays by the score.

The clackety-clack noises of that old machine had so thrilled me as a child that I used to run around our backyard pretending I was starring in whatever movie Dad was writing. I was "Moon Princess," leader of a smuggling operation between Gelethel and Cherubtown! I was a Zilch giant, riding my viperbike through the dunes of Bellisaar, terrorizing wayfarers! I was the old god of Gelethel, whom the angels ate right up!

Dad was nothing if not prolific. A mechanic in his former life, he was also—thankfully—more than adept at improvising broken typewriter keys, re-inking ribbons, replacing rubber feet with wine corks, substituting shoelaces for carriage pull straps, and bending the typebars back into position whenever the alignment was off. His pile of movie manuscripts by this point was higher than my head.

"Movies," he'd say in his smiling, melancholy way, "that will never see production."

The whitelight of Gelthic noon dazzled me the moment I stepped out from under the awning's shade. In this part of the world, just south of the Bellisaar Waste, even our winters were twice as hot as anyone else's summers. And at the moment, we were far from winter. I stopped on the salt-brick porch, raising my arm to overhang my eyes.

I'd left the Celestial Corridor right after Betony's canonization. Her brother's was the first petition of the day, but I'd had enough—

enough of starving fanatics, golden bathtubs, invisible angels, everything. I wanted my parents, even though I didn't plan on mentioning the sacrifice to either of them. Dad, because it made him sad and sick, and he was already both. Mom, because she no longer understood me. And even if she could, her relationship with the angels had always been so complicated, I probably wouldn't have dared.

Dad's desk was, unusually, cleared of all manuscripts. A single mug of cooling tea sat on the mosaic surface. His chair was empty. I squinted into the brightness towards the stand of verdy trees, and sure enough—there sat Mom, enthroned on her wheelchair. She was draped in a lightly crocheted shawl of kidney-pink yarn shot through with bronze, the same colors as the armor worn by the Holy Host.

One of my mother's brothers sat on a chair near her. His face was turned away. I couldn't tell what kind of uncle he was today.

Then he saw me, and grinned.

A bad uncle then. My good uncles never grinned, only smiled. Always with their mouths closed. Always beatifically, as though through a veil.

"Ishi!" Uncle Zulli leapt up, looking guiltily relieved to see me.

A second later, I found out why.

"Watch your mom a sec while I take a piss, okay? Your dad had an appointment with the doc, so I'm a man short of a tag team. About to burp up my bladder. When you called out just now, I almost lost it. Nearly hosed down the back wall. Would've, too—but for Broszia here."

If Onabroszia Q'Aleth had still been herself, she'd have slapped Zulli till he peed out his nose for such vulgar talk. Mom wasn't the oldest of a horde of siblings for nothing. I folded my arms.

"Don't just stand there talking about it, Zulli. Go, go, go!"

"Don't say 'go,' Ishi," Uncle Zulli groaned. "You tryin' to bust me?"

Then, not hurrying at all, and so lightly he barely crushed the lovegrass beneath his feet, Uncle Zulli minced his way across the yard and went into the house. I took his place in the hard wooden chair beside Mom and covered her hand in mine. Her circulation was terrible. The texture of her skin was like torn tissue paper over hard rubber, and her arm was not only bruised in several places but punctured here and there with scabs. She kept hurting herself—usually in the middle of the night, just when Dad finally dropped into a frail sleep. She'd forget where she was, and that she was barely mobile, and all too apt to fall into or out of things. Like doors. And beds.

"See, Mom, if you'd've given *me* a younger brother," I said, "I'd've made sure he was potty-trained before setting him loose on the world. Uncle Zulli forgets his bladder is the size of a pea. He's always drinking gallons of tea—inevitably before visiting places that have no public facilities. Or places that have private ones that he can't get to for one reason or another."

I peered into her eyes. Cataracts clouded the irises, once dark and dagger-sharp. Now she was trapped behind those opal anchorholds. Mom stared at the backyard wall like it held visions. Dad interpreted that filmy far-off gaze as tranquility, but I wasn't so sure.

Still patting her hand, I blurted, "Alizar the Eleven-Eyed has a new saint."

Mom turned her head and, almost, looked at me. "I am a saint," she said serenely. "I was Kalikani's saint, before Kirtirin stole me."

Parts of my body tingled. Others went numb. It had been so long, so very long, since my mother had talked to me.

"Right," I whispered, then cleared my throat. "Right, yes—I re-member you saying that once. Tell me about that, Mom."

She continued with queenly graciousness, "Kalikani chose me when I was eight. I was wearing my green dress, with the sparkles. I was so excited. It was my birthday and they took me to see the Heraldic Voice. They asked me if I saw the angels. I did. I saw them all and named them all, right away. The Heraldic Voice asked me to describe them. I said they were tall and beautiful, with flowing hair and flowing gowns. Kalikani wore a green dress, like mine. Green as, as this, this . . ." she pointed to the trunk of a verdy tree, not knowing what to call it.

"Her hair was green, and her teeth were green, and her eyes had roots growing out of them. But Kirtirin, her twin, wanted me. He was green too, but like a lizard, with a lizard's tongue, and a long green lizard's tail. So he said, 'You cannot have her, sister; she is my saint.' And Kalikani smote him with her branches, and wrapped three branches around his throat and squeezed. And the Heraldic

Voice told me that they were very sorry, but the angels would each have to choose their own saint, and for the sake of peace in the Celestial Cenoby, it could not be me. So they sent me on my way."

I nodded. "That must have hurt your feelings."

Mom nodded back, and to my surprise, started weeping. Great clear tears rolled from the clouds in her eyes.

I kept patting her hand, helplessly.

Her story about how the angels had rejected her changed every time she told it. The truth was, Mom had never been able to see angels, and everyone in Gelethel knew it.

From the time she was tiny, Mom was fixated on angels. She told stories about the Invisible Wonders to her friends, hosted backyard tea parties purporting to be graced by their attendance, and drew endless reams of pictures depicting—what she insisted were—angels. Her notions of their faces, forms, characters, temperaments, and relationships were as wild as her stories and as changeable. None of it matched existing canon. But that never made any difference to her. Mom just *knew* she was right about the angels—more right than any of the saints who'd ever recorded their observations in the Hagiological Archives. Onabroszia Q'Aleth knew best.

At age eight, Mom had stood in the Celestial Corridor, and publicly—*at her own insistence*—declared herself a saint. She spoke with such force and determination that the hundreds of Gelthic laity gathered there that day, the Heraldic Voice included, listened enraptured for the better part of an hour.

But in the end, none of it was true. Mom couldn't really see the angels of Gelethel. She was not a saint.

What *was* true was that the angels (particularly Kalikani and Kirtirin, the Enemy Twins) were impressed with Mom's great faith in the Invisible Wonders, motley mix of grand delusion, self-importance, self-deception, and powerful imagination that the faith of a precocious eight-year-old was. So impressed, in fact, that they offered her—filthy gamine daughter of no-account parents—a scholarship to one of Gelethel's best schools.

Onabroszia quickly rose to the top of her class and went on rising. She won scholarships for private schools that were usually reserved for the extended families of past and present saints (privileged among the laity). Then, she landed an angelic grant to start her business right out of school.

All that time, she was working enough odd jobs throughout the fourteen districts of the Angelic City that her barter-cache was stuffed with "benzies"—the benisons each angel manifested for its particular district. Soon, she had enough stock, both liquid assets and IOUs in the form of notarized benzie slips, to put her younger brothers through school as well. When they were old enough, she sent them on to the Empyrean Academy, where they learned to surrender their bodies to the angels. After that, Mom had eyes and ears in the Celestial Corridor: eyes and ears that were loyal to *her*.

Her brothers may have given their bodies over to the Invisible Wonders who ruled Gelethel, but when they were at home, they were ruled solely by their eldest sister. They were Broszia's boys, mind and soul.

And Onabroszia Q'Aleth had a bone to pick with the angels.

If Mom could not live as a saint in the Celestial Cenoby, then she would work as a devil within the Angelic City's walls. She would undercut the authority of the fourteen Invisible Wonders by bringing in benisons of her own, from out beyond the serac. And she would distribute this contraband to the Gelthic populace.

By day, Mom and her brothers were blessed amongst all people of Gelethel. By night, they ran the Angelic City's underworld: a smuggling operation that spidered throughout the fourteen districts still extant within the Gelthic serac, and without it too. If they were ever caught, they'd suffer the same fate of all dissidents. First, they'd spend a period of penance in the saltcellars, while the angels worked them from within. Last, they'd take a short walk and a swift fall down the Hellhole in the Fifteenth District.

This was why Mom was the number one reason I could never tell anyone I was a saint. Even now, it just might kill her to learn it. If she didn't kill me first. I wouldn't put it past Onabroszia Q'Aleth, even in this state, to throttle me cold.

"Ishtu," Dad's light voice came from behind me. "I didn't think you'd come by today."

CLOSE UP ON MY FATHER'S FACE

*T*ITLE *C*ARD: "YOUNG MECHANIC GOES ROGUE!"

Dad starts out, fresh from trade school, as a mechanic for a film production company called Elixir Entertainment. Elixir is based in King's Capital, Koss Var, its studios converted out of old aeroplane hangars: huge concrete caves containing sound stages and construction bullpens, temporary offices, living quarters, community kitchen, laundry, and of course a shed out back for the costumes, all in different shades of pre-Pankinetichrome gray.

He works with Elixir for a golden few years, right before the Koss Var Air Force re-requisitions the studios for hangars. Dad smells the rats of war and is pissed right off. Not only is he out of a job he loves, but he's also an avowed pacifist.

But, surprise! Mechanics being worth their weight in iron, when the KVAF "invites" Dad to stay on with them as a tactical aircraft design and maintenance specialist for their new fleet of bombers, it's an offer he can't refuse. Not if he wants to stay out of prison. Pay's okay, but that isn't the point.

By day, Dad's working for the KVAF, a mechanic for the Empire of the Open Palm. By night, he's a *filmmaker*. He's producing a stealth documentary—gathering intel, digging for gossip, following trails to undisclosed filling factories, interviewing similarly beleaguered colleagues under conditions of anonymity. Filming everything.

The night *Mystery Munitions and Hidden Hangars* releases, Koss Var's secret police come to Dad's apartment. But he's gone. He's just made it across the border when the bounty on his head is blasted all over public radio and newsreels.

Too late. Dad's anti-war documentary has blown the whistle on the Empire of the Open Palm's intentions for the Bellisaar Theatre. And while his film doesn't stop the New War from rumbling over the horizon, it sounds a fair warning.

And when the first KVAF bombers fly south to strafe the great city-states of the southern desert, Rok Moris and Sanis Alis aren't unprepared.

Title card: "Welcome to Gelethel!"

Tracking shot on Dad. His mustache is luxuriant. His brow is expansive, intelligent. His spectacles are crooked, and though he is a hunted man, his brown eyes twinkle.

He arrives at the Gelthic serac after crossing the desert in a rusted, half-wrecked jalopy. He has heard of that godless place southeast of the Bellisaar Waste called Gelethel—that mythical city that has never heard of motion pictures.

In the bed of his dilapidated deathtruck, Dad carries two projectors, as many cans of film as can be crammed, and a scrim. In those days, Cherubtown isn't a refugee camp yet. It's still just a shrine for actual pilgrims seeking congress with the angels, plus a little way-station selling food and drink and rental tents outside the western serac, where the Holy Host lowers Gelethel's bridge on petition days.

Dad stops at the shrine, asks some questions, gets his bearings. Then, bold as a fighter pilot, as soon as the bridge is lowered, he drives straight up to the ramparts, over, and down the other side into Gelethel.

He and his jalopy follow the train of pilgrims all the way to the Celestial Corridor. He parks right outside, on a stretch of salt pan, and strides forward.

He will be the man who brings movies to the angels.

Title Card: "A Foreign Entrepreneur!"

Fourteen Invisible Wonders sit enthroned, watching Dad with perhaps more interest and curiosity than usual. Dad, a pilgrim petitioning for citizenship, tells them that he is a filmmaker, formerly of Koss Var. He says "filmmaker," not "mechanic," nor even "projectionist"—though he is both of those things too. He does not mention exile or criminal activity or the price on his head or the war he knows will come. Some instinct tells him the angels would not be interested.

But *films* interest them. The angels like stories. They demand an explanation.

Instead of explaining, Dad gestures to his rig: projectors, scrim, et cetera, that he has hauled in. He is ready and willing to give them a picture show.

The angels accede. In fact, they *demand* a picture show: if he does not oblige them, he will eternally regret it. Emphasis on "eternal."

Dad obliges. He needs an electrical source for the lamp; would the angels direct him to the nearest outlet?

Zerat Like the Lightning extends his hand in blessing over the rig. The Celestial Corridor is suddenly illuminated. The scrim begins to flicker: shadow, silver, shadow, silver, white, black, gray.

Miracle of miracles! It is just possible for the petitioners gathered in the Celestial Corridor that day to behold, in the flickering light, a rare sight for their naked eyes: fourteen eager outlines leaning forward in their thrones.

Mom is there too—Onabroszia Q'Aleth, Garbage Queen of Gelethel—twenty-four years old and the richest woman in the city. That day she sees what she has never seen before. She sees the angels. They are not as beautiful as she has imagined.

Title Card: "The Angels Are Pleased!"

The Invisible Wonders agree that this foreign filmmaker may stay in Gelethel. He will have a movie palace of his own, where he will proudly display his sacrifice: all the films he has brought with him to edify the angels and their worshippers.

But he must *never* leave Gelethel, they warn him. If he is caught trying to leave, the Holy Host will execute him. He is a citizen of Gelethel now: he must marry a Gelthic woman and produce a line of children who will protect and guard the magic of his movie palace.

Title Card: "Free Motion Picture Magic For All!"

When the Heraldic Voice, speaking for the angels, informs Dad of his new obligations, Dad protests. (He does not yet know better.) He tries to explain that silver nitrate degrades over time, that there is always danger of fire—it is not uncommon for entire archives of celluloid film to go up in flame and poisonous plumes and be lost forever—and that, most importantly, it will be *absolutely necessary* to provide new cinematic material for Gelthic cultural consumption on a regular basis.

The angels cut him short.

The fourteenth angel, Imperishable Dinyatha, breathes upon the cans of film, granting them the grace of her own longevity. As for the rest, the Heraldic Voice informs him, Dad need not import any new films into Gelethel; the angels believe that his films will enthrall audiences throughout the ages.

In their great benevolence, the angels evict—on the spot—the current tenants of the Gelthic Opera Hall. They bestow the building on Dad for use as his nickelodeon. He is to show his films to the people of Gelethel (and any angels who happen to drop by) free of charge.

Title Card: "Foreigner Finds Love!"

Dad begins work. Since he isn't allowed to barter movie tickets for other benzies, he does the next best thing: decides to barter the Quick's concessions instead.

The citizens of Gelethel protest.

Citizens: Give us snacks! Angelic gifts should be free for all!

Dad: How is that? Every district is provided a variety of benisons by its ruling angel. Shuushaari fills the fountains in her district with fish the first day of every fortnight. On thirteenth day, the angel Beriu makes the flakes fall that, when gathered and set to soak, will rise into dough for baking. Zerat, on the eighth day, recharges all batteries, big and small, that fall within the lines of his district. None of these benisons manifest outside their zones—yet all of Gelethel eats fish, bakes bread and cake, and powers their houses with electricity. Every district trades their specific benisons with every other district. That's the basic economy of Gelethel. I'm doing nothing wrong.

Citizens: But before the angels gave you Quicksilver Cinema, we never needed movie concessions! Now that popcorn exists, it must be ours!

Dad: Then let the angel Olthar provide you popcorn outside Quicksilver Cinema.

Citizens: (resentful silence)

Dad: But he won't, will he? That's not how benisons work. My concessions are for the Quick alone. I prayed for them *specifically*, imploring the angel Olthar to add value for patrons of the movie palace. In return for his beneficence, Olthar receives more visitors to his district, is remembered fondly in their prayers, and, in this way, worship of his name increases. He gains power and favor among the angels. Meanwhile, I must live—and to live I must be able to barter. I *will* declare my concessions as benisons worthy of trade.

Citizens: What do you need benzies for anyway? The angels gave you a job, a movie palace to sleep in, all the food you can eat!

Dad: I cannot live on popcorn alone.

Citizens: How does a dirty pilgrim like you become such an expert in Gelthic economy?

Dad: (dryly) I'm a quick study.

After they are evicted, the dispossessed owners of what used to be the Gelthic Opera Hall (and is now Quicksilver Cinema) go to squat in Nirwen's Hell. Despite rumors of the Holy Host using the abandoned fifteenth district to "disappear" certain of Gelethel's criminal element (i.e., apostates), most days Hell is empty as a fossil in the salt pan. The area, having no official angelic oversight, is the least policed zone in Gelethel.

The aforementioned owners could have slept far more comfortably in Alizar's Bower, where fruit and veg hangs ready to be freely plucked off vine and tree. They could have stayed with friends and family, or even huddled for shelter in the halls of the Celestial Corridor. But in their desire for revenge, they want complete secrecy to plot against the pilgrim with his newfangled machines and fancy ideas, who in a single day took away what was theirs.

What follows is no secret anywhere in Gelethel. Everyone knows who is vandalizing the Quick each night, but nothing is done about it. At least, not outright.

(Later, much later, Dad learns all. How Onabroszia Q'Aleth reported the conspirators to the Holy Host; how one night the Host marched into the fifteenth district and rumbled those Hell-dwellers in their tents; how, when the Host left the fifteenth district again at dawn, they bore no prisoners with them. In Gelethel, Dad is told, this can mean only one thing: that the bodies lay somewhere in the secret recesses of Hell, where no one living can reach, nor any mourner recover them for burial. But, as I said, Dad comes to know about this much later.)

But before all that, when the vandalizations at the Quick are still happening, Dad is at a loss. Still scorched by his near-miss with the Koss Var secret police, he is, understandably, leery about reporting to the authorities. He wants to maintain a low profile, behave like an ideal citizen, and keep the doors of his movie palace open, as prescribed to him by the angels. But no sooner does he fix one defacement but another window is smashed, another door kicked in, another imprecation smeared (with paint and other less benign materials) on the salt-white walls, slogans like:

GO BACK TO KOSS VAR, DOGMAN!

"Dogman," Dad begins to intuit through repetition and context, is a common slur for foreigners. It derives from "dogma," on the assumption that everyone outside the Gelthic serac is a staunch theist who has unilaterally rejected a purely angelic rule.

Now, Dad has always been an *atheist* himself, but considers converting to some brand of theism on the strength of spite alone.

At least no one dares steal or destroy the equipment inside the Quick. It is, after all, blessed by the angels. But the movie palace is not a safe place to visit—not even to see the strange new pictures Dad has brought in from outside the serac. Not even for the snacks.

But hark!

One afternoon, Mom—AKA Onabroszia Q'Aleth, radiant and blessed—surprises the entire Angelic City by attending a matinee with her younger brothers in tow.

The Q'Aleth family, everywhere watched and emulated, are observed strolling into Dad's empty movie palace at forty-five minutes before showtime. They are espied waiting in line at the concessions stand, where Dad, in a starched soda jerk cap and black-and-gold striped apron, stands eager to serve them.

The Q'Aleths pay for their movie snacks (mountains of them) in an array of barter: benzie slips of all kinds—the officially notarized IOUs from Tanzanu's district—that Dad can trade in for meat, fabric, bread, fish, batteries, craft trade, municipal services, water lots, etc. All transactions complete to everyone's delight, the Q'Aleths cart away their spoils into the theatre: buckets of popcorn, bags of peanuts, pretzels wrapped in cloth napkins, small paper cones stuffed with mint sticks and hard caramels and chocolate bullets scooped out of the large glass jars at the candy buffet, a frosty bottle of beer for Mom, ice cream sodas for the boys.

Emboldened by Mom's example, and salivating for the angelic concessions found nowhere else in Gelethel, citizens come flooding in.

By showtime, all seats are full: eight hundred seats in the orchestra, three hundred in the mezzanine. There is some double-stacking: parents with children, lovers cuddling. Standing room only. The concession stand looks like no man's land between two enemy trenches. But that's fine; the angel Olthar's next Feast of Excess is in two days' time, when all stores in his district—the OlDi—will be automatically and lavishly replenished.

Dad, now with cap cast aside and sleeves rolled up, plays movies for his audience all day. He is tireless, elated, sweating spigots in the projection room. He doesn't notice when Mom comes in and sits quietly behind him, watching him work. He doesn't notice until after midnight, when everyone else has left the theatre, and he is shutting everything down, wrung out from nervous exhilaration. He turns around, and . . .

"Anyone ever tell you, Mister," says Mom, taking a long, lipstick-stained drag on her cigarette, "that you look just like an angel?"

Dissolve
to
Present

MOM STARED AT THE BACKYARD WALL LIKE IT WAS A DISTANT star. Behind me, Dad was waiting for an answer. I wiped my face quickly, smiled brightly at nothing, and then, still smiling, turned around.

"Hey, Dad. Of course I came. Why wouldn't I?"

I visited them almost every afternoon. If I couldn't make it, I'd find some cheeky street g'lark and slip them a benzie as payment to run a message to their house with my apologies and rescheduling plans.

"Well," Dad explained now with patient Dad-jokiness, "you know, it's fifteenth day, Ishtu."

Slowly—too slowly, he started crossing the sun-blasted yard.

"Yes," I prompted him, "and?"

"*And,*" he went on, "we save fifteenth days for only our most loathsome chores. I thought you loved us more than that, Ishtu. You might have visited us on third day, the Feast of Excess, to show your excessive love. Or on thirteenth day, when we all strive to do impossible things with cheer and vigor. But you. Our only child. Beloved of her uncles. Heir to all our fortunes. You visit us on *fifteenth* day."

He shook his head sadly as he approached. But I could see the twinkle in his eye, and I knew him; Dad liked showing off his thorough knowledge of his adopted city's traditions. And also to mock them.

Rolling my eyes, I stood up from the chair to hug him. "Nice to see you too, Dogman." Then, leaning close, I whispered in his ear, "Sorry I made her cry."

"Yes, she does that. It must be a very confusing state for her sometimes. But remember, Ish, she was talking too," Dad said, pleased. "I watched you both awhile, from the back door. She'll still talk to me, sometimes, especially just after I sing to her. It only works with hymns, though. Well, and drinking songs. A complicated woman, our Broszia."

He took my seat, then. He endeavored to make it seem a hospitable gesture, as if he were merely settling in for a comfortable visit, but I saw it for what it was. A collapse. The gray exhaustion in his face, the blue cast to his lips.

His face had thinned down these last few years, but his mustache was luxuriant as ever, worn like a set of ivory tusks, well-maintained and lavishly drooping. I loved his bald head, his big ears, those faded brown eyes that watered as they gazed at me.

I sat at his feet in the dusty lovegrass, hugging my knees. My knees creaked. I wasn't the child my parents made me feel like anymore. I wasn't any kind of child at all.

"Dad, what did the doc sa—"

He beat me to it. "Heart disease."

He wore that little fatalistic smile that bespoke a lifetime of regret and resignation—and a mordant sense of humor about it all. I squeezed my knees hard, crushing them together.

Keep it together . . .

"If you asked the bad uncles for help, they—"

Again, Dad interrupted, "—could probably smuggle me in some S'Alian drugs, yes. At huge cost—even with the family discount. Worse, at considerable danger to themselves. But benzies and bad uncles aren't really the issue, Ishtu."

His smile grew at his slant rhyme. A man in love with words, my dad.

"The issue," he went on, "is a life in its eld. One of high stress, high fatigue, indifferent diet, no exercise, and constant internal moral strife. No drug imported from Sanis Al can cure that. I'm done for, I'm afraid. I could drop any minute."

"That," I said flatly, "is unacceptable."

Alizar! Alizar could cure him. He'd just resurrected Betony, after all—rose her right up from the drowned dead, and . . .

In front of the other angels, Alizar whispered.

If his voice had been an actual sound, he would have sounded as weary as Dad. As it was, it manifested as an ache in my bones, a trembling in my extremities, the hard burn of lactic acid in my muscles—as if I had climbed too high on the serac and now—exhausted, untethered—had only to fall.

Betony was already dead, the Seventh Angel went on. *I broke no laws to resurrect her. But I cannot give your father a new heart—or your mother a new mind. I could not keep such a miracle secret; the others would sense it; they would know. We all agreed, when the war began and the pilgrims came, that we would no more heal the people of Gelethel of their ills—lest they prove too fruitful, live too long, and burst the bounds of the serac to our destruction.*

"We" agreed, he'd said. But I remembered the day when all the angels sang up that issue. Alizar the Eleven-Eyed—with me silently backing him at every moment—had strongly disaccorded with the choir. But he was sung down, forced to abide. I'd never salted the wound by praying he would help Mom, even when she lost the ability to read and write, even when she stopped walking and talking—even when she forgot my name. But now, Dad . . .

"It is what it is," Dad said mildly, after too long a pause, too long a struggle for breath. He shrugged deeper into his stooped shoulders, lost his smile. Shaking his head from side to side, he began rubbing rhythmically at his knees, which always pained him as mine were starting to.

"The Quicksilver Cinema was *my* dream, Ishtu, not yours. It makes me sick—sick!—that you're stuck with it. It's like living inside a corpse, playing the same fourteen-damned movies over and over again . . ."

I interrupted him, "It's fine. I like running the Quick. I love all those old movies."

"Ishi." Dad leaned forward. He didn't touch me, didn't place his palms to either side of my face, or grip my shoulder like Mom would have done when she was driving home a point. Dad rarely instigated touch.

"Ishi—what you love, what you know—it's only a shadow of what is actually out there. Not even a complete silhouette—a scrap of shadow. Cinema alone . . . out past the serac, think where it's gone. Talkies, Pankinetichrome, and now, home movies. The world is moving on. And I want . . . I want *you* to move, to move on . . ."

His breath was coming in short, shallow, rapid. I took his hands in mine.

"Dad, Dad. It's okay." I laid my cheek against his cold knuckles. "It's better, isn't it, that I don't know what I'm missing?"

He sighed deeply, and after a time grew calm again. Sitting up, I tried coaxing a smile out of him, but his whole forehead had collapsed into a ravine that could not be remade smooth. There were parts of the serac like the look on his face.

"I should have walked out," he said. "When you were a baby. I should have walked out with you then, right over the ramparts on the fifteenth day, as the pilgrims were coming in. A capital punishment for a pilgrim made citizen, but who knows, in the crowd, I might have made it. If I were caught, they'd never have harmed you. And if I'd succeeded—you'd have had a chance then, at least. I understood Gelethel enough by the time you were born. I knew what it would mean to stay and raise you in this place, knew that no child, *no child*, should ever be so trammeled by her geography . . . But then, the war—and all the roads from here to Sanis Al or Rok Moris so salted with mines it was a death sentence either way, and . . ."

And, he did not say, *there was your mother.*

We both knew that Onabroszia Q'Aleth would have killed Dad the moment he tried to smuggle me out. But the war was a convenient scapegoat, so I shrugged, and stretched, and said, "Oh, well. Yet another reason Koss Var can go right off and fuck itself, eh?"

He grunted.

Slapping my thigh with exaggerated finality, I struggled to my feet. "Well, you two! Enough of this maudlin old nostalgia talk. I'm a working woman—and I have a cinema to run."

"Yes. Yes, of course." Dad nodded, rubbed his knee one last, troubled time, and smiled at me—or tried to.

Leaning down so I could drop a kiss on his sun-mottled pate, I looked into his eyes and said, "We're showing a double-feature tonight: *Godmother Lizard* and *Life on the Sun*. Want to come? I'll spring for a chariot and send it off for you two when it's time."

"No, thank you, Ishtu," Dad replied, awfully polite. "I'm just a little tired tonight. I think Broszia and I will stay in. I still have some of that vegetable soup you made us from Alizar's bumper crop benison in the Bower."

"What," I asked, only half-pretending to be aghast. "The one from *last year*? Dad! That was good soup! You should eat it!"

He managed to send one of his patented twinkles my way. "Well, you know, Ishtu, I've been saving it up for a rainy day."

"This is *Bellisaar*," I reminded him. "Even the angels can't make it rain. The best they can do is raise wells and divert rivers."

"Good for me, then, that angelic vegetables never go off. Now," he said, clearly doubling down on my farewell and dismissing me in turn, "I told your Uncle Zulli to take a break while we had our visit. He's napping in the great room. Working tonight, so he needs rest. Will you wake him up before you leave, tell him I want to see him?"

"Sure thing, Dad."

I bent to kiss Mom, a double-tap on each cheek, Gelethel-style. "Bye, Saint Broszia," I said cheerfully. "Put in a good word for me with the Enemy Twins." I glanced at Dad. "See you both tomorrow?"

"How about the afternoon?" Dad placed his hand lightly over Mom's. "Broszia and I have been sleeping in till about ten or so. Sometimes it takes us a while to get going."

This, I knew, was code. Their nights, already horrific, were getting worse. Mom never slept for more than a few hours; she'd always been most active from eight in the evening to four in the morning, even when she was well.

"Of course. I'll bring lunch. *Not* soup." I grinned down at them both like a bad uncle, all audacious swagger and one-sided dimple, one hand cocked on my hip. "Maybe a nice big salad!"

Dad's eyes bulged in mock alarm.

"Oh, no, Ishtu. Not another salad! If you love me . . ."

"Come on, Dad. Have to keep you strong, don't I? Your only daughter, beloved child, heir to all your fortunes, et cetera, et cetera. And just think of all those lovely, lovely leafy greens. So cool. So fresh. So good for you!"

Dad muttered something about "rabbit food." But I, as if he were the angel Alizar and I the other thirteen, blithely overrode his protests.

"By the time I'm done quacking you, Domi LuPyn, you'll live another hundred years under these angelic skies, hale and hearty as a Holy Host."

"God forbid," Dad muttered under his breath.

That was plenty blasphemous, even for him. There hadn't been a god in Gelethel since the fifteen angels ate Her—oh, millennia ago.

"On that note, Dogman," I said, "I'm off. Sleep well!"

ZULLI'S
TAKE

I DASHED BACK INTO DAD AND MOM'S HOUSE SO QUICKLY THAT the dimness caught my eyes like a velvet hood. Swaying at the sudden blackness, I stopped, my dark mood plummeting to crush-depth, the tears I'd hidden from Dad returning.

Then, straightening my shoulders, I marched down the hall and into the great room, right up to that ratty old yellow sofa with the stains and spills of generations, and the stuffing and springs poking out of every cushion, and I shook the youngest of my uncles awake.

"Zulli! Uncle Zulli!"

His eyes popped open. "Wha—?"

"We need to get Dad and Mom out of Gelethel as soon as possible. It's urgent." I took him by both shoulders and shook him. "It's a matter of life and death."

The words came out of my mouth with such force that I almost didn't recognize my own voice. I meant what I said—every word. But I couldn't believe I'd actually said it. I was raised to obey: my mother first, then the angels, then my father and uncles, and then maybe my own conscience. The only secret I'd ever kept was the angel Alizar's, and that had made me quiet all my life, not confident.

Under my grip, Uncle Zulli's shoulders were relaxed as two cats. His expression became so serene, so implacable, that for a moment I thought he was Irazhul, my good uncle: warrior of the Holy Host, porous and shining with angels, ready to transmit a report of any misdeed committed within his hearing. Then he blew out his breath.

"Yeah," he said, sitting up and scratching behind his ear like a g'lark's gutter mutt. "Yeah, it's about time, isn't it? We been expectin' it for years, but the war, y'know?" He shrugged. "Disrupted all our big plans."

My knees and breath gave out. I squatted, inhaling deeply, and began to talk. "It has to happen soon, Zulli. Dad said, he said that, that he might . . . any minute." I cleared my throat. "Look, I can take them to Sanis Al myself. But you and the Razman and the others have to arrange things for me. I . . ." I hesitated. "I remember where to go, from that one time. But . . ."

Zulli's face betrayed nothing, so I continued, "I just don't know *when* I need to be there, or what to do once I get there. And once I get us . . . out . . . I don't know *anything*! We'll need a guide, a . . . what do you call them?" I snapped memory into my fingers. "A possum! And I know Mom used to trade goods for foreign currency, so I need to get my hands on that—except I don't know where she stashed it away."

I had a few ideas though, starting with the benison flake bin—which Dad, not being a baker, never touched. Uncle Zulli regarded me steadily, and then his neutral expression broke out into one of his rubber clown looks: black brows arched comically, eyes stretched wide, nostrils flared. He held up his hands to slow me down.

"Hey, Ishi, hey. Possum first. One thing at a time." He rubbed his chin sleepily, then tapped a finger against his jaw. "We'll put word out right away we want a rendezvous with Nea. Great lady. Trustworthy. Knows Bellisaar like the crust up her crack. Has a viperbike the size of, like, if a camel fucked a tank—even has a nice cozy sidecar. Should fit you all with room to spare."

"Nea," I repeated. The name was not familiar, but then, Mom had never let me near this side of the business. "How long have you known her?"

Zulli shrugged. "Known her since the start—from back when Broszia started tappin' the serac for weak spots. Nea was already there, tappin' right back. She's an ace possum—piggyback you all the way to Sanis Al, hook you up with her contacts there. Hates Gelethel, loves helpin' people leave it. We send out word we want her—you know, the way we have"—he waggled his eyebrows. Sometime things "fell" from the ramparts at certain spots when Zulli and the bad uncles were patrolling— "and soon enough, she shows up. She'll send us a time and a password, we pass it to you. In the meantime, Ish—"

The next moment, he looked so intent, so preternaturally serious, that I drew back, once more expecting my good uncle Irazhul to come shining through. He did not.

"—be on the beam," he finished. "You gotta be ready at a moment's notice to pick up and leave. That's the deal, or it's off."

"I'll be ready," I promised.

Zulli nodded, and then, throwing back his head, gave a mighty and insinuating yawn. Taking the hint, I stood up.

"Voice like an angel," I teased him.

Zulli stopped yawning long enough to award me that bad uncle grin of his that never failed to invoke its match in my face. "What d'you expect, you come prayin' to me for benisons?"

Reaching down, I scruffed the wooly brown curls of his head. "Thanks, Uncle Zulli. Sorry I came on so strong right off your nap. It's just—" I gestured toward the back of the house, the backyard.

Zulli nodded, his goofy, happy-go-lucky demeanor flickering off, then on, then off, then on again. By which I understood that he was as worried about my parents as I was.

"It's all killer-diller, lil dynamite. About danged time you up and blew this popsicle stand. If I weren't bound by circumstance," he gestured to his circumstance, his body, "I'd go haring all up and down the globe. Somewhere," he said dreamily, "*cold*."

"I'll send you a snow globe. But," I added, leaning over to kiss him, "you'll have to smuggle it over the serac yourself."

"Right." Zulli looked wry. "Anyway. They say S'Alian medtech is outta this world. If anyone can give Broszia and Jen their right and comfortable twilight, it's the docs in Sanis Al. As for you . . ." He rose from the couch and looked at me fondly. "Me, Jen, Razman, Wuki, Eril—all we ever wanted was you out and over the serac since about forever. Even before Broszia stopped knowin' your name. We just thought *you* didn't."

My chest cracked open on the inside. Only my skin stopped all the panic and hope from pouring out over the floor. I shook my head, over and over. "I—I wasn't ready."

Nor had the angel Alizar been ready, I thought. Nirwen hadn't yet returned. She hadn't yet sent him her sign—his second saint. How could I have left him all alone *then*, surrounded by enemy angels? But now he wouldn't be alone, what with Betony . . .

We will speak more of this anon, Ishtu, Alizar promised, his voice—for an angel's—very gentle.

"Well, you're more than ready now," Zulli was saying, though I hardly heard him for the singing in my bones. "I could tell right away. Never saw you look so much like Broszia than just now, stompin' in like one of 'em thunder monsters from days of yore. Loomin'. Makin' demands. Spittin' image. Terrifyin'."

His eyes a-flash with sudden tears, he set his forehead to mine and whispered, "You know we'd all walk through fire for her, right?"

And so you do, I thought. Every day. Every night.

"You may have to," I warned him. "You ever smuggle two seniors and a cinema-owner out of Gelethel before?"

He waved his hand. "Easy as seein' angels."

That was total Zulli. How every kid brother would have answered a dare.

THREE
VIGNETTES
I WISH I HAD
MADE
(WITH THE SUPER 8 CAMERA MY UNCLES GAVE ME)

VIGNETTE I

L AST YEAR IN ALIZAR'S DISTRICT. THE DAY THE MIRACLE HAPPENED. It was my birthday. In this instance, my birthday happened to fall on the seventh day of the fortnight. The seventh day was Alizar's feast day, Bloom, and the ridiculously abundant bumper crop he manifested in his district for all of Gelethel that day was in fact his birthday present to me. Our own secret celebration.

Instead of being zoned for residence, the angel Alizar's district, Bower, was a butterfly-shaped patch of public parkland consisting of six hundred forty acres. It was situated in the center of Gelethel. Citizens from all over the Angelic City could stroll Bower's rock paths, climb its hillocks, explore its mosseries. There were many kinds of gardens to enjoy: fragrance gardens and herb gardens, orchards and berry brambles, stretches of vegetable gardens, swaths of grassland. A person might promenade the esplanades in high fashion, or sit quietly beside the bog pavilion, or bathe naked in one of the terraced pools, or sweat contentedly in the house of succulents.

On the Feast of Bloom, every citizen of Gelethel was invited to harvest whichever of Alizar's benisons they needed from Bower— fresh fruits, herbs, honey, and vegetables; the rest of the fortnight, the trees and bushes and hives and grasses all quietly cycled through their season.

But last year, on our double birthday/feast day, Alizar outdid himself.

All day long, every hour on the hour, all six hundred forty acres of Bower flowered and fruited, fruited and flowered. The trees bent double with their bounty; the hills were carpeted with plump drupes. Vegetables grew so large, they had to be carted away on chariots. The air was fragrant with wintergreen, white sage, thyme, lavender, lemon balm, rosemary, basil, chamomile, yarrow, marjoram, gentian, sandalwood, hops. The hives overflowed.

Everyone I'd ever met in Gelethel—in the Quick, the Celestial Corridor, out and about in the other districts—seemed to be in Bower that day, wandering the Seventh Angel's dream: mouths sticky with sweet juice, hair yellow with pollen, eyes struck with a wonder I'd never yet seen in this city ruled by Invisible Wonders.

And the wind, smelling of wine and wildflowers.

And the light, supersaturated with kaleidoscope colors.

And the bumblebees, only just heavier than the breeze.

◆ ◆ ◆

VIGNETTE II

O UR HIKE THROUGH HELL, ME AND THE BAD UNCLES—SIX, seven years ago?

They'd descended en masse on the Quick, storming up the mezzanine to my rooftop apartment and rattling me awake at an unangelic hour. They all had a rare day off together, they informed me—and they wanted to show me something.

Dark outside yet, as we ventured onto the streets and hopped into Uncle Wuki's chariot.

Wuki and Eril both called out, "Steed!" at the same time, meaning that they both got to sit up front. This also meant that they were the ones operating the push-pedals, a chore I was glad to concede. Wuki took the wheel and handbrakes—since it was after all (as he was fond of pointing out) *his* chariot.

On the back bench, the Razman and I contented ourselves doing nothing. Zulli stood behind us on the tailboard, grasping the canopy poles and leaning far forward whenever the mood seized him, sticking his head between ours and making joyous whiplash sounds, crying, "Whoa, boy, whoa!" every time Wuki squeezed the handbrakes even a little.

I asked where we were going.

Uncle Raz glanced at me, smiled slightly (he only ever smiled slightly), and said, "Nirwen's district."

"We're going to *He-ell!*" Zulli whisper-sang behind us.

Like his brothers, he seemed to have no desire to rouse the OlDi betimes, but there was a nervy mischief in his voice that made him seem much noisier than he actually was. The Razman turned around and hissed him quiet.

Hell was Nirwen the Forsaker's district. Back when she was still Nirwen the Artificer, it had been called Lab. In diamond-shaped Gelethel, which was divided into fifteen equal allotments, Hell took up the southmost tip.

With no official angelic oversight and only sporadic patrolling by the Holy Host, it was an area let to run wild. All the old industrial parks and university satellites were still there, long since converted to unauthorized tenements where citizens new to Gelethel tended to squat till they got the lay of the land. But with no benisons incoming and a stigma attached to anyone who gave Hell as their forwarding address, few stayed long.

The roads changed the instant we rolled over the western border of Mews—Tanzanu's District—into Hell. Here, the salt-pan was cracked. The weeds ran rampant. But it was greener than I'd expected. Green as if the angel Alizar himself, missing his friend Nirwen, regularly wandered the streets, weeping seeds into the dirt from all eleven of his eyes. It was breathlessly, eerily quiet. Even the g'larks and others of Gelethel's roofless population preferred to rove elsewhere than Hell, camping each day in a different district to kipe benisons on the sly without having to trade for them. But here, the ditches and gutters and doorways were empty of sleeping bodies. Nothing rustled, nothing stirred.

Wuki and Eril pedaled us further and further in, heading south. The blue shadow of the serac loomed above us on both sides of the road, dovetailing into the southmost point of the city. As at the other cardinal points of Gelethel, I knew that there should be a stair there, at the bottom of Hell, leading up from the street to the ramparts atop the serac, where Tyr Hozriss, the southern watchtower, stood. This stair, like the others that led to the watchtowers of the north, west, and east, would be much wider and more ornate than the access ladders and lifts that ran up the serac at kilometer intervals all around the city. It would have carved railings following the vertical zig-zag of the shining white steps, both made from the same compressed salt-and-starch bricks that most of Gelethel was built from.

When we came to the place, Wuki parked the chariot in no very neat way, then turned around on the bench to face me.

"You've never been here," he told me.

"No," I agreed with him, puzzled. I hadn't been. My uncles knew that. These days, I was pretty much confined to Olthar's District where I lived and worked at the Quick, to the north side of Kir where my parents lived. I visited Bower when I could, and the Celestial Corridor when I couldn't help it. But that was pretty much it.

But Wuki didn't release me from his gaze. "You were never here *today*."

"Oh." Now I understood what he meant. "Yes, all right, uncle." At his expectant eyebrows, I elaborated, "I slept in today. Till noon. Never stirred."

"We never showed you this."

"Of course not."

Satisfied, all my uncles spilled out of the chariot, me in their wake, and led me to the steps.

Unlike the other cardinal staircases, the southern stair was gated off from the street. A ten-foot high cage braced the bottom of the steps, iron stakes driven into the ground in a wide semi-circle that ended flush with the serac itself. There was no way through unless we climbed the fence, and even in my early thirties I wasn't what you'd call athletic.

At my imploring look, the Razman smiled a little, drew a key out of his pocket, and put it to the lock.

"Captain's privileges?" I asked, eyebrow raised.

Smile vanishing, he warned, "Do not say 'captain' here, Ishtu," and pushed open the gate.

Zulli wriggled past us to bound up the steps. He was the youngest of my uncles, but still a good fifteen years older than I was, with the energy of a puppy. Eril followed, slightly hunched, as if a winter wind blew for him alone. It was coolest in Gelethel at this pre-dawn hour, and this close to the ice of the serac, probably just around freezing. But Eril's winter wind was not external.

Uncle Raz gestured that I go next. Wuki came to bear me company, offering me his arm, patting my hand reassuringly.

"Six hundred forty nine steps to the top, Ishi," he said. "You ready? Ready to burn some calories?"

I groaned. "Uncle Wuki, why do you torment me?"

"Because I love you."

Up and up and on and on we went. The uncles stopped, finally, just about midway up the staircase, and for the first few moments, I didn't even know why, nor even care, because I was bent over my knees, catching my breath.

When I straightened again, I was surprised, for we had not reached the top. And then I was surprised again, because I saw that we could not. We could go no further.

Above us, the wide staircase had been sheared off as if by some great sky hammer. Not only had the whole top half of the stair crumbled, but behind where it had been, exposed, the serac itself gaped open like a wound. The deep blue wall of ice that surrounded our city on all sides, two hundred meters high and fifty meters thick, showed here a dark fissure. Even in the brightening light, I couldn't see all the way to the bottom. Just a cool blue drop into darkness.

But I knew what was down there. I'd heard the rumors all my life.

Bodies. Countless, frozen bodies. Those who had displeased the angels. Those who had fallen afoul of the Holy Host. Gelethel's criminals and apostates. The ones the angels could not bring to penance in the saltcellars. The irredeemable.

Their icy grave was at the bottom of a breach that extended almost all the way to the top of the serac. A few meters short of the ramparts, it thinned to a hairline crack, thence to a line like spider silk, thence to smooth blue ice once again. The salt-brick walkways built atop the wall ran uninterrupted into the arched doors of Tyr Hozriss, the southern watchtower.

Staring down into that lapis-dark drop, I thought:

Does that breach run all the way through? Is that a doorway, Alizar? Is that *our* door?

But the Seventh Angel didn't answer then. Neither did any of my uncles, who had brought me here to show me just this. So I repeated the question aloud.

"Does the breach run all the way through?"

Alone of my bad uncles, Eril turned to stare directly into my eyes. "What breach, Ishtu?"

I stared back, silent, until one by one, without another word, each of my uncles turned and headed back down the stairs.

The Razman was last. As he passed me, he took my hand and pressed it warmly, comfortingly. He did not meet my eyes. I stood still, waiting until all my uncles were far, far ahead of me.

And then, I opened my hand.

In it, the key to the gate.

◆ ◆ ◆

VIGNETTE III

O NABROSZIA, BAKING CAKE.
It was not long after our chariot ride to Hell. Maybe a year? Anyway, more and more pilgrims were flooding into Cherubtown as the war raged on in the Bellisaar Theatre. Badness came in waves, the periods of peace never lasting more than half a decade, and never enough to completely rebuild. On petition days in the Celestial Corridor, human sacrifices had already started.

At first the war had disrupted the smuggling side of Mom's business, but recently it had picked up again. Couldn't keep Onabroszia Q'Aleth down for long. Temporary disruption was one thing, but Mom maintained that war was good for business.

Cherubtown consisted of two types: pilgrims and cherubs. The former were desperate to get into Gelethel. The latter were just desperate for basic necessities that only Gelethel could provide: food, water, medicine, blankets, clothes. For those, they'd trade everything from family heirlooms to junk scavenged from the roadside. Whatever it was, it was sure to find its market on our side of the serac. There were many collectors in Gelethel who'd pay top benzie for trash simply because it was not of Gelethel.

Legally, the Angelic City forbade commerce with any individual, corporate body, or government outside the serac. After all, whatever the citizens of Gelethel needed, the angels would provide, magnanimous in their benisons! *Legally*, Gelethel traded only in benzies, which no pilgrim could offer from the outside.

In other words, if it weren't for the universal human desire for the exotic, illicit, and forbidden, the cherubs would've been shit out of luck. But humans were pretty much the same on both sides of the serac, and an infrastructure promoting the amicable flow of contraband—thanks to Onabroszia Q'Aleth—was already in place. In trading smuggled goods with cherubs, Mom saw yet another chance to spite the angels, and took it. Gleefully.

Every fifth day—the Feast of Whispers, sacred to the angel Murra—was trash day. Each dawn of Whispers, Q'Aleth Hauling Industries would send out their fleet of push-pedal chariots—the ones that required four pedalers, with the big beds in the back—into the districts to collect Gelethel's scraps and castoffs. The carts would then haul their loads over to an area of Nursery, Hirrahune's district, where a gracious land grant from the Ninth Angel had allowed Mom to build a series of elevator platforms along the southwestern wall of the serac. QHI workers went in shifts, loading trash onto the platforms, hoisting it up to the ramparts, and dumping it off the side— into Cherubtown.

We hadn't chosen to dump our trash into Cherubtown. Cherubtown had grown up around our dumpsite, because cherubs and pilgrims were constantly scavenging the middens for anything useful to wear or eat or make things out of. But benisons from Gelethel quickly deliquesced outside the serac—and there was never enough to begin with.

Which brings us to the cake.

Mom's whole thing with the benison cake wasn't her idea originally. It was Zulli's husband's.

One day when we were all over at Mom and Dad's for dinner, Mom had sidled up next to Zulli's beloved, his night sky, the cinnamon in his apple tea, and asked him idly, "Madriq, why are you throwing out a ton and a half of perfectly good bread every fortnight?"

When Mom got all idle and casual like that, it behooved the interrogatee to answer promptly and honestly. Madriq was no fool.

"I'm, um . . . Well, I was trying to feed the cherubs."

"Angelic benisons are for Gelthic citizens," Mom said piously. "Pilgrims and cherubs are not your concern."

He shrugged, looked sideways. "Zulli said he saw a bunch of kids down there, last time he patrolled the ramparts. No parents. No tents. Hardly a rag to their backs. Starving. So." He shrugged again, and while he didn't say, "Angels be damned," there was a tightness in his face that Mom could read like a scroll.

Madriq was a baker. As far as he was concerned, anyone who was hungry had a right to be fed, preferably by him. The fact that he was happiest stuffing pastries down Uncle Zulli's bottomless gullet was a cornerstone of their marriage.

"Carry on then," Mom said. "Q'Aleth Hauling Industries is happy to collect whatever waste you deem fit for the middens, regardless of content. Ishtu, my only begotten child," and her eyes glinted at me, "why don't you drop by tomorrow and I'll teach you how to make benison cake. My mother's special recipe. I saved it all these years to teach you."

Now, she knew, and I knew, and all the uncles knew, that Zaripha Q'Aleth had never baked a day in her life. But Mom was born with an ineffable talent to make herself and everyone else around her believe her every lie, and if she wanted to teach me how to bake our ancestral benison cake from a recipe that didn't yet exist, who was I, merely her daughter, to argue with her?

Turned out, Mom's "benison cakes" were so dense with lard from Rathanana's district, Abattoir, they were practically meat. She stuffed them with every conceivable kind of candied citrus, dried fruit or berry in Bower, and then dropped a coin in the middle—Mom was something of a numismatic, and enjoyed collecting currencies from outside the serac she'd never be able to spend—before slathering the top with honey and shaved almonds, then dumping them into the trash.

As for me, Mom's minion, I added only one thing: Alizar's blessing.

I prayed to the Seventh Angel that the cakes intended for the pilgrims and cherubs outside the serac would last longer than the other trash we dumped haphazardly into Cherubtown. I prayed that they would courier his blessing of health and healing rapidly and directly into their bodies.

Alizar was more than willing to try. He poured everything he had into the blessing. I felt it when the cupola-shaped cakes swelled with his intent. I heard the dough humming as it cooked, and the slight singing hiss as the cakes cooled. Even the sacks we loaded them into, which were to be hauled out by the QHI chariots, seemed plumper, shinier, and more sentient than sacks should be.

Alizar thrummed excitedly as the chariots drove away. He and I knew that a single bite of these benison cakes would bestow upon its gobbler a blast of necessary vitamins, minerals, and phosphates. They would cure scurvy, replenish deficiencies, boost the immune system, ease dehydration, whisk away nightmares, impart new vigor, and enhance reflexes with every bite. They were our small, beautiful rebellion, and one, moreover, that I had shared with my mother.

But alas.

It was my good uncle, Host Irazhul Q'Aleth, who commanded the patrol atop the ramparts on that Whispers morning. He happened to be making his inspections near the QHI dump-lifts when the sacks with Madriq's bread and Mom's cakes went over. He stood, looking down into Cherubtown, and watched the pilgrims and cherubs stampede toward the food.

Later, stopping by Mom's after dinner, Host Irazhul reported to us that at least two children and an elderly person had been trampled to death in that desperate scramble. He stood at the head of the table, behind Mom's chair, his hands resting lightly on the carved back, and stared expressionlessly down at all of us. Mom alone could not see his face; she sat staring straight ahead. And so she did not see the wolf teeth and hawks' beaks studding the flesh of his face, submerging and surfacing in moving patterns, indicating the presence of at least two angels.

"Furthermore," Host Irazhul went on, "there is only one baker in the Angelic City who produces loaves of such size and splendor that even I, from the heights of the rampart, could espy them and name with certainty their provenance. Madriq Urra," he said to his husband, "I am arresting you in the name of the fourteen. You are sentenced to an indefinite period of penance in the saltcellars, and when your penance has been deemed enough by the angels Tanzanu and Rathanana, we shall release you again into your family's custody."

"Zulli," Madriq whispered.

But Zulli wasn't ascendent that night. Nor would he be for all those long months that Madriq was imprisoned in the saltcellars, put to the question by the angels who dwelled in Host Irazhul. And even when Madriq finally walked free, Zulli wouldn't be at home in his own skin, or even his own home, for far longer than that. It was a long road of raging and baking, and walking, and talking, and a million small gestures of atonement and tenderness, before forgiveness between them became less a daily practice than a stunning reality.

All of that came later.

From that night on, however, a detachment of the Host watched the dump-lifts every Feast of Whispers, in case another deluded Gelthic sympathizer tried to pull a trick like that again. No one did, so far as I knew.

What I do know is that after her good brother Irazhul took Madriq away, Mom broke every dish in the house. And then she sat right back down at the head of the table, and seized snarled fistfuls of her own hair, and sawed them off one by one with the bread knife at the table. Dad and I watched her and dared say nothing, lest Onabroszia Q'Aleth turn the knife on us.

It wasn't long after that that Mom's memory started to degrade. It happened rapidly. A year hadn't passed before she'd forgotten almost everything she'd ever known: her desire for vengeance, her business concerns, her baking recipes, her daughter's face, her own name.

All Onabroszia Q'Aleth could remember, and that only sporadically, were the angels. And how much—how very much—she loved them.

◆ ◆ ◆

FADE TO BLACK.

AERIAL:
QUICKSILVER
CINEMA

D AD'S MOVIE PALACE, FORMERLY THE GELTHIC OPERA HALL, was three curvy tiers of compressed halite. A section of the first tier was topped with a glass dome—the roof of the lobby. The third and smallest tier, which sat well above the actual theatre, was my apartment, with balcony and roof garden attached.

Opera had been around about a century before I was born, but it had never enjoyed more than a lukewarm reception in Gelethel. This was probably the reason the angels had conferred the building upon Dad. We Gelthic citizens had a sort of national aversion to singing. Maybe we thought that music always had to sound like angels, and, over the years, our operas began to reflect this. By the time Dad took over the GOH, operas had become three-hour shrieking events, full of discordant high-pitched whistles playing no melody whatever, huge glass objects shattering from great heights, flash explosions, stink bombs, and stroboscopes. Increasingly ambitious composers did their best to induce migraines in their audience, going their length to replicate the "music" of angelic voices raised in chorus.

Anyway, Gelethel decided it liked movies better.

On the inside, Quicksilver Cinema was what you might call shabby-deluxe. The lobby was lined with glass cases, only half of them sporting movie posters behind the panes. Dad had brought everything he had to Gelethel, but it wasn't much. Twenty-three feature-length films, four newsreels, twelve cartoons, sixteen shorts, and his documentary—which he'd never shown to anyone except our family in private viewings. He'd owned just seven movie posters in all, and three of them weren't even for movies he'd brought with him. Over the years, he'd pasted drawings that the children of Gelethel (myself included) presented him based on movies he'd shown. The other vitrines he sometimes used as gallery space, to showcase any Gelthic artists who expressed interest.

But when Mom got sick, Dad didn't have any more time or attention to sponsor artists. That's when he sold me the Quick.

Under my apathetic watch, the vitrines were getting dusty. So were the candy jars. And the chandeliers. I never vacuumed the deep red carpet. I often forgot to scoop out the old, stale popcorn from the bottom of the bins before Olthar topped it up with fluffy new stuff on his next feast day.

I did still sweep the actual theatre after shows, and occasionally mopped up sticky spots, but my heart wasn't in it. I was afraid of washing the painted silk curtains that framed the big screen; they'd probably disintegrate into moths and despair. Or maybe I would.

Every time I passed under the grand marquee and through the murky double doors, it felt like cannonballing myself into quicksand. My lungs filled with suffocating mud. Darkness closed in on my skin, my eyes, my ears, deadening and pressurized. Even my clothes hung heavy and soggy on me in those moments, as if I wore the angel Rathanana's mantle of flayed flesh, no matter if I'd just come in from the hot dry afternoon air.

But we do what we have to do, we Gelthic citizens. No one could accuse us of shirking our duties. As we abided within the serac, so we obeyed angelic law, and angelic law stated that nobody and nothing must stop me from opening the Quick—for the glory of the Invisible Wonders who ruled Gelethel—tonight and *every* night.

Not even the body on my threshold.

◆　◆　◆

THE BOY ALIZAR LUZARIUS STIRRED. AND MOANED.

Not dead, then.

"Hey," I said. "Hey, you. Kid. Get up."

Not astonishingly, Alizar Luzarius stayed where he was.

"What happened to him?" I asked the angel Alizar.

We proclaimed his official status "ghost" to the Heraldic Voice an hour ago. The Host released him from the saltcellars and left him for dead. He is neither citizen nor pilgrim. He has no rights in Gelethel. If he lives till next fifteenth day, he will be allowed to cross the bridge back into Cherubtown.

What he didn't say, what I already knew, was that most ghosts died in the gutter, left to desiccate for as long as the fortnight lasted, and then were taken out with the rest of the trash at the Feast of Whispers.

"But Alizar," I asked with trepidation, "why is a ghost—and a saint-killer—on *my* doorstep?"

The Celestial Cenoby was three districts over. The boy didn't look capable of dragging himself half that distance. Besides, how would he even know to come to the Quick—the one place he wasn't likely to be kicked into the curb, no questions asked? Even without a healthy Gelthic paranoia regarding the prevalence of angelic intervention in our daily lives (the Seventh Angel's in mine, in particular), this was too big a coincidence.

"Alizar! Did you bring him here?"

When at first he didn't answer, I turned on my heel as if to leave the boy where he lay. But the Seventh Angel stopped me with one of his patented see-sawing "Awwww, come on" sort of non-sounds, the angelic equivalent of twiddling his thumbs and toeing the dirt—which felt a bit like plate tectonics along one's cranial sutures.

You don't really want to leave him like this? Alizar asked gently/earthquake-ily. *Not your sister-saint's own brother?*

"The saint you had to *resurrect*," I reminded him. "And speaking of which, I thought you'd still be recuperating your strength, not . . . meddling."

Actually, I feel fine! Alizar said brightly. *I just needed a nap.*

I bent my thoughts into a vulgar gesture and then, dismissing all eleven of his eyes to the back of my mind, took a step closer to the boy on the ground. I lowered my voice still more.

"Alizar?" I whispered. "Alizar Luzarius?" Then, after a moment, "Ghost?"

No answer. Kid was cooked. Literally cooked, if he'd just dragged himself all the way here under the Bellisaar sun on his hands and knees. I gingerly stepped over him, unlocked the Quick's doors, jogged over to the soda fountain, and filled a dusty pint glass with seltzer. After a moment, I scooped a few shovelfuls of nine-day-old popcorn into a bag, and brought both water and popcorn outside again. It wasn't Mom's benison cake—but then, what was?

I paused, put my hand over the popcorn, and said a prayer to the Seventh Angel. Mom's cake, after all, had only been the vehicle. And in Gelethel, anything could be a vehicle.

Outside, I stood and stared down at the boy, who still hadn't moved. He was like a cricket some kid had poured diatomite over. He was a murderer. A fanatic for the angels. Worse, a teenager. And now his sister was a saint of the Seventh Angel, which in Gelethel made her more *my* sister than his. And the Seventh Angel had given him into my care.

For what? For what?!?

No answer from the other Alizar, so I left the boy lying in front of my door. I also left the benzied-up popcorn and soda water. I had a business to run. I was showing a double feature in an hour and a half, and my projectors weren't going to load themselves.

◆ ◆ ◆

An hour later, having done the least I could get away with in order to open the Quick tonight, I dragged myself back into the lobby and unlocked the doors for the evening show.

The boy was conscious again. Not only conscious, mobile. Vigorously. He was, in fact, polishing my glass doors with his sleeve, which he'd wet with the water left in his cup. My doors needed it. But maybe not like that.

He flinched when he saw me, his tar-colored eyes very wide. I nodded at him, handed him another pint of water, and a push broom from a closet just off the front doors.

"Drink that. Sweep that." I pointed to the vestibule. "And then I'll give you a hot dog for dinner."

He opened his mouth—probably to announce he was a breatharian, or solar scrupulist, or some other ascetic something—then shut it again, returned my curt nod, and took the broom.

I went back inside.

A few dozen patrons trickled in over the next twenty minutes. Everybody in Gelethel knew that the movies changed every fifteenth day, so I hadn't bothered to advertise my double feature. Everyone had already seen both movies anyway. I'd only just changed the lettering (and a few of the lightbulbs) on the Quick's marquee this morning before petitions began. Till then, it was still advertising *Winds of Vicissitude*, which had been last fortnight's feature. We'd managed to fill half the house for that one—on the first day, at least. Our theatre sat eleven hundred at capacity. People still got excited about our sav-nav films, even after the whatever-hundredth time they played.

Maybe because we lived in a desert and movies about water worlds were alien and fascinating? Or maybe it's just great filmmaking. I mean, what's *not* to like about sentient psi-ships piloting themselves through panthalassic planets? Besides, it was refreshing to root for a non-human protagonist.

When it was clear that no one else would be coming, I called the kid inside.

He crept into the lobby as if afraid his scab-cracked feet would disintegrate onto the carpet. But the moment the Quick's erstwhile splendor frayed his attention fourteen ways, he forgot all about his feet, and turned around and around, staring at everything with hungry eyes, ending by looking up at the domed ceiling, mouth agape. His arms hung at his sides, only his fingers pointing straight out. His eyes were lit by the thousand crystal pendants dangling from the chandelier.

"Is that," he gasped, "the angels?"

When I didn't answer, he dropped his head, smiled at me like a saint, and said shyly, "I always thought that was what the angels would look like. Beautiful. Like starlight and sunlight and snow. Just like that."

I shook my head, but he was no longer looking at me. The crystals had caught his eye again, and then the brass fixtures, the red carpet, the vitrines, the curving staircase to the mezzanine.

Instead of following him around the lobby like the owner of a naughty puppy, I walked behind the concessions counter and cleared my throat.

"Come here." I used my Onabroszia Voice. The boy snapped to as if I were the High Commander of the Empyrean Academy. "Hold out your hands. Here. Take these."

He obeyed, and I passed him a stack consisting of Dad's old uniform—a set of maroon livery with gold piping, tunic and trousers—a black and gold striped apron, and a black and gold cloth cap.

"Bathroom's that way," I said. "Wash up, put those on. They won't fit, but they're better than what you're wearing. Then come back here." I pointed to the precise spot where I was standing.

"Price directory is by the till—a list of things we accept as barter for concessions. No haggling. I'll start the first film at seven.

You watch that clock." I indicated the handsome wind-up on the wall. "Every twelve minutes or so, I'll run a short promo while I change out the movie reels.

"Sometimes people will come to you for concessions. Barter away. Benzie slips only—they're kind of like our currency. Make sure they're notarized; it'll be an embossed sigil of a hawk's head for the angel Tanzanu. If we accepted straight trade, we'd be up to our hips in livestock and old boots. Anyway, tonight, we'll do a cartoon between features but skip the serial short. Before we run the cartoon, we'll have a longer intermission—about fifteen minutes. I'll come out and help during that one, but not during the promos. Once you've taken care of the line, wait a bit, then come on into the theatre—if you want."

I looked at him doubtfully. "You can stand at the back and watch the movies. Or . . . sit if there's a seat open."

There would be, I knew, and also that he might very well collapse if I kept him on his feet.

"But, mind you, leave a seat open between you and any paying customer. Oh, and," I added, "if I catch you with your hand in the till, you're done here. Apparently the angels have declared your status ghost, so I can't pay you with benzie slips even if I wanted you. So. Anything you need, you come to me and we'll work it out. I'll see you don't starve, and have a place to sleep, and fulfill any reasonable request until we get the rest sorted."

I glared at him, because with every word, every order, the boy stood taller and brighter, looked more alive and eager and desperately attentive. Alizar's benison in Olthar's popcorn was still increasing in its effect. Or maybe it was hope. Both.

But I remembered, every second we stood there, that he had walloped his sister on the back of the skull and brought her over the serac to die. And she was *my* sister. Beloved of Nirwen. Beloved of Alizar. Our sign from beyond. The only reason I'd be able to rescue my dying parents and take them to safety somewhere away from here.

"Any questions, ghost?"

"You can call me Alizar," said the boy breathlessly. He was not smiling. His face was painful with gratitude.

"No," I said. "I really can't."

If crestfallen could have an identical twin, that twin's name would be Alizar Luzarius.

"No one in Gelethel calls their spawn after any of the fourteen," I heard myself explaining, and the comforting tone in my voice I neither recognized nor approved of. "It's bad luck. The angels might get jealous."

"Oh," said the unlucky bastard who'd been named after an angel. He shifted. He scratched behind his dirty ear. He yearned for something else, something beautiful, to look at in his shame. His gaze glazed over with chandelier crystals again, then focused on me, still glittering.

"What about Ali?" he asked. "Can you call me Ali? My sis—. . . I mean . . . some people call me Ali."

"Ali will do." I grasped him by the shoulder and spun him toward the bathroom. "If I can remember it. Now, go, ghost. I don't have all night."

When he was gone, I glanced up at the chandelier. The crystals were trembling slightly, stirred to rainbows by some invisible breeze. Some of the pendants opened and closed like shining white eyes. A few loosed a sharp, whistling chime, like wine glasses at a wedding toast.

"You and I," I told the angel Alizar, "are going to have a little chat. Later."

The chandelier sang back.

I was to meet my angel on the roof at midnight.

THE DOUBLE FEATURE WENT OVER PRETTY WELL. THERE WAS even a smattering of applause at the end.

The first film I showed was *Godmother Lizard*. It's the epic tale of a lowly clerk working for the Koss Var occupation in the desert nation of Rok Moris. She finally twigs the fact she's grafting for the bad guys, and risks everything to join the oppressed Bird People in rebellion against Koss Var's Empire of the Open Palm. She has some help from a little desert god named Ajdenia, the "Godmother Lizard" of the title.

The second film was *Life on the Sun*. Chronologically, it's an immediate sequel, but cinematically *Sun* was made ten years later by an entirely different writer/director team. Both films fall under the same broad histo-mythical war movie category. *Life on the Sun* is a highly fictionalized account of how the rebel Kantu and her Bird People won the Old War. It begins where *Godmother Lizard* ends: with the first uprising in Rok Moris against Koss Var. The grand finale is the big battle wherein Rok Moris—with the help of its neighboring desert nation Sanis Al—finally drives the occupying forces of Koss Var out of its city-state and into the Bellisaar Waste.

Sun was made almost forty years ago. It had been released to coincide with the actual, non-mythical nation of Rok Moris celebrating its bicentennial: two hundred years of liberty from the Empire of the Open Palm. Halfway through that month-long celebration, fighter jets from the Koss Var Air Force flew south and bombed the holy temple of Ajdenia in Rok Moris to smithereens. Thus, the New War began. And had been going ever since.

In very recent years, a sort of smothered détente presided here in the Bellisaar Theatre. At the beginning of the New War, Koss Var had had global ambitions. Too many of them. Demoralizing and conquering the nations south of the Bellisaar Waste was merely its opening gambit. But eventually, Koss Var stretched itself too thin. Now the Empire of the Open Palm was back to crouching resentfully in the north, licking its wounds. I hoped it got sepsis from its own filthy tongue.

A long-running fantasy of mine, as I'm endlessly cranking my projector, is about the tiny studio apartment in Rok Moris where I'll someday live when I finally leave Gelethel. I'll make bookshelves out of planks and cement blocks. I'll keep my clothes in baskets and sleep in my closet, cozy as a nest. I'll have a galley kitchen, a small refrigerator barely big enough for my daily needs. I'll paint the walls myself, all different colors.

I've always wanted to move to Rok Moris. Dad thinks I'm crackers; he's all about Sanis Al. It's the largest nation south of the Bellisaar Waste. According to Dad, "the Red Crescent" is graceful in its plans, generous in its services, technologically and medically advanced, boasts incredible universities, and is just generally bursting all over with the arts. I think he's always regretted choosing Gelethel instead of heading further west.

But Rok Moris—smaller, scrappier, bombed-out, with her taped knuckles and broken nose and chipped teeth—is mine. She's *feisty*, you know?

And soon, very soon, maybe I'll get a chance to see her. If the bad uncles can get this possum Nea word in time. If Nea can smuggle me and my parents out of Gelethel. If we can make it to Sanis Al alive—despite roads salted with mines, and Zilch roaming abroad, and all of us so naive about the world outside. If I can settle Dad and Mom somewhere, see them comfortable. If I can scrape up the wherewithal to do some traveling on my own. Then, maybe, just maybe, my daydream of that hole-in-the-wall studio apartment in scrappy Rok Moris might one day come true.

That's a lot of "ifs."

◆ ◆ ◆

D AD SAID THAT, OUTSIDE GELETHEL, IN THE DAYS BEFORE talkies, movie palaces would hire full orchestras to play what he called "soundtracks." But like I might have mentioned, if you want to insult a Gelthic citizen, just call them a musician.

Music was angelic in nature. It meant possession, invasion, lack of consent. Silence was autonomy. We didn't mind title cards—they gave us structure: text, dialogue—because they were quiet, and because we could fill the flickering silences between them with our own stories.

Or we could, after the twentieth viewing, use that time of storied darkness to eat some concessions and take a very comfortable nap in the company of our friends.

That night, after the last of the moviegoers sauntered out, sleepy and replete from three hours of snacks and silver shadows, I met the kid—the ghost—Ali—in the lobby.

"That," he breathed, "that was, that was just . . ." He spread his trembling hands, held the silence of the movies between them.

"First film?" I remembered mine too. One of my earliest memories, from before I had speech.

"Well, no, I . . ." Ali frowned. "But it made me remember something. From maybe, when I was little? My sis—someone took me to see that one—the second movie you played—a long time ago. It was cold. The building had air conditioning, I think. Very dark, black, I couldn't see anything. And there was this monster, this huge bird, blotting out the sky."

He flung out his arms, demonstrating. The gawkiest young roc the Bellisaar desert had ever seen. "And she had a white jewel in her forehead that flashed with lighting, and horns, and when she screamed, there was thunder. And everywhere she flew, rain, rain beneath her wings. And people were dancing in the streets, because it had been so dry for so long. They played big drums to celebrate, but . . . it sounded too much like, like the explosions back home, and I began to cry and, and . . . and then someone took me outside again, and yelled at me for being a baby."

He was describing the final scene from *Life on the Sun*—but as a distant memory, not as the movie he'd just finished watching. I wondered if he'd fallen asleep and dreamed the memory as the reels played out.

"It does sound frightening," I said carefully, uncomfortably aware of how loud my voice had been earlier when I was issuing commands at him. It wasn't now.

Ali paused, looked down at his feet. Dad's were clown shoes on him. "Maybe she bought me an ice-cream later, though, to say sorry."

"That was . . . nice . . . of her."

To my horror, the boy began to cry. Just folded up, completely and suddenly, and sobbed.

"Hey," I said. "Ghost. Ali. Stop. Stop it." I knelt beside him, put my hand on top of his head, a benison. "She's in a better place now. Your sister. You know that, right?"

It wasn't a lie. Just because I'd never wanted the silken sheets and salt-walled libraries of the Celestial Cenoby didn't mean it wasn't a million times better than Cherubtown. Or ten million times better than floating face-up in the Sacrificing Pool. But the kid was not to be comforted. A guilty conscience was like having a skull full of broken glass.

"Stay here," I muttered, and left him to sob himself out.

I had to find this boy a bed, and I didn't want him anywhere near my apartment tonight, where he might overhear me in conversation with my angel. The only place I could think of was the cry room. These days, I kept it locked, using it for storage and the Quick's lost and found. Back when Dad ran things, it had been fully equipped with everything a harassed parent needed when their kid had a meltdown in the middle of a movie. For my part, I thought parents could just quiet their babies in the lobby if they had to, or go to Nirwen's Hell, or home, or stay and make the other patrons suffer. I didn't care.

Betony might've appreciated a cry room though, back in the days she was taking young Ali to the movies. She must have wanted a place to escape, just for a moment, the terrible war outside. I wondered what it had cost her, those precious ninety minutes in the air-conditioned dark. I wondered what it had cost her to leave again, with an armful of screaming toddler in need of soothing and ice cream.

Inside the cry room was a padded bench. Not only that, but the lost and found box yielded a light jacket, a baby blanket still smelling softly of spoiled milk, and a broken parasol. The last I cast aside, then rolled up the jacket for a pillow, and laid the blanket on the bench.

There. The kennel was ready. Now to herd the puppy into it.

Ali didn't fight me; he was exhausted—despite the Seventh Angel's amped-up popcorn. I left a steel milkshake blender cup full of water, and a well-wrapped hot dog (fully blessed) nearby, in case Ali woke up hungry or thirsty in the night. I was no kind of saint for the Celestial Cenoby, but I was Alizar's own—and he fed all of Gelethel from his Bower and allowed no barter for it. And Madriq, my uncle's husband, had tried to do the same for the pilgrims and cherubs outside the serac. I could do no less for this ghost.

Then I was ready to go up to my roof garden and meet my angel.

But it was not Alizar the Eleven-Eyed awaiting me there.

It was Betony.

JUMP-CUT
TO THE
SAINT

THE SEVENTH SAINT HELD MY PENKNIFE LOOSELY IN HER HAND—
for all the world as if her being discovered here by the Holy
Host wouldn't get me buried up to my neck in salt, and her confined to the Celestial Cenoby. The other angels, already suspicious
of Alizar, would question me closely as to my involvement with his
saint. And his saint? She would be cloistered again, this time more
thoroughly: bricked into her room, fed through a slot, and if they let
her out at all, it would be on the tightest of leashes, under full guard.

But Betony looked rather cool about it all, perched on the edge
of one of my lounge chairs, waiting. Stripped of her outer robe, she
was swaddled in a quilted silk vest the color of moonlight, its short
slashed sleeves tied off above the elbows with silver cord, a white silk
shirt billowing beneath that, with equally billowing trousers lashed
to her legs below the knee. The braided platinum crown still haloed
her brow, though her hair had been cut and styled since this morning. I could see all the old piercings in her ears, now ringed in silver
hoops or filled in with jeweled studs. She was trimmed, plucked,
coiffed, made up, salt-scrubbed-clean—like all saints, whom the laity
only ever saw at a distance when they were paraded through Gelethel
on extremely special occasions.

I stopped at the doorway, eyeing the penknife. "Returning my
property?"

Betony slithered off my lounge chair and stood to face me. Losing some of her cool, she flipped my knife nervously in her hand.
Nervously but, I noted, expertly.

"Not yet." Her voice was rougher and deeper than I remembered
it. Perhaps a result of being drowned then resurrected. "Where is
Alizar?"

"The angel?"

She snorted. "No, the treacherous little terg. Only got two eyes.
Which I'm gonna carve out."

"Oh, you mean Ali," I said. "My new employee."

Betony looked at me with swift appraisal, surprise only sharpen-
ing her. "Yeah? You hire mugs on the regular this side of the ice?"

"I wouldn't say regular. Ali's a . . . mug . . . who merits special treatment. Brother of a saint and all." I pointed behind me. "He's downstairs.
Probably still sniveling—if he didn't already cry himself to sleep."

Her gaze drifted to the distance beyond my shoulder, as if trying to pierce dark rooms, hallways, stairways, and several floors to see if her brother was weeping or soundly sleeping.

"Never stays down long," she murmured.

"Nightmares?"

Betony shook her head: not in denial, just returning to the room and the present. "Wets himself to this day. Used to call him Geyser."

"So much for my cry room," I replied. "But it's probably seen worse. Anyhow, I can show him where the cleaning supplies are in the morning."

She stepped forward, still gripping my knife. "He don't have till morning. Gonna eat his terg heart tonight. Swear to the god Nirwen, he'll wish those Zilch got him that time."

I was startled by her blasphemy, and recalled how her half-brother had accused her of following the false god of Cherubtown. But Nirwen was an *angel*, last I'd checked, not a god. Time enough to question Betony later though, I hoped. For now, I stepped through the doorway and to one side of it, gesturing for her to enter the building.

"These stairs lead down from the roof to the balcony just off my bedroom. Go through the apartment to the kitchen, where the door takes you to more stairs. Those'll get you to the mezzanine, whence you'll head down to the first floor lobby. Your brother's in a little room between two of the bathrooms. Door isn't locked."

Betony, glaring suspiciously, demanded, "Why you helpin' me?"

I grinned at her like a horned viper at a lizard hatching, shoving my hands into the pockets of my coveralls.

"I am a citizen of Gelethel. We're very helpful. Or, at least," I added, "complicit."

She still didn't move.

"Go on," I urged her. "The angel Alizar gave you your life and my knife. He must've shown you how to sneak out of the Seventh Anchorhold, shepherded you all the way to the Quick. It can be no coincidence that he also led young Alizar Luzarius here earlier today. Practically gift-wrapped him for you, didn't he? How typical of angelic cruelty, to give the boy food and drink, a place to sleep, a promise of honest work, and then deliver upon him the wrath of a vengeful saint in the darkest hour of night. How utterly righteous it would be, to murder the boy who martyred you. Tomorrow, you can write an account of tonight's adventures, make it part of Gelthic canon; you'll be hailed as a hero. Go on. Do what you will. No one's stopping you. No one can, *Saint* Betony."

The tip of my penknife gleamed, and so (to my relief) did Betony's grin. "Big liar, ain't you?"

I relaxed as she went on in her voice like sharkskin, "Could be I might believe all that dungball 'bout any other angel. But Alizar Eleven-Eyes is a little sugarbug. Wouldn't murder a kid—even a murderin' kid—even if you promised him big worship, blood-out, bone-in. And even if *he* would, gethel"—she pointed my penknife at me—"I don't think *you'd* let him."

I didn't believe she was being truly aggressive towards me, but I considered removing the knife from her grasp nevertheless, just like Uncle Raz had taught me.

But maybe Betony would've fought me on instinct. Probably would've won too, despite lessons from both my bad and good uncles. So I just held out my hand instead, open-palmed. She relinquished the knife gracefully into it.

We stared at each other.

"You feedin' him?" she asked at last.

"Popcorn and hot dogs," I said, "along with Alizar's blessing—which is better than nut butter and enriched cream via feeding tube when it comes to malnutrition. The Seventh Angel is . . . is excellent at food."

"That's good." Betony sighed and sat again, heavily. Whereas before she had been spring-loaded and thorny, now she retracted, unwound, seemed to curl in. "Fucker's starved to death."

Dropping her head to her hands, she encountered the impediment of her crown, and cussed. I laughed softly; she reminded me of Mom. Or, not exactly Mom. Someone from my family. Some new family member I was just now meeting.

She glanced up, grinning wryly. "Still kinda wanna split his jug."

"Understandable."

"Why I came here."

"Not really, I think."

"Nah. Not really." Taking off her crown, Betony tucked it into one of her inner jacket pockets and plunged her fingers into her thick black hair, rubbing her scalp vigorously.

I flopped to the lounge chair next to hers.

"Actually," she confessed, bringing her legs up to hug her knees, "been dyin' to meet you. All day." That wry grin again. "I mean, *dyin'*-dyin'—not just lofty-talk. Saw you through that glass tub when they dunked me. Before that too, when you palmed me the shiv. Coulda sworn I met you before, or dreamed you . . ."

I tossed the penknife on the side table between us and stuck out my hand. "Name's Ish."

Immediately releasing her knees, Betony reached out and shook it. Her grip was firm and forthright, all calluses and confidence: the handshake of a woman out to prove at first touch that no scammer could scam her, no fraud defraud her, no marksman make her his mark. A lot of power in that grip. It seemed such a fragile defense against landmines and mortar shells, dysentery, starvation, angels.

"Just Ish?" she asked me. "That slang-bang for something? Secret-in-the-rhyme? Your mama a fishmonger, you a squishy baby, what?"

I released myself of her thin and crushing fingers. "No mysterious alternate meaning. Ish is just short for Ishtu Q'Aleth. I think 'Ishtu' means 'potato soup,' which my mother craved when she was pregnant with me. That was one of the stories I was told anyway, but there are hundreds just as plausible. My mother was, as you put it, a big liar. A storyteller."

"She dead?"

The words were curt and her expression didn't change, but Betony's clear eyes flooded with sympathy, as if her own recent, intense intimacy with death had opened her right up to the mourning of the world. Or maybe she'd always been like that, even before Gelethel.

"Not yet," I said, and received into my body her solace—just for a moment—before I turned the subject. "So that's me. Ish. Mistress of motion pictures and proprietor of Quicksilver Cinema: Gelethel's one and only movie palace now and forevermore."

Betony scrutinized me from under her eyebrows. They were formidable, thick and black. Already her skin was losing that iron oxide look, regaining a rosy-brown glow.

"Slurred a part, Q'Aleth," she said.

"Oh yeah?" A frisson of excitement mingled with fear shot through me. Betony was giving me a look that I'd wished all my life to see on Onabroszia Q'Aleth's face. Recognition. She saw *me*.

"Yeah," she replied. "Slurred right over those thirty-odd years you spent playin' crypto-saint to the Bug."

"Who?"

"Oh," she said, "uh, Alizar. The angel. Eleven-Eyes. I call him Bug, 'cause of all those little wings on him. He said it was okay. Wyrded me, callin' him by 'Alizar,' you know?"

"I know," I said, remembering my earlier conversation with the other Alizar: Alizar Luzarius, her brother. "So . . . have you two been chatting all day? Since . . . since this morning?"

Betony shrugged. "Gotta lotta bones to crunch, me and Bug. See, I blame him and Nirwen—if she's even real, which he says she is—for gettin' me killed. Now, Ali ain't clean of blame by any means. But Zilch-balls, Q'Aleth!" she suddenly shouted, "Don't tell me my little hairshirt brother got all spunked up to murder me on his own, not when he could barely move for lack of vittles or cloud ale."

"Cloud ale?" I interrupted.

Betony gave me a look like I was half Ali's age and maybe just dumped in my pants. "You gethels'd call it water, I guess."

"Oh. And . . . have you decided to forgive him? Alizar, I mean. I mean," I amended, "the angel Alizar. Um . . . Bug."

She laughed suddenly. "Poor Bug! Keeps apologizin', makin' food appear, not to mention patchin' me up like a dollywyrd. I was so full of holes, Q'Aleth, even after he raised me up from corpsitude. Bruised like bad fruit. Hard to hate him when he's poppin' all my blisters like soap bubbles. Nothin' pangs now. Wasn't doin' so good, before."

Betony held out her arm to me, and I took it, tracing the branching red scorch mark from the angel Zerat's lightning strike. It took the shape of a tree incarnadined on the back of her hand, its roots disappearing under her sleeve.

"Only mark he didn't patch. No," she said, almost to herself, "not *patch*. What's his lofty-talk for it? Oh! 'Meliorate.' It was the only mark he didn't *meliorate*." Betony pronounced the word with evident satisfaction. "Said it was too risky—might draw attention from that staticky assface angel—you know, thunderbolt guy."

I wanted to kiss that bloody tree until it vanished from Betony's hand. But though we were sister-saints, I did not yet know her well enough.

And besides, one could not lightly banish a birthmark of the angels.

"Zerat Like the Lightning," I supplied, even though I personally preferred "staticky assface angel" myself. "And, yes, meliorating this wound would be tricky."

"Why?" she challenged me.

Liberating her arm, I explained, "Zerat's scorch mark was a deliberate tagging of his territory. Removing it has repercussions. On the one hand, Zerat and the other three angels claimed you for their sacrifice. You were theirs; they drank your death. On the other hand, Alizar—Bug—in resurrecting you, gave them a purgative. *You* got your life back, *they* got a hangover, and *he* got a new saint. As well as his sign from beyond the serac that Nirwen stands ready to . . . to do whatever the two of them promised they'd do, a hundred years ago. But the mark remains."

Betony muttered something that sounded anatomically impossible—especially for angels, who didn't have anatomy.

"I know," I said. "It isn't fair. It's fabulous fucking Gelethel."

If I interpreted her next mutter correctly, Gelethel was doomed to get the same anatomical treatment as its angels. At length.

But presently, having cussed herself calm, Betony leaned back again in her lounge chair and asked, "Hey, Bug! Wanna weigh in? You been crypto this while. What're you and Faceless Nirwen hatchin' on the other side of the ice?"

We both awaited a reply from the Seventh Angel, who did not indulge us with one.

So by mutual consent, we waited some more.

When it became painfully clear to Alizar, eager eavesdropper that he was, that *we* wouldn't speak until *he* did, he deigned, reluctantly, to contribute to the conversation. Not in dialogue, no, but as a sort of shimmering, bewildering

{*shifty*} {*silence*}

"Aaand . . . he's not saying," I interpreted out loud. "I swear, some days, you can't shut him up. Everything is bells and twinkles and chitinous wings. The rest of the time, it's like, if your name's not Nirwen, you don't even register with him."

"Might be, he's a shy Bug," Betony mused. "Might be, Bug's got a secret so gloomdig he can't trust us with it."

"Is that true?" I asked Alizar.

{*shiftier silence*} {*slight apology*} {*hint of maybe–yes?*}

"Pike it," Betony shrugged. "Bug's keepin' his bones in the cup. As for me and my murder tree"—she rubbed the scorch mark with her fingertips—"might be I get used to it. Or better," she brightened, "I'll find a tap-and-scratcher to ink me a new tree right over it. Load it with fruits, flowers, climbin' ivy, like that dollopy great garden Bug keeps rappin' on about. Hey, Q'Aleth, you gethels have any tattoo parlors in this city?"

"I . . . yes." I paused, imagining the ruckus in the streets if a saint from the Celestial Cenoby suddenly showed up one day in a tattoo parlor.

And then I began to smile.

"Why, yes," I repeated, "yes we do. Actually, there are several in this very district. There's one just down the street from the Quick. But," I warned, "you'll want to get it done in the OlDi if you're going to do it at all. Most of the real artists live here. Go anywhere else, you'll end up with a hack job."

"Hack job," Betony cackled. "I get it." And she patted her emblazoned hand one last time, then pulled her sleeve down over the mark, done with it for the time being.

We relaxed into our respective lounge chairs, allowing a new but familiar silence to string itself between us, like an industrious spider dancing her trap between two trees. Gradually, but very naturally, we started breathing in sync. We realized it about the same time, caught each other's eye, and burst out laughing—in wonderment. But both of us kept quiet yet, hoping to spur the angel Alizar into volunteering actual speech.

He didn't, so I decided to help him along.

"I have to say, Saint Betony," I said with a predatory idleness that Onabroszia's brothers would've recognized, "Alizar's been incredibly

profligate with his healing powers today. I'm not talking about resurrection—which angels aren't supposed to be able to do at all. But
fixing you up afterwards? That's a big no. Angels laid down the law
a long time ago about healing the people of Gelethel. If the others
found out that Alizar's broken that law, they'd tear him apart and
scatter his pieces through the acres of Hell."

This—finally—provoked the Seventh Angel to reply: *We have*
special dispensations to heal our own saints!

"As if you wouldn't do the same for, say, a ghost—via, say, a
bucket of stale popcorn," I retorted. "It's not even your feast day! I
never saw you act like this, out of turn—except that one time with
Mom's benison cakes. How do you expect to get away with it?"

But it was Betony, not Alizar, who replied. "Already got away
with it, didn't he? And that's just the start, right? Bug's showin' his
grit."

"What grit?" I stretched my legs out and crossed them. "Alizar is
not known for his . . . puissance, as it were."

"His what?" By this time, Betony was lying flat on her back,
knees up, hands behind her head. I was on my side, facing her, chary
of copying her gestures too closely even though my body kept wanting to imitate hers.

"His prodigious and unparalleled powers. No offense, Alizar,"
I put in quickly, "but everyone in Gelethel knows that among the
angels, you're considered the weakest. They all bully you. They sing
you down. They—"

Betony flung out a hand to stop me. "Wait up a cut. Bug's been
showin' me how things work here. Gethel barter system and all. Your,
whaddya call 'em—'benzies?'"

"Benisons, yes," I said, "what about them?"

"So Bug told me how he doesn't let all you gethels chaffer your
benzies for his stuff. Forbids it in his district. His, what do you call
it, 'Garden'?"

"Bower."

"Told me he just gives it away."

"Yeah," I agreed. "The angels call that weakness."

Betony scoffed. "That ain't weakness, Q'Aleth. Weakness is killin'
someone for their bread. Strength is splittin' your last loaf with them.

At least," she took a deep breath, "that's what I always told myself. And Bug's like that too. Big grit."

I stared at her, imagining her life thus far. Twenty hard years, out in the thick of the New War. Born into it. Grown to maturity in its blood-soaked sands.

"No wonder he loves you so," I said.

Betony squirmed a little, and turned her face to the sky.

I thought of her brother, Alizar Luzarius, who had sacrificed Betony to the angels. I thought of the angels, accepting death as their due, sucking it up, whilst Alizar the Eleven-Eyed gave only life and kept giving it, without demanding anything in return. I reflected on how Alizar Luzarius would have been rewarded for his blood sacrifice: citizenship, a home, work, all the benisons of Gelethel that he could earn or trade. And then I recalled how Alizar the Eleven-Eyed was scoffed at, sung down, treated like a worm amongst dragons—when in fact all of Gelethel benefited from his blessings.

I thought it all through, for the first time, and assumptions that I'd held as canon my whole life long began all at once to fracture.

"It's . . . true," I stumbled for the right words, "that angels amass power through . . . through the prayers of those who live in their districts. An influx of prayer—usually in response to a certain need, like electrical power or benison flakes or the silk thread that rains from the sky—results in a stronger angel. One who, ostensibly, is then better able to provide more and more lavishly to their worshippers. But—"

I scrubbed my face with both hands, my momentary glimpse of revelation eluding me. "But that's where Alizar cuts his own throat, right? Because he gives it all away before anyone can pray for it. No one even *lives* in his district, so how can he ever amass enough—"

"But everyone comes," Betony said, eager now that my attention was firmly fixed on something other than her. "Don't they? Not just on his feast day. Bug made his place a public park, right? Gethels go there just to nest out."

I blew out my breath. "Yes, right, but—"

And then I stopped, remembering my birthday last year. That look—the same look—on everybody's faces, from newborn babies to the bent and old, as Alizar the Eleven-Eyed gave and gave and gave unto them, until even *they* couldn't ignore the miracle of plenty anymore.

"Alizar," I asked the air suspiciously, willing him to manifest, "How many prayers of thanks do you get each Feast of Bloom?"

{*sheepish shrug*}

"Yes, but the number?"

The Seventh Angel intoned a number that I knew was roughly the same size as the entire population of Gelethel.

"Every *fortnight?*"

Every day, Alizar said, so quietly that he might have been Murra Who Whispers. I could barely hear him, and only if I listened all the way down to my feet.

I sprang to my feet. "*What?*"

Why didn't he tell me before? Why didn't I *know?* And what was wrong with me that I had never observed, never comprehended, the vastness of my own angel's strength? No other angel received that kind of prayer. They boasted of their numbers to each other in the Celestial Corridor every petition day, and mocked the Seventh Angel for keeping silent, singing that he had so few worshippers that he was ashamed to sing the number out. I'd listened so long to that rotten bilge that I absorbed it. I'd *believed* it.

It had to be secret, Ish. Until now.

Alizar's love and concern rushed over me like a beeswax breeze, and he manifested before me, his flickering gold-green figure bursting with flowers and tendrils, a thousand wings fluttering frantically, eleven jewel-like eyes beseeching me.

Do not be angry, my saint. I have longed to tell you your whole life long. But none of it mattered till this morning. Whatever powers I have amassed these years, I could not have used them to act. Not without Nirwen's signal. Not without my second saint, who has come among us now.

"But," I implored him, "what about the other angels? Aren't they more powerful yet? They've been taking sacrifices all these years while you've been abstaining. They're all . . . *engorged* with force and potency."

Betony broke in, in a very dry—almost Dad-like—way, "Tell me somethin', Q'Aleth. Does watchin' a bunch of invisible jackasses get high on dead refugees make you *more* or *less* likely to praise their names? Not talkin' 'bout out loud now. Talkin' 'bout in here," she tapped her breast bone, "in your hiddenmost."

"In my hiddenmost . . ."

Betony waited, listening. The breeze that was Alizar bent around me, listening.

"In my hiddenmost," I repeated, "I drowned all the angels of Gelethel in their Sacrificing Pool long ago. And then I burned the Celestial Corridor to the ground." I grinned weakly, frightened by my own audacity. "In my hiddenmost, salt can burn."

"Anything can burn," Betony said, "that kinda hurt gets hot enough. I seen that." Lowering her voice (as if *that* would prevent Alizar from overhearing), she asked, "Does Bug know? How you feel about the other angels? Think he's scared you'll turn on him?"

She hadn't yet learned how to sense the Seventh Angel lurking in her own skin, her mind, in the words of her mouth. But she would, and swiftly.

"No," I said. "There's no turning on him. I'm his saint. Alizar knows my thoughts, even when I don't always know his. Whenever I speak, he's there in my mouth, sitting alongside the words." I added gently, "Your mouth too. Can't you hear him singing? It's clear to me," I said, "whenever you speak."

Betony gave another of those head shakes that didn't mean denial. We were both, I thought, operating on information overload and in dire need of refreshment, stat.

"Saint Betony," I asked, "do you want a beer?"

"Oh *fuck* yeah!" Betony blurted, and we both laughed.

And then we both got really drunk.

Alizar's Diegesis

"**S**o, Saint Betony . . ."

Betony lolled her head to the side. She was lying on her stomach on the lounge chair, the angel Alizar sort of hovering over her shoulders, giving her a massage with a few of his trumpet-like blossoms and golden tendrils and wing tips. Being massaged by flowers may not seem substantial, but I knew from experience that the Seventh Angel's attentions could penetrate the knottiest of muscle clusters.

"Mmnphlmph?"

I took a long slow sip of benison wine—or, as the laity liked to call it, beer. "Tell me, are the angels shitting themselves in the Celestial Cenoby over your resurrection?"

She flashed her half-lidded raptor eyes in my direction before lifting her head from her arms and nose-diving into her own tankard.

"Yup."

"And what does that look like?" I pressed.

Betony emerged, bearded with foam. "Looks like a buncha saints in fleeky trim rammin' up my door and demandin' answers for their angels." She snorted. "Mostly stuff like, what's the Seventh Angel doin' with godhead powers anyway? And who the filthy fuck are you, cherub, that he pulled you from the deadwater?"

I was impressed. "Cloistered saints say fuck?"

"Not in so many words. But . . ." She took another drink. "Yup."

"Saints can be such little shits," I said.

Betony flopped over onto her back to stare up at the hovering wing-and-eyeball figure that was the angel Alizar.

"I'm *your* shit, Bug," she told him solemnly. "And so is Q'Aleth."

The best two shits an angel without an anus could wish for, replied the Seventh Angel fondly.

I laughed so hard I almost rolled off my lounge chair. But as the empty cup I was holding had spontaneously begun to refill itself, I very carefully sat up straighter and held onto it with two hands. And I was amply rewarded for my care.

Alizar was all about the benison wine tonight. The drunker Betony and I got, the more gleeful he became, and his glee bubbled over as beer. Amber lager foamed and fountained out of our cups. It was perfect, crisp and tangy with notes of molten caramel and ripe red cherries; it practically purred. I licked my lips.

"It ain't . . ." Betony hesitated, turning to me. "It ain't *bad*. Where I'm at. My new stake. Saints aside, it's thump swaggy. I don't mean to bellywhistle about it. I mean, I'm clean. New kit." She gestured to her clothes. "Servants. Food. The *food*, Q'Aleth—forget beer, I could get drunk on food alone. The Cleno . . . the Cnoby . . . that place they put me—"

"The Celestial Cenoby," I said grandly, not at all over-pronouncing all of my vowels and consonants. At all.

"Yeah, that." Her eyes became huge, luminous with wonder and not a little fear. "I'd live there forever, sure. Gladly. Part of me didn't even wanna leave tonight. Not even to meet *you*, Bug-kin." She smiled at me, tiredly, as if knowing I would understand. "Know the last time I got a bed to myself—one I didn't pay ass over teeth for?"

I shook my head.

"Me neither. Part of me . . ." Betony broke off, swinging her legs over the side of the lounge chair and heaving herself to a sitting position. Her shoulders crunched forward desolately.

I panged for her, then realized, a bit startled, that I'd sat up at the exact same time she had, in a mirror position.

"Part of me wants to thank that little hairshirt for whackin' my cap and draggin' me here to die. Because—without Ali and his sweetsmoke dream of," she slid a sideways glance at me, "fabulous fuckin' Gelethel, I . . ."

I leaned forward, breaking our symmetry to take her hands in mine and squeeze them. "Without him, you wouldn't be here."

"Yeah. That's it. Why?" Betony whispered. "Why am I here, Q'Aleth? Why me? Anybody else, they get drowned in a bathtub, they stay drowned. Why'd *I* get the regalia?"

The answer seemed obvious. "Nirwen chose you, didn't she? You're her holy sign. You're who Alizar's been waiting . . ."

"I'm no kind of holy. I'm not even religious!" Betony protested. "And if I were, I wouldn't worship *Nirwen*. Back in Cherubtown, there was all this talk about her bein' some kind of new god among us. You heard Ali mention it, yeah?"

I nodded.

"Well, I never saw a rag of her," Betony confessed. "My friend Scratch—she's a war vet, got her face burnt off in the fire bombin' of

Sarro Ranch—me and her used to go 'round the tents, sort of takin' the pulse of Cherubtown, you know? Place is a powder keg. We were out last night, and . . . was it last night?"

She looked around, confused, as if freshly astonished that only a day had passed since then. I waited, and Alizar hovered nearer, patting Betony's head gently with various of his protrusions until she regained her bearings and continued:

"Last night, we came upon a tent meetin' of the new religious. Watched all the preachers preachin' and the converts praisin' Nirwen's name, and I turned to Scratch and said, 'Got no use for a god who walks around this trash-fire without takin' the trouble to fix it. I'd sooner worship the God-King of Koss Var, may his dick fall off.' And Scratch said, 'Hells, Bet, it's enough to make a gal a goddamn atheist.' And then we left early. That's all I can remember about . . . about last night. Guess Ali saw me leavin' that tent and took me for some angel-defilin' heathen. Then cracked me."

When she realized she was crying, a slow-seeping weep, Betony rolled contemptuous eyes at herself. I stroked her hands with my thumbs until she sniffed it all back in and wiped her face on her shoulder.

"Anyway. That's why I'm here. Didn't do nothin' special but raise a brother ready to murder me or martyr himself at a pin's pull. The other saints—they're right to look at me like I'm a sand-leech suckin' the dark side of their thongs. I don't belong here. But Q'Aleth," Betony leaned in, all the way in, "I'm *stayin'*. I'll eat their food, wear their clothes, stare at them fourteen fuckin' angels till somebody decides to toss my dead body off that ice wall. I ain't goin' back."

A faint thrum in the air, a coruscating disquiet, alerted me that Alizar was overwrought. All glee gone, all beer evaporated by his anger and anxiety, he shimmered and buzzed, busy with emotion.

He wanted to reassure her—badly. But he was stymied by his own secrets, by his and Nirwen's longstanding ambitions, by all the ineffable things mere mortals cannot comprehend. So he said and did nothing to comfort Betony in her doubt.

Well, fuck that. Alizar, just like the rest of us, sometimes wants a bit of prodding. Especially now, when Betony needed answers so badly.

Angels are suckers for repetition and ritual. I knew just what to do. I reflected the question back at my sister-saint, and brought all my own saintliness to bear, going down on my knees before her and squeezing her hands even more tightly.

"Why you?" I asked, my upturned gaze on her and her alone. "Why did Alizar the Eleven-Eyed, Seventh Angel of Gelethel, reeve of Bower whose feast is Bloom, defender of the Diamond of Bellisaar, choose *you*, Saint Betony? Answer me that."

She began to shake her head in that way she had, so I demanded again, urgently, "*Why* did Alizar choose *you*?"

"Because I am not of Gelethel," Betony answered promptly. And I saw, shimmering on her lips, the fluttering of tiny, crystal-chip wings.

Casting a quick glance about, I smiled in satisfaction. Alizar had vanished from sight, only to have re-manifested in the mouth of his newest saint.

Betony clapped a hand over her lips, but that didn't stop him. Alizar kept on talking through her mouth. He even used one of her hands to pluck the other from her lips and hold it in her lap, giving it the occasional avuncular pat.

"Because I've walked this world with my own two feet," Betony went on, faster and faster, speaking with the fervent tenderness her angel held for her. "Because I've seen the worst and broken for the better. Because I'm fast. And sly. And can lie quicker than thought. Because I'm good with a penknife. And . . . he, he likes my hair? Because I kept my shitty baby brother alive even when it cost me everything. Because I can infiltrate the . . ."

She stopped short, shook her head once, sharply, then blurted, "Because I can infiltrate the Celestial Cenoby!"

I sat back on my heels—my knees creaking—and loosened my grip on her hands. She did not pull away and I did not let go.

"And why," I lowered my voice, "does the angel Alizar want you to do that?"

This time, I felt the fluttering of wings on my own lips, a flickering glow in my throat, and we both answered together:

"Because he is making his bid for godhead of Gelethel."

"The angels are falling," we said.

"They began to die the moment they ate their god," we said.

"Alizar and the angel Nirwen knew this," Alizar-in-Betony told us. "They could *see* it. They knew that if they did not act, this would be their fate too. That is why Nirwen the Artificer left Gelethel. A hundred years ago, she walked out into the world to learn how to become a god. Alizar promised to stay and do the same—for the good of all Gelethel. For the good of the angels, who are rotting like cankerous fruit on a once-thriving tree."

"The angel Nirwen knew that once she left, she could never come back," Alizar-in-me finished. "Once apostate, citizen no more. Once apostate, outsider. And no outsider whom the angels consider foe may breach the Gelthic serac. That is hieratic law; it is canon; it is written in the Hagiological Archives in the saints' own hands. It was the last law of god before She was eaten, and it holds true for humans and angels alike. Nirwen left Gelethel. Her face was erased from all our graven images, her title revoked, her district left barren. She has no way back *in*."

Betony and I gaped at each other, listening to ourselves speak with Alizar's voice, our breath beery and warm. Strong golden fumes that I associated with the Seventh Angel—honey, pollen, warm berries, savory herbs, cherry blossoms—seeped from our skin, our mouths, mingling to form a mirage between our bodies: shimmering and vaporous, a gleaming bubble shaped of wings and eyes and twinkling lights.

"And *that* is why," Betony and I said together, staring at our own faces reflecting off Alizar's rainbow-slicked bubble, "there are *two*."

The Seventh Angel fell silent.

"Two?" Betony repeated, frowning at me. "Two what?"

"Two of *us*," I whispered.

The soap bubble between us popped. Alizar vanished from the space he had occupied—to go back to wherever it was the angels went when they were not with us. Our cups disappeared too, and with them, the last of our drunkenness. We stared at each other with clear eyes, shivering in the aftershock of angelic possession.

A second later, Betony and I leapt from our chairs.

We stood back to back, facing out, listening. The hairs on our arms were bristlingly erect.

"Somebody's coming," we both announced.

I shook my head to sever the connection between us, but it was like trying to disengage from a cat's cradle made of molasses. Betony thunked the heel of her left hand against her temple and looked at me ruefully.

"Can you climb?" I asked.

"Got up here, didn't I?" Betony returned.

"Then go over the balustrade, now—take the jasmine trellis to the streets."

She didn't argue. It wasn't like she couldn't listen in on my life whenever she wanted, or that I couldn't do the same with her. We were sitting inside each other's skulls now, right where Alizar the Eleven-Eyed had put us—two halves of the same saint.

"Be safe, my sister," I murmured to her. "Be swift and sly!"

Betony's grin was like a searchlight illuminating my worry as she slipped over the balcony. She nodded at my little penknife, now folded neatly on the side table.

"Blessed Q'Aleth," she whispered back, "thanks for the loan."

"Anytime, Saint Betony."

I pressed myself against the roof garden's railing, keeping my back to the door that led down to my bedroom balcony, masking her descent. Betony had only lowered herself a few feet when she beamed up at me.

"Always wanted a sister."

My heart belled within me; I became a cathedral. "Me too."

And then she was gone.

REVERSE ANGLE: WUKI AND THE RAZMAN

"**H**ELLO, MY UNCLES," I CALLED OUT CHEERILY, MY BACK STILL turned to the door. "Did you come singly or in battalions?"

"Little of this, little of that," replied Uncle Wuki's adenoidal tenor from just inside the stairwell. Uncle Wuki may have been puffy and brown and big like a bear, but he always sounded like a seven year old with a bad head cold.

Rotating until my back was to the railing, my elbows resting on the white brick, I nodded a casual greeting at him where he loomed in the doorway. His face was in shadow, but I could still feel him grinning at me—a dopey grin, big and childlike.

"Hey, Ishi," he said. "Zulli told us your latest plans. We came over to chat about 'em. He'd've come too, but . . ." He shrugged his broad shoulders.

"That's right," I recalled, "Uncle Zulli had to work tonight."

"Got called up for rampart watch. Drew the graveyard shift." Wuki giggled. "Poor slob. Always has the worst luck."

I nodded with mock sympathy. "Which you, his brothers, all exploit without ruth or mercy."

"Well, of course," Wuki replied guilelessly. "Zulli *is* the youngest."

Standing on tiptoe, I glanced to the silent shadow waiting behind him on the stairs. Not a bear. A colossus. The last time I'd seen him, three angels were riding him all the way to Betony's death. I softened my voice away from its teasing edge.

"Hey, Razman. You had quite the morning at the Celestial Corridor. You sound?"

"For now."

Uncle Raz sounded unutterably tired. He gave Wuki a light push, then stepped out after him onto my roof garden. As he passed under the threshold, he reached up and removed a small box from a hidden cache in the lintel.

The box was stuffed with cigarettes. Raz took two, passed one to Wuki, and put the box away, sliding the door of the cache closed so that it was imperceptible to a casual observer, or to a good uncle.

Both of them simultaneously lit their cigarettes and held them loosely in their hands, letting the phantasmal plumes drift up into darkness.

None of Onabroszia Q'Aleth's brothers actually smoked; that had been Mom's sole domain. Cigarettes were her favorite vice long before she'd discovered a secondary use for them: tricking the angels in regards to her younger brothers.

Wheresoever one of the warriors of their Holy Host abided, there too might the angels dwell. In this sense, Hosts were barely more than receptacles to be engorged or engulfed by angelic attentions depending on a given angel's needs and moods.

And angels were capricious, self-concerned, often inattentive.

Fortnights could go by of my bad uncles going to work, dressing up in their Holy Host armor, and performing perfectly normal patrols. And then, without warning, I'd suddenly have to endure weeks, months—half a year!—of never seeing my bad uncles at all. The shadow side of Q'Aleth Hauling Industries would grind to a stop; nothing would come in through the serac or go out over it clandestinely, and certain citizens of Gelethel who had grown accustomed to their choice of non-angelic perks would get very uppity indeed. But I didn't care about that: I cared that Zulli, Eril, Wuki, and the Razman were vanished from my reach, and that the good uncles had taken their place: Host Irazhul, Host Hosseril, Host Wurrakai, and—of course—Host Razoleth, Captain of the Hundred-Stair Tier.

My good uncles were good uncles whenever they were wholly or in part possessed of angels. A trained eye could tell them apart at a glance—for all that they shared bodies with my bad uncles. But my good uncles were unmistakable—with their patient, gleaming faces, their bland, blancmange lawfulness, and their tendency, at any time, to manifest angelic attributes: a bloat of pearl, a hawk's head bursting from knuckles or neck, a child's tiny hands jutting from their shoulders like small, helpless horns.

It was easiest, of course, to recognize a good uncle when he was barbed with attributes. But the cigarettes were still my first and best clue.

They were Mom's idea. Warriors of the Holy Host did not pollute their bodies with depressants, stimulants, or anything considered a traditional offering to the gods who reigned outside the Gelthic serac. As tobacco fell under two of these three prohibitions, my bad uncles lit cigarettes as a signal to me that all was clear, that their bodies were their own. Of course, they couldn't keep cigarettes on their persons, lest the good uncles suspect rebellion, but we had hidey-holes all over the Quick, and at Mom and Dad's house too.

Raz came to stand with me at the railing. "Zulli says you want out. With Broszia and Jen LuPyn."

He always called Dad by his full name whenever he was himself—to make up, I thought, for all the times when he was a good uncle and never referred to Dad by name at all, just "the immigrant your father."

"I'm taking them both to Sanis Al," I announced. "There's no medical infrastructure here, Razman, and they're deteriorating fast. Dad came home after his doc's appointment this morning and he was . . . he just . . ."

I shook my head, remembering how Dad had seemed like a degraded film of himself, leached of color, just shades of quiet gray, flickering out.

Clearing my throat, I continued, "So . . . Uncle Zulli says he'll put the word out, and this Nea woman—your possum?—will make contact with us when she's back in the area?"

Wuki laughed. "Well, aren't you in luck, Ishi? Zulls dropped by the barracks to pass on what you told him—just as we were on our way to Broszia's to tell him *our* news. Because *we'd* got word just this afternoon that Nea's in Cherubtown. Some pilgrim passed on her message at the petitions today. Said our possum paid him to stick it under the brick."

He was talking about a certain loose brick near the gigantic pink salt-crystal doors of the Celestial Corridor—right beneath the faceless image of the Fifteenth Angel, Nirwen. It was how Mom used to communicate with her brothers when they were working the tier. She'd piously attend every petition day, and piously walk away with a full roster of whom among the Hosts was patrolling the ramparts for the whole upcoming fortnight, how they would be distributed amongst the watchtowers, and when the changes of the guard were scheduled.

"Said Nea paid him in *benzies*," Uncle Wuki was going on. "No lie—he had slips for meat, cloth, water, even a hotel voucher so he wouldn't have to squat in Hell when he got his citizenship. Notarized by Tanzanu and everything. Wonder if Broszia maybe smuggled a wad of 'em out years ago. Ha! She'd've done it too, mark me!"

I made a little "go on" noise in my throat.

Wuki slung an arm around my shoulder. "We let the pilgrim keep his benzies in the end—after we threatened to take them away, of course. We'd caught him in the act, see—brick in hand. The Razman arrested him for vandalization. Man almost pissed himself. We squeezed him, got the buzz, then told him we'd let him go, ha, *this time*, with a warning. No more pulling bricks up in the Angelic City! Welcome to Gelethel, Citizen! May the fourteen bless and keep—"

Raz held up a hand, cutting Wuki off from his flow of speech like a guillotine. He turned to me.

"The note contained your passphrase," he said, handing me a folded slip of paper. "Memorize it. Destroy it. This is how it works: yours is the call, Nea's the response. If she does not respond, retreat immediately. Tomorrow midnight is the rendezvous. You know the place."

He could only mean one place—the one neither he nor the other uncles had ever mentioned again after taking me there in secret all those years ago. That broken southern stair, fenced off from the streets. The key I'd never used. The crack in the serac.

Nirwen's Hell.

"Ishtu," the Razman said clearly. I looked up at him. "Do you understand me? Do you have the *coordinates*?"

And he cleared his throat twice.

I nodded, understanding his meaning. The Razman did not lightly clear his throat—and never twice without good reason.

"I have the *coordinates*," I repeated, emphasizing the word as he did.

His shoulders relaxed—well, for the Razman, which wasn't much.

I glanced at the paper with my passphrase. Four words: call and response. I committed them to memory, then took Uncle Raz's proffered cigarette and used the lit end to burn the paper with the password, before handing the cigarette back to him.

Wuki, who was taking surreptitious whiffs of his own cigarette, didn't see Raz's hand flash out and lightly slap the back of his ear.

Resigned, he tapped a few ashes onto my railing, leaving little piles like bird droppings.

I enjoyed seeing them there. Small offerings to the new godhead. Both new godheads, maybe.

"Any news from the Celestial Corridor?" I asked. "Since this morning, I mean."

I wanted to know if word of Betony's recent extra-cenobian activities had gotten out. Saints rarely left their anchorholds, and never unaccompanied.

A sensation like a pair of ears pricking up on the insides of my ears startled me. Just my thinking about her had bound up our thoughts again. Betony wasn't anywhere near—she was, in fact, more than halfway across the city by now, loping boldly through the streets of Gelethel, made invisible by her own Invisible Wonder. My hands folded into fists, my thumbs stiffened and shot out: her way of giving me a thumbs up. Good thing my hands were in my pockets.

I flicked her off, then had to smother her smirk on my mouth.

"News?" Wuki replied. "Sure there is." He started drawing random shapes in his ash piles. "The whole Celestial Corridor's been dancing the light shambolic ever since this afternoon. After things got weird on the ramparts."

"The ramparts?" I stood up straighter. "Which part?"

"Hirrahune's district. Nursery. Just southwest of Tyr Valeeki," said Raz.

"That's . . . QHI's dumpsite, isn't it?"

Wuki rubbed his chin, where there was always a shadow of a beard even if he'd just shaved five minutes ago. "Yup. There's unrest in Cherubtown."

I swallowed, nodding, trying to look nothing more than interested. Ten percent curiosity, ninety percent pure Gelthic insouciance.

But . . . whatever was happening in Cherubtown, it of course had something to do with Nirwen and Alizar—therefore with Betony and me—and if so, why hadn't Alizar told us about it?

Here was a wonderful opportunity for the Seventh Angel to jump in, irritatingly meek and deflective, and say something like, *Well, Ishtu, there's been rather a lot happening at once . . .*

But he didn't.

So I laughed a little, and asked Wuki, who was dying to tell me, "Unrest? What kind? I didn't think Cherubtown had the calories for unrest."

Then again, I thought at Betony, *if they're all like you, I'm surprised the cherubs haven't laid siege to the serac.*

We yakked about it, Scratch and me, Betony replied. *But we didn't have the ladders and stuff. You need a lotta ladder to climb that ice.*

She was approaching the walls of the Celestial Cenoby now, contemplating her ascent. She thought briefly about asking Alizar for a boost, then decided it was more fun to jam her bare hands and feet into the nooks and crannies available to her.

Oh, to be nineteen again.

I withdrew my attention, not wanting to distract her, and focused on the Razman. He was standing to my right as Wuki was to my left, his hands folded together on the railing—all but the fore- and middle finger of his right hand, which pinched the steadily shrinking stub of cigarette between them.

"The cherubs were throwing a festival," he murmured, so softly it might have been a prayer. "There were fireworks. The angels were . . . distressed."

"I'll say!" Wuki put in. "I was on duty at the ramparts when it went down. We of course sent word about the festival—the long way, with a runner," he explained, "since none of us were activated as Hosts at the time. Apparently, when our message reached them at the Celestial Corridor, the angels started issuing so many contradictory commands that the Heraldic Voice fainted dead away from interpretive stress. They took to their bed with a migraine—haven't emerged since. So, lacking an instrument, the angels themselves joined us at the western serac."

"What, all of them?" I asked. "Joined . . . all of you . . . Hosts?"

Wuki nodded, momentarily grim. I reached out, grasped his hand, and silently squeezed it. If he'd been angel-ridden today, it meant he was probably feeling just as sore and used as Raz. No wonder he was chattering so: Wuki always got maniacally cheerful whenever he was in pain. Uncle Eril sunk into melancholy; Zulli tended towards dramatics, overeating, and long naps; Raz got quieter; but Wuki . . .

He was practically dancing. He spread his arms. Smoke swirled around him.

"Now you might ask, Ishi: where did those cherubs get all their fireworks from? They don't have bread, water, or medicine, but they're setting off sparklers like it's the Feast of Zerat? Big ones too—thunderbirds, flowering trees, mushroom clouds, the lot. And the answer is: who knows? Miracles, they say! The new god of Cherubtown provides, they say! And not just *fireworks*, Ishi, but a *feast*! Dancing! Bonfires! *Bonfires burning on bare sand*—no fuel to feed them. The multitudes sated. Wine and cake. And even the scrappiest beggar wore ribbons in their hair!"

"What . . ." I cleared my throat, "what was the occasion for the festival? Did the angels ever find out?"

"Our newest saint," Raz said.

This, of course, was no surprise. But it still felt like a surprise. Right in the center of my chest. I couldn't speak, only stare.

Wuki gesticulated another wild rollercoaster of smoke. "Think about it, Ishi! First: Saint Betony isn't a Gelthic citizen but a *pilgrim*. From Cherubtown! Second: she's no child, not like all *our* saints are when first they're plucked. She's a woman grown. Third: she was *dead*—a sacrifice. And she was brought back to life!"

"*Reputedly* dead," Raz corrected him.

I frowned at the warning note in his voice, watched his hands open and close, clench into fists. Betony had died by those hands, which the angel Thathia had turned into eels. He knew it, and he knew that I had witnessed it. The murder of a saint.

His gaze met mine but cut away too quickly. Wuki waved off his brother's qualifier.

"The *cherubs* think she was dead," he said. "And if dead, then raised. They're taking her resurrection as a sign that the sacrifices must stop. No more pilgrims, they say. No more petitions! No more angel fodder!"

"So, you see, Ishtu," Raz concluded, in his deep way, "the angels have some reason to be upset."

"And did they . . . how did the angels respond?"

Wuki couldn't contain himself; he practically howled, "We trumpeted their answer down from the ramparts! We shouted it from the skies! We spoke in angel voices and were heard!" He was shuddering, his lips trembling, his brown face gray behind his stubble, but at the last his outburst seemed to calm him.

Steadying himself with a deep breath, he said, "The cherubs want an end to petitions, sacrifices? Very well, the angels proclaimed: the serac is henceforth closed; the bridge shall ne'er again be lowered on fifteenth day. More than this: the angels shall double—nay, treble—their patrols on the ramparts; they themselves shall ride the Holy Host day and night, making certain no illicit commerce, communication, or pilgrims can creep through. Gelethel is at capacity; it has all it wants of the outside world. Let Cherubtown choke on itself."

I exchanged a glance with the Razman. We were both thinking the same thing: that Nea's timing that afternoon was extraordinary. Providential, even.

I crossed my arms over my chest to keep my hard-beating heart trapped in its ribcage. "It sounds like . . . if I don't get Mom and Dad out tomorrow, I might not get another chance."

"Well, yeah, that's why we . . ." But there Wuki stopped. He began to cough uncomfortably, like the smoke was irritating his throat. I reached out to pat his back, but he jerked away from contact, still coughing, holding out his hands to stop me from coming to his aid again. The cigarette fell from his fingers he flashed the sign of the angels at us: a 1 with his left hand, a 4 with his right.

Raz moved quickly, pushing me aside and taking Wuki by the shoulders to whisper in his ear. Wuki's eyes slowly unfocused as Raz's words did their work.

I couldn't catch the actual phrase this time; I was too busy kicking Wuki's cigarette through the open space between two white railings. It fell like a tiny meteorite, blinking out somewhere between the roof and the sidewalk three floors down. Raz's cigarette followed it, sailing over the ledge. We both hastily brushed piles of ash off the railing before turning around. Wuki's coughing had stopped.

I knelt immediately, and kissed my uncle's instep. "Hail to thee, Host Wurrakai. And to the angel enthroned in thy flesh."

The angel was Childlike Hirrahune. I knew it by the baby-faced tumescence bursting from the side of my uncle's neck.

"Niece," said Host Wurrakai mellifluously, helping me to my feet. His high, nasal voice was now sweet and flute-like, pure as a boy soprano singing anthems in the acoustic perfection of the Celestial Corridor. "We have been listening on the night winds for talk of saints and angels. Now. What is being spoken of here tonight, O Brother?"

He peered, bright-eyed, white-eyed, from me to the Razman. No sign of Wuki remained; he was completely subsumed.

Raz stepped up to my side. "We came to take record from a witness," he reported. His voice and face were relaxed, but I felt the bunched muscles of his arm tense against my shoulder.

"While at prayer," he continued, "I recalled that our niece Ishtu was present this morning for the events in the Celestial Corridor. Wishing to secure her statement, but reluctant to interfere with her cinematic vocation, I betook myself and you, Host Wurrakai—then, unactivated—to the Quick once her work was done. The sworn oath of a Q'Aleth—one who is among the most respected business owners in Olthar's district—will go far in quelling the rumors of the new saint's supposed demise and resurrection. It would not do, after all, to have our citizens believe the gossip from Cherubtown."

Childlike Hirrahune's round-eyed likeness blinked agitatedly at me from Host Wurrakai's throat.

I blinked back. The protuberance was about as like the actual angel Hirrahune as a plaster cast was of its model. But it was an extension of the Ninth Angel nevertheless, a sign of her engaged presence, and she would think it odd if I did not stare. Any devout citizen so privileged as to witness even the smallest physical manifestation of an Invisible Wonder would drink in the sight and dash off to tell all their friends at first opportunity.

"Ah!" Host Wurrakai nodded, the attribute in his throat bobbling like a bit of stuck pudding. "An inspired notion, Host Razoleth! Should diamonds and pearls fall from her lips, Domenna Q'Aleth could not speak better value than to swear by what she saw today."

Raz glanced at me, adjuring me with his eyes to agree with his every word. "Our niece was closer to today's events than we two are standing now, Host Wurrakai. She saw the young saint sink into the Sacrificing Pool. She saw her sink to the bottom of it—*but not drown.*"

I had seen it all.

How Betony fought. How she struggled and reached and cried out to her angel. How Host Razoleth held her down with his arms that were eels. How the light in her luminous eyes blew out.

I thought about screaming.

If I opened my mouth right now, I'd have no choice but to scream.

But behind my eyelids, eleven other eyes opened inwardly. A soft feeling petaled apart in my skull, as if I stood in the very heart of Bower, in Alizar's Moon Garden, with jessamine and albatross and angel trumpets loosening all around me, and nectar-sipping night moths fluttering to feed in the falling night.

This deception can harm neither me nor your sister-saint. No lie they make you tell can abrogate the miracle. No lie can undo the resurrection. Nothing can.

Betony chimed in: *And it's totally fine by me if you lie to these fuckin' angels, Q'Aleth. Might even be fun.*

And so, with their permission and blessing, I perjured myself in a voice that was strong and clear.

"True, the girl did lose consciousness briefly." I cupped my hands together at my breastbone in prayer. "But all saints must undergo some trial before canonization; that is tradition. We are gentler, of course, with our own Gelthic children, but surely this feral cherub required some sterner induction? After all, what kind of saint runs *away* from the Sacrificing Pool? Rather than staging such a coy escape, should she not have rather dived into it willingly?"

I shrugged. "But what can you expect from a saint of the Seventh Angel—known to be the weakest, the meekest, the most disregarded of the Invisible Wonders who rule Gelethel? Surely, Host Wurrakai, such matters are beyond my mortal ken."

Host Wurrakai leaned closer. "And you will swear by this, Domenna Q'Aleth? You will swear that the saint was not dead when the Seventh Angel plucked her from the water?"

"It was clear to me," I continued importantly, "that when the saint was lifted and levitated before us all, she needed only a minor resuscitation, not a resurrection. Any child would know the difference."

Host Wurrakai paused, gazing down at me with radiant fondness. "You are a good child, Niece."

I did not remind him that I was but two years shy of forty. My uncles were all in their sixties—still buoyant and youthful, in the prime of their manhood. The warriors of the Holy Host, so often infused with angelic essence, enjoyed what used to be the privilege of all Gelthic citizens before the New War: a decelerated aging process, immunity to disease, the assurance of attaining supercentenarian status, and an easy death at the end of it all, dignity intact.

Mom, who was only seven years Uncle Raz's senior, looked like she could be his grandmother. In appearance, I looked to be around Uncle Zulli's age, or slightly younger, more like a little sister than a niece. Alizar, upon my request, was allowing me to age naturally. But he balked at the idea of me dying any time before I reached twice eleven times seven—which was old even for a Gelthic citizen. I was working on bringing him around, not keen on spending the last fifty years of my life being mistaken for a cricket.

"Thank you, Host Wurrakai." I beamed at him but leaned ever so slightly against Uncle Raz for support.

Against my shoulder, his arm grew tense, then tenser.

No—not just tenser. Bulkier. Stonier. His muscles were growing muscles. His skin began to crackle and shine.

So.

Zerat Like The Lightning, again.

Of all the angel-damned angels, the bully Zerat! That strutting, arrogant scourge of helical discharge. No other angel disdained Alizar the Eleven-Eyed the way Zerat Like the Lightning did. The other self-styled "strongest" angels followed his voltaic lead—even Rathanana. Even Thathia.

But there was no time to glare at my uncle's charioteer like he was some kind of coiled viper of ionized plasma I'd happily crush under my heel—no time to speak the word Uncle Raz had given me earlier—for I was dropping to my knees and kissing my uncle's instep.

My voice caught in my throat when I tried to greet him. My poor Raz! To have been possessed of multiple angels already that day—and then to be seized *again*, in the black hours before dawn, before he'd had a chance to sleep! Brutal.

"Hail to thee, Host Razoleth."

The eldest and most honored of my good uncles, Razoleth, Captain of the Hundred-Stair Tier, placed a beneficent hand upon my head.

"Niece. Greetings. We thank you for bearing witness to the truth about this morning's proceedings. Now we must ask you once again to knock upon the door of your heart, and speak the truth that opens there."

I stared at him with all the vacuous adoration I could summon. Host Razoleth's pupils were spirals, sparking with Zerat's high-current charge.

"Now, Niece. Were the circumstances surrounding Saint Betony's resurrection *all* that we three—" he gestured to himself and Host Wurrakai— "were speaking of here tonight? For as I cast my mind back, aided by the Invisible Wonder within me, I recollect— as but through a lens dimly—some talk of . . . Cherubtown. And . . . gods."

Fulgurating fuckhead.

I bowed my head and said, "Yes, Host Razoleth, you recall correctly," all the while furiously thinking how to thread the word that the Razman had given me earlier into the conversation—and do it in such a way that neither my good uncles nor their angelic parasites would suspect it.

Host Razoleth's expression was one of such supreme complacence that I bitterly wished to rip the angel from his flesh. To let my uncle slumber peacefully—just once!—without fear of occupation or metamorphosis.

"Remind me. What was it?" His eyes searched mine, white and radiant as Host Wurrakai's, but shot through with veins of snapping blue. "Something about . . . *tomorrow*."

There were always a few moments of muzzy shift as a bad uncle became a good uncle. A few moments to redirect the mind of a good uncle down a path predetermined by the bad one—a path that avoided certain pitfalls of memory that would expose a good uncle to his own worse nature.

Raz had used Wuki's shift to whisper the keyword at him that diverted his attention down their agreed-upon narrative. They had come to question me about Saint Betony's resurrection, *not* to give me Nea's coordinates for tomorrow.

But though Uncle Raz had given me his own keyword earlier, and made sure I'd understood it, I hadn't been quick enough to speak it. The trap that Raz had set for himself during his daily "prayers," deep meditations in which he constructed mazes for his better nature to wander around in, remained unsprung.

Gooseflesh ripped through my skin, but I kept my face upturned and eager. "We were speaking of the serac," I prompted him helpfully. "You told me of the unexpected festival in Cherubtown. Some nonsense about the saint who didn't drown. And you mentioned . . . *coordinates?*"

"Coordinates?"

Wrong. Something was wrong. His was an awful excitement: the Eighth Angel's electric elation.

"I'm sorry," I corrected myself quickly, "I misspoke. You were explaining to me how perhaps the festival was an early sign of Cherubtown's intention to coordin*ate* an attack against the serac."

Whenever a given keyword did not work, or had the opposite-than-intended effect of clarifying instead of obscuring near memories, a close variation to the keyword might re-ignite the misdirection. My mind skidded forward giddily, ready to split "coordinates" into its parts and roots, explore its conjugations, perhaps spout a slant rhyme . . .

But the infinitive form, in this case, tripped the trap.

The excitement—and the dangerous blue spark—faded from Host Razoleth's eyes. His shoulders slumped silkily—the only time I ever saw Uncle Raz slump like that was when he wasn't Uncle Raz. I could see his memories begin to re-write themselves, keeping the angel Zerat busy examining and analyzing them.

And then Host Razoleth did that thing I hated. He cupped my face in his massive hands. I tried not to flinch from the static shock. Failed. He smiled.

"Do not trouble yourself about the serac, Niece. Within its icy diamond, Gelethel is safe from all enemies who come slouching from the sands of Bellisaar. Tomorrow, perhaps the day after, we the Holy Host shall ourselves be coordinating a strike on Cherubtown. The Invisible Wonders desire that we rain down fire and salt from atop the ramparts. We are to punish those ungrateful trash-eaters and false pilgrims—and show the agitators among them the extent of our power."

Everything in me shuddered except for my body. I turned my head and kissed one of his rough palms, receiving another bright shock for my devotion.

"Obliterate them, Host Razoleth," I said softly, "for the glory of Gelethel."

"We shall do so. And so, to that end, I must ask you, Niece, to stay away from the serac for the time being." His voice was very deep, very terrible and tender. "We suspect the cherubs have allied themselves to a new benefactor—whom they call god—one who has been building secret siege engines for them, seducing them with provisions and weapons, inciting them to swarm the Angelic City with promises of the paradise they will find herein. Perhaps they think to slaughter us. Perhaps they merely mean to scatter throughout the fourteen districts and hide in the crevices like the cockroaches they are. We will not allow neither, nor any other act against Gelethel.

"For the next fortnight at least," he continued, "the ramparts and watchtowers of the Gelthic serac shall be safe for no one but the Holy Host—as we smash the infernal engines of Cherubtown, and their Dogmanic architects, to dust."

"The ramparts and watchtowers hold no interest for me, Uncle," I promised faithfully—lying like a feral cherub, like my beloved angel, like I'd been lying every day of my life for thirty years. "I will turn my face from the outward ice and direct my contemplations inward to the Celestial Corridor: as all the devout of Gelethel should do."

Host Wurrakai laughed. Not his own silly little giggle, but sharper, higher, a child's piccolo yip, a sound that might have been a cry of pleasure or pain.

"Very wise, Niece!" he praised me. "For we shall smite their verminous heads with fire, and salt the bloody furrows of their wounds, and cover their tents in smoke and sorrow."

"Yes, Brother," agreed Host Razoleth. "We will show them the righteousness of the fourteen."

At last my good uncle released my face from his shocking hands.

"Farewell, Niece. Give my fond regards to your mother, my sister, and my enduring hopes for her health. And," he grimaced slightly, "greetings to the immigrant her husband."

"Yes, Host Razoleth, I'll see them tomorrow."

He stopped, cocking his head slightly, as if "tomorrow" had sent him reaching for another memory. Tomorrow had brought him here in the first place. *Tomorrow.* The possum Nea, her password, my apostasy. *Tomorrow*, a bell ringing faint but sure. *Tomorrow*, midnight, in the very heart of Hell . . .

But the Razman's keyword had done its dirty work. The more Host Razoleth sought for that elusive *tomorrow*, the more it retreated. Other memories crowded in to sew dust and discord across the pathways to revelation, and instead of lingering to pursue them further, Host Razoleth just nodded at me again, advising, "Stay away from the serac."

Then he walked across the roof to the stairwell that would lead him down to my bedroom balcony, Host Wurrakai in his wake.

They passed under my lintel, one after the other, but they never looked up at the cache of cigarettes hidden there.

LONG SHOT:
THE SERAC

O N OUR MAPS, GELETHEL WAS THE CENTER OF THE WORLD, A large white diamond outlined in a thin blue diamond that was labeled the Gelthic serac. This was the wall enclosing the Angelic City on all sides, two hundred meters high at the jagged tips of its peaks, fifty meters thick at the base, all of it pure compressed ice.

From its foundation, Gelethel, rhombic in shape, was fifteen kilometers long on each of its sides, with a total area of two hundred twenty five square kilometers. Most citizens assumed it was the shape that earned Gelethel its nickname, the "Diamond of Bellisaar," but the saints, who studied such things, knew that the origins went back much further than that. In ancient times, what later became our city was an inland lake fed by the Anisaaht River: Lake Amoula was its name, sometimes called, for its glimmering, the Diamond of Bellisaar.

Angelic revelations came piecemeal to the saints, but over the centuries, a picture of Gelethel's pre-history began to emerge. The saints recorded their findings slowly and painstakingly in the Hagiological Archives, but only a privileged few of the laity were ever permitted to study there, and so the whole story was not well known.

I knew it, of course, because Alizar the Eleven-Eyed had told me.

Lake Amoula had once been a shining, shallow, saltwater plane. Only brine shrimp and brine flies lived there; most living things found the waters undrinkable and for this reason, humans never lingered long in its vicinity. And because gods did not go where their worshippers could not, it was a godless lake, content to be so.

But millennia of quiet contentment were shattered when one day, from out of the burning depths of Bellisaar, a god did indeed flee to Lake Amoula, pursued by an army of demons.

With her fifteen angelic companions she ran, from some war-ravaged realm beyond Bellisaar. An army of converters had upended her reign; its sorcerer-priests with their stronger gods had unleashed untold demon horrors, who sought to devour her and hers. Harried through the wastes, the god bolted at all speed, until she came to the edge of that deathly, glittering basin, Lake Amoula.

And, springing from the salt-rock shores, the god dove into the very heart of the shallows.

She made such a splash that the lake waters flew up in all directions, like a startled flock of birds, like a rainstorm in reverse.

Then, from the epicenter of her own quake, the god reached out in all directions and wrenched the waters rising around all her—billions of tons of brine, a vasty saline ring of waves—into the shape of her desire: a rhombus.

Which is to say, a diamond.

A diamond, after all, pierces in four directions at once. No matter which way her foes came at her, within the four walls of that diamond, the god and her fifteen angels would be safe.

And so, into this shape the god froze the waves of Lake Amoula, enormous fortifications of compacted ice. These she set as palisades of protection for herself and her angels. As long as her precious ones remained within the prescribed boundaries—her unmeltable, unevaporable, impenetrable ice walls, smooth as volcanic glass, hard as adamant—then, the god promised, the walls would protect them. Nothing that crawled, flew, limped, or slithered out of the desert could harm them. Not even demons. Not even other gods.

With the very last of her strength, she pulled a palace out of the drying salt pan that had been the floor of Lake Amoula. (Salt, the philosophers say, is a substance especially dear to the gods, being as it was, anathema to demons.) The god's new palace was dazzlingly white, a kilometer-long corridor crowned in colossal domes, its walls and halls of compressed halite, its honeycombed chambers shaped like shells of all different varieties, and all its doorways arches.

But now the god had spent herself, spilling out almost unto self-emptying. She was everywhere in the pristine ice of the serac, and she was at its salt-white center too, and being everywhere, was also diminished.

More tired than any god had ever been tired, she beseeched her angels to make a home of her palace.

It was theirs now, she said, to guard and be guarded by while she rested.

So declaring, she stretched out on an altar of sparkling rock salt: not white like the rest of the palace, but glowing like the gigantic doors of the main corridor, pink and damp as the flesh of the inner lip, and finally—*finally!*—on this crystal bed she slept.

And while she slept in tender form, the angels descended upon her, and devoured her.

Thus perished the god Gelethel.

And thus was born Gelethel, the Angelic City.

♦ ♦ ♦

"ANGELS," I'D TOLD ALIZAR WHEN I WAS EIGHT AND FRESHLY appalled to discover I was his saint, "are *assholes!*"

And always *have been, Ish,* said Alizar. *You have no idea.*

And then he proceeded to tell me how a hundred years ago, the fourteen angels—of their own free will—had accidentally cracked the serac.

♦ ♦ ♦

A HUNDRED YEARS AGO, RIGHT AFTER THE FIFTEENTH ANGEL Nirwen forsook Gelethel, the remaining angels attempted to shrink the city.

They hated that its dimensions honored a false number. The angels were not fifteen anymore, but *fourteen.* Should not, therefore, the area of the Angelic City be squeezed down to a more divine one hundred ninety six square kilometers? Yes! And could not this feat be accomplished by reducing the serac by a mere kilometer on each of its sides? Yes again!

However, not being gods—no matter how they styled themselves—the angels could not quite manage it. A great trembling rolled throughout the Angelic City. Fissures opened in the salt-paved streets. Worst of all, a crack began to appear almost at once in the immaculate blue ice—starting just beneath Tyr Hozriss, the south-point watchtower.

The angels left off their attempts. The city remained—in shape and in scope—as the god had originally intended it: except godless, and a little worse for wear. The serac still stood strong, but part of the southern wall had been compromised. This was an easy deficiency to conceal from the people of Gelethel, as it had occurred in the district of Hell, formally Lab, abandoned when Nirwen took her Lesser Servants and departed the city.

The broken stair that no longer led up to Tyr Hozriss was caged off and locked away. Long-term squatting in the fifteenth district was strongly discouraged. Nothing more was officially said about the crack in the serac—or the dark drop into an icy death awaiting anyone curious or stupid enough to trespass into this most disgraced and forbidden corner of Gelethel. Awaiting also any criminals the angels desired to disappear.

I didn't know how the Razman had come into possession of the key he gave me. I'd bet Mom had passed it along to him when she started getting sick. Or he'd taken it from her, recognizing when she was no longer able to do so.

I *did* know that throughout her shadowy career, Onabroszia Q'Aleth had, in fact, smuggled dozens of apostates—former citizens of Gelethel—*out* of Gelethel. I didn't know the number exactly, but from what little Uncle Zulli had told me, Mom's association with the possum Nea had begun years ago.

Mom would get word—she *always* got word, somehow—of someone wanting out of the Angelic City. She would arrange the exodus—clandestinely—with Nea, and then anonymously alert the apostate to time, place, and password. She would make sure the gate was unlocked when they arrived. The apostate would rendezvous as directed, never knowing it was the respectable and devout Doma Q'Aleth who so gleefully guided their path astray from the angels.

And then Nea would just . . . spirit them away. I didn't know *how* she did it. I don't think even my bad uncles knew how she did it. I doubted even *Alizar* knew.

The problem was the ice. The Gelthic serac was divine in nature; it resisted hook or axe, crampon or screw. Even the angels could not build *into* it, just atop it—the watchtowers, the ramparts that ran between them—from bricks of compressed salt and starch. And even these chemically anathema structures could not melt the unmeltable ice.

How, then, did this outsider "possum" of my uncles manage to pass so easily between the impenetrable ice walls?

And how, I wondered, arriving in Hell on the appointed mid-night, with my wheelchair-bound Mom and my heart-weakened Dad, was the possum Nea going to tote us all up the better part of six hundred forty-nine steps, down a hundred-meter crevice of impenetrable ice, through the glacial labyrinth of the southern wall, and into the Bellisaar Waste?

I didn't express any of my concerns aloud. Dad was well aware of what we faced. Mom—as usual—said nothing as we disgorged ourselves from the covered chariot in which I'd puffed and pedaled us and all our luggage across the several districts composing south-eastern Gelethel.

But despite my doubts, despite the stubborn silence my angel had maintained on this matter, assuring me merely that all was arranged to his satisfaction, I approached the gate caging off the southern stair and called out the first part of the passphrase Uncle Raz had given me.

"Mother Scratch."

Beyond the cage, from the deep shadow of the stair came the response, so low it was practically seismic.

"Father Bloom."

And Nea rose out of the darkness, where she had been crouched and waiting.

The moment I saw her, rising up and up, all my doubts and questions and theories crashed away in a fresh avalanche of panic.

Nea was Zilch.

♦ ♦ ♦

"**Y**OU'RE ZILCH!"

Dad, who'd been trundling Mom's wheelchair close behind, lurched into me. I was carrying everything. All he had to do was push Mom. Even that, I feared, was taking its toll on his blue-beating heart. But he'd assured me that he'd be peppy as prickly pear jelly: so long as we didn't go too fast.

Fast be damned, I thought. The shock of seeing the giantess before us just might kill him.

Then Mom yelled gleefully, "Angel-sucker! Fucking Zilch! Baby-eater!"

For a woman who, for the past twelve hours, had been doing the best imitation of moribund I'd seen outside a morgue, Mom's decibels were alarming. Her voice echoed off ice and darkness, salt and stone. All of abandoned Hell seemed to hear her.

I cringed beneath the weight of our packs.

Nea looked down—way, way down—through the cage that separated us. "We don't use Waste-cant for ourselves," she said thoughtfully. Her voice was quiet, very deep, like the Razman's—only with more vitality, a green vein of youth and hope.

"'Zilch' is, anyway, inaccurate," she went on. "Not that a Gelthic shut-in could conceive the difference at first glance, in the dark, with no other frame of reference."

Nea moved out of the shadows, coming closer to us, until her hands wrapped the bars of the cage. Her hugeness loomed. She clinked softly; from the intricate full-body harness she wore swung all kinds of straps, clips, grips, and other tools I didn't know the names for. They glinted in the darkness, but they did not look like any kind of metal I could name. Several coils of slim, black rope dangled from loops on her belt. Her hair was covered with a dark helmet, her hands with dark gloves.

"I see we have offended you," said Dad with weary sweetness.

"Please—I'm sorry," I said quickly before he could apologize further. "I was very rude."

I moved forward and jammed the key Uncle Raz had given me into the padlock securing the cage. It popped reluctantly, but as the gate swung open, the tension in the air seemed to slacken.

"You *were* rude," Nea agreed dispassionately. "But then, you have lived in Gelethel all your life. The technical term for what we are," she added, standing aside to let us in, "is 'nephilim.'"

Dad turned to her, startled. "Half-angel?"

"After all," Nea said, seeming surprised at his surprise, "it was the angel Nirwen who created us. We are half her own material, half the material of mortals."

"Where do the Zilch come in?" I couldn't help asking, which set Mom off on another happy howling diatribe against the Zilch.

But Nea's voice, so deep and cool, so instantly soothing, hushed Mom's tirade like a lullaby. "'Zilch' is a philosophy of despair resulting from an occasional mutation in our code. It is not a species. Many genetic outliers live quite happily amongst the nephilim majority, and do not subscribe to the Zilch credo. Take me, for example. I will not live a tenth as long as most of my community. I may not live out the year. But I do not, I assure you, go around barbecuing babies."

I saw the outline of her hand move to her shoulder and tap something there. Suddenly, a small light flicked on, radiating from a tiny button on her lapel. The intense pinprick bathed her face in eerie blue twilight, like the heart of a star or a glacier.

That button was S'Alian spell-tech; such gadgets were often featured in cloak-and-dagger-type movies set in Sanis Al. But no film I'd ever seen told the story of what Nirwen the Forsaker, former angel of Gelethel, had got up to once she'd left the serac behind her. No news reels spoke of Nirwen's get, the nephilim—her greatest experiment. All I'd ever heard—mostly from traumatized former pilgrims—centered around the Zilch: gangs of bandit giants terrorizing the wasteland interior on their viper bikes.

I never knew they were *Nirwen's*.

Nea went to one knee in front of Mom. Kneeling, she was almost three meters tall. That was bigger than Uncle Razoleth, even when swollen by angels. Her large, long face glowing like the aegis of an ancient knight's shield, she engulfed Mom's hand in hers.

"Onabroszia Q'Aleth. Greetings. Do you remember me? We met when I was a child. Nirwen sent me to test the serac, looking for cracks. You were doing the same on your side, searching for a better way to move contraband through the ice. You'd had some success— but you hadn't yet managed to smuggle *people*. But you'd discovered the Hellhole, and sent secret messages out into Cherubtown letting it be known you wanted a way to climb the ice, to explore a possible egress. Night after night you came to this place, waiting for answer. And one night, I climbed out of the dark, and we spoke."

Mom stared, her brow wrinkled.

"Nea," she said.

"Nea, yes." The giantess smiled reassuringly. "We are old friends. Now," she became suddenly very businesslike, "I need your attention, everyone. This is the plan."

Her gaze encompassed mine, making sure I was with her, was hearing and comprehending everything. I nodded. She did the same with Dad, who also nodded. She turned back to Mom, radiating complete attention.

Mom watched her like a moth watches a lamp, transfixed.

"Doma Q'Aleth," she began, "I am going to lift you from your chair and strap you into a cradle harness, so that I may carry you up the steps with my hands free. It will perhaps make you feel like a child, but there is no other way."

Nea unsnapped a small bag clipped to her belt and unfolded it into what looked like a piece of reinforced canvas dangling a snake pit's worth of straps. Squatting before Mom's chair, she began working the canvas under and around Mom, weaving her limbs into the chaos of straps, adjusting here, tightening there, making certain her neck was supported by the canvas, until she was bundled like a babe.

When she was finished, she said simply, "Now I will lift you and secure your harness to mine."

Mom sat, placid, as Nea hoisted her up, clipped the cradle to a loop on her chest, and adjusted a few more straps so that she could carry Mom freely and easily. Nea was not even breathless. She appeared even more enormous now, with Mom, doll-like, cradled against her. Mom stared up into her face, suddenly bewildered.

"We will climb the steps together, you and I," Nea told her. "You will be very safe, Doma, I assure you. For all my size, I walk quite lightly. When we reach the Hellhole, we will take a few minutes as I harness up Domi LuPyn."

She gestured to Dad, her hand just brushing his elbow. "When he is secure, I will lower him down first to the bottom of the serac. Then it will be your turn again, Doma. Your husband will have your tag line. He will use it to help you slide over the edge, and also keep you well away from the cliff wall. I hope it will be as pleasant as being rocked to sleep. When you reach the bottom, your husband will unclip you from the rope, and tie the second rope—the tag-line—to the first, so I can gather both ropes back up. Then I will harness your daughter, Domenna Q'Aleth, and lower her down. All of this will take less than twenty minutes. After that," she concluded, breaking eye contact with Mom to check in with Dad and me again, "I myself will rappel down the serac using the naked anchors I have left in the ice. I will hitch Doma Q'Aleth onto my back again, and we will all depart the serac the way I came in, beneath the ice—and leave Gelethel to its angels."

She said the last with a great tranquility, but I sensed that beneath that calm, she hated this place. She couldn't wait to crawl under the labyrinthine serac and escape out into the open blast of Bellisaar again, trailing three refugees like trophies from an enemy encampment she had successfully infiltrated.

Which, I suppose, was exactly what she would be doing.

I closed my mouth, which had fallen open. My heart was skidding triple-time. "How did you get in at all?"

"I told you. I climbed," Nea replied patiently. She drew from her belt two axes. The heads were long, thin, curved, serrated like the skulls of pterodactyls. I also saw that what I'd at first mistaken for a strange metal was not metal at all. It was ice.

"You *climbed*?"

"Yes. You know—kick, pick-pick?" she explained, as though it were a rhyme every child should already know.

My throat swelled with disbelief. I forced a breath to hush my voice, which otherwise would have bellowed out. "But how did you leave your anchors in the serac? No tool can pierce the ice!"

Nea beamed with pleasure. Now it was she who looked like a child. A very large, very intimidating child.

"A hundred years ago," she began, almost in a sing-song, "when fourteen angry angels cracked the serac, shards of ice splintered off, and fell to the far side of the southern point. Nirwen the Artificer was lurking outside the city, in the long shadow of Tyr Hozriss—at last beyond the range of the other angels' senses. She gathered up the pieces of ice and took them with her into the Waste. From them, she made these. And these. And those."

Sliding the ice axes back into her holsters, she pointed to an array of what looked like long, hollow screws of various sizes dangling from her belt: all translucent as crystal, all a deep vivid blue.

"Ice screws," she explained. "They make holes in the ice—I thread my ropes through to make my anchors."

She directed my attention to the toes of her leather boots, from which two profound spikes of blue stuck out like teeth. She opened her mouth to expound further, but Dad beat her to it.

"Crampons!"

He'd been watching everything keenly; he'd never been one to interrupt or speak out of turn. But now he glanced at me. "Do you see, Ishi?"

"Nothing pierces ice from the Gelthic serac," I said slowly, "except ice from the Gelthic serac."

Nea slid a hand over her belt lovingly. "Nirwen made these tools long ago. When I discovered that I . . . that I had the mutation, rare for my people, I went to her. I confessed I felt the despair that might drive me to the Zilch. She told me I needed to give my life meaning, and to that end lent me these tools to wield."

Turning abruptly, she pointed to Mom's wheelchair. "Does that fold up?"

"Uh, no," I said, trying to keep apace.

"We must leave it then. You will have to get her another in Sanis Al. The chairs are all spell-tech there. They fold up on command, go where you direct them, are durable but paper-light. Some of them fly. S'Alians have such sorcerers, such physicians! Perhaps trying to make up for years of child sacrifice."

She dismissed my startled expression and the wheelchair together. "Don't worry; they don't do that anymore. Unlike the angels of Gelethel, the Fas of Sanis Al evolved. But until we get you settled in that city for good, never fear: I will carry her. And so, are you ready, Doma Q'Aleth?"

Mom mumbled something from her canvas cradle. Her expression was quickly melting from bewildered to tearful.

Dad reached up and patted her ankle. "It's all right, Moon Princess. It's a throne worthy of you."

Mom smiled tremulously, and Nea smiled down at Dad with approval. Without another word, she began hiking up the white brick steps to Tyr Hozriss.

Dad and I stared after her a few moments, stricken with something like awe. He cleared his throat, but I was the one who spoke first.

"You go on. I'll stow the chair and chariot and be right up."

Dad nodded and started slowly up after Nea and Mom. I first wheeled Mom's chair, then pedaled the chariot, into the deep shadow beneath the southern stair. When they were hidden, I hurried to re-lock the gate that caged off the steps to Tyr Hozriss. These tasks done, I ran up after Dad. It did not take me long to reach his side.

When I offered him my arm to lean on, he looked at me, raising his wire-bush eyebrows. "I shall have to buy a special cane in Sanis Al, I see." He sighed, his stooped shoulders heaving with exaggerated melancholy. "So that my daughter may walk unburdened again."

"Yeah, what a burden," I teased him. "It's not like I owe you my existence, my cultural education, and whatever vestige of a moral compass that remains to me or anything."

I could barely see his face, now that Nea's blue button was far ahead of us and masked by her bulk. But Dad's smirk had always had an unmistakable air.

"A moral compass can get you lost in Gelethel," he noted.

"It's getting us out now."

Well, a moral compass, a new saint, and the help of a rebel angel.

Dad shrugged a little. "We're not out yet, Ishtu."

WHEN I'D GONE TO DAD'S EARLIER THAT AFTERNOON AND told him my plan—basically, that I was taking him and Mom to Sanis Al tonight, willingly or *un*—he hadn't argued. He'd looked, briefly, astonished.

After that, a fierce focus possessed him. Dad turned from me and right away began packing, slimly for himself, bulkily for Mom.

I left him at home so I could wrap things up at the Quick, where I spent the afternoon giving Ali a crash course on the projectors and changeover system, teaching him the cues to look for, how to unload and reload the feed and take-up spindles, and telling him that he'd be in charge, because I'd be busy the rest of the night. Our last exchange went thusly:

"You're to look after the place for me, Mister Ali. You're my manager, okay?"

The glow on his face. The radiance. How he'd basked in the hon-orific, in the blessed respite of a new title.

"Yes, ma'am. Yes, Doma Q'Aleth. Thank you."

I wasn't a Doma; I'd never married. But to him, I probably seemed too old to be called Domenna. Instead of arguing, I gave him my keys, saying, "Eat whatever you want from the concessions; the angel Olthar replenishes the snack counter biweekly—on third day—the Feast of Excess. That's day after tomorrow. Make sure you clean out all the old stuff before he does—we don't want bugs."

I was mindful that I never bothered with any of these chores anymore—but, really, why should Ali be idle? He came more alive with every demand I made of him.

"What else?" He clasped thin, imploring hands before him. "I found your carpet sweeper. Shall I vacuum?"

I strove to sound authoritative, not guilty. "Of course! Once or twice a fortnight should do nicely, unless there's a spill."

He looked at me with a hint of disapproval, a little lift of the chin. I had a feeling that Mister Ali was going to be sweeping the Quick's carpets nightly, and possibly daily too. And why should he not?

I cleared my throat, which seemed, suddenly, full of briny toads. "QH Industries picks up trash every fifth day before dawn. Oh, you'll want to know: that's the day after Feast of Meat, when Ratha-nana manifests megabovids in his district for slaughter. You take your benzies over to Abattoir, and they'll trade you for your portion."

"I don't have any benzies," Ali reminded me politely.

"Never mind," I assured him, moving rapidly past the sinking feeling in my chest. "After this, I'll show you the safe. As a ghost in Gelethel, you can't legally trade benzies yourself, but as an employee of the Q'Aleths, you can trade in our name. You'd be surprised how much bovid you can get for a few buckets of popcorn."

He nodded, his eyes wide and solemn. "Yes, Doma Q'Aleth."

"Fifth day," I continued, "is trash day. The angel Murra's feast day. We call it the Feast of Whispers, or just Whispers. Everyone in the city must speak quietly on that day, Ali, so bear that in mind. People would look at you askance if you yelled. The noisiest thing around will be the QHI chariots pedaling the city's trash to the dump-lifts."

Something flashed across Ali's face that reminded me strongly of Betony, his skeletal features suffusing with something far older and sadder than his years.

"That's when we ate." He looked down, knuckled the corner of his mouth, his whole body crying out though his voice was very quiet. "We didn't call it Whispers. We called it Vittles—in, in . . . Cherubtown. No one whispered then. There were fights over what came over the ice—I mean, the serac. We'd all be waiting at the dumpsite, lined up since dawn, looking up. And when the dumping started . . . it was like bombs dropping."

He passed a hand over his eyes. "I'm glad. I'm glad to know its real name. Murra's Day. The Feast of Whispers. It's . . . right."

This boy, this murderous boy. Living off the rot of Gelethel and still in love with the angels.

I took his chin in my hand almost helplessly, but then I didn't know what to do with his face. He waited. Utterly trusting. Utterly faithful. He wanted only more chores, every task an anchor in his new life, making him less a ghost.

"Come on," I said. "I'll show you the safe. Put all the benzie slips from the till inside it every night after the show."

He trotted after me, absorbing everything I said like a cactus in a once-a-year rain. "Also, you know, Mister Ali, the Quick is dark all day. We don't open till after sundown. So in the morning and afternoon, you're free to do whatever. I recommend going to the library. It's called the Shush—in Shuushaari's District. We missed it today—but in a fortnight on the Feast of Fish, take some benzies over to Shuushaari's fountain square, and fill a bucket with whatever the First Angel has manifested. Swordfish is my favorite, but cod and tilapia are great too. If you think ahead, you can go to Bower and harvest a bunch of lemons from Alizar's orchards. Lemon and fish are great together. Shuushaari's salmon is good and fatty—sometimes it arrives pre-smoked! Oh," I added, "my library card is in my sock drawer. Use it."

"Your s-sock drawer?" Ali stammered.

"There's nothing dirty about my socks, gh—Mister Ali. I prom-ise. Good Gelthic socks. Borrow a pair if your feet get cold. And use the library. Books are good for you. All Q'Aleths are educated, so you have to be too."

He started glowing as soon as I said this, and stopped asking questions, which was why I'd said it. I was worried about him, but I knew I shouldn't be. He would inherit everything once I was gone. He'd have the Quick . . .

But I thought I'd drop by Uncle Zulli's, last thing before I left for Mom and Dad's again. I'd ask him and Madriq to keep an eye on the boy. They'd know what to do.

"All right," I said. "I'm off. Think you can handle things tonight, Mister Ali, while I go on my hot date?"

"Yes, ma'am! I mean, yes, Doma!"

"Maybe I'd better start calling you Domi Ali, eh?" I teased him. "You're just that important."

He beamed, and his mouth was missing too many teeth from too many years of deprivation and malnutrition and who knew what other abuses? I wanted to embrace him. But this was all the goodbye the kid was getting. One misspoken word, and I'd wager half my heart he'd go straight to the angels. And why shouldn't he? Loyalty to me would mean him losing everything all over again.

When I returned later to my parents' house, I found Dad ready and waiting. Mom was napping on the couch, and Dad was reading an old textbook about Gelthic architecture called *Salt and Starch: The Stuff of Angels*. He'd left his stack of finished screenplays in a teetering heap by the trash pile, and never said a word about them, so I didn't either.

But I lingered on the back porch those last few hours to mourn them. His screenplays! I reread a few of my most beloved favorites. I even read one I'd never seen before—and it wasn't my favorite, but it was still so good, so very good, so *Dad*.

The urge to empty my backpack and stuff it full of his scripts leapt like flame in me. It itched in my fingers, my palms, the soles of my feet. So rash. So ludicrous. Such obnoxious urgency. I almost thought the angel Alizar was trying to tell me something. But it was only grief. And I didn't have time for grief. I had time to do the last of Dad's dishes, and that was all.

Then, when the angel bells rang midnight in, I loaded my parents up into the chariot I'd chartered for the purpose, and we set off for Hell.

◆   ◆   ◆

"**Y**OU SAY SOMETHING, ISHTU?" DAD ASKED ME.
   "Nah. Just my knees creaking. How about you? You good?"
"Never better."

But he sounded winded, tired. And no wonder. We'd been climbing the beard of Grandpa Forever and hadn't even reached his chin yet. I didn't remember the stairway seeming this long when the uncles took me up. But then, I'd been six and a half years younger, and had my ageless uncles to buoy me along. Now, what with worry for Dad, and our frequent stops to catch our breath, I was constantly checking the night sky for signs of dawn.

Not that I'd let on for a single second.

"When we get to Sanis Al," I told Dad in a conspiratorial whisper, "if you ask very nicely, I'll take you to see a *talkie*."

In the dark, Dad's deep-eyed smile deepened. "Pankinetichrome, even?"

"All the colors of the rainbow." I flared my hands and shook them like a burlesque dancer. "Full orchestra!"

"Don't think they do those anymore. But now that you mention it," he mused, "I might fancy a musical after so many years of Gelthic drought."

I groaned. "*Music*! Okay, Dogman. If we must."

"A musical," Dad continued, "with dancing. *Tap*-dancing, Ishtu."

"Oh, bells. How about . . . tap-dancing and sword fights?" Dad didn't like fighting movies, but I loved them.

"Mmn," he countered, "tap-dancing and sav-nav?"

I loved sword-fighting, but I *adored* sentient psi-ships with an agenda. "Very well," I agreed. "A musical might just be about bearable if tap-dancing boats are involved."

Dad leaned sideways into my arm, heavy with affection. "Then we'd better get a move on."

We didn't. We continued at our tortoise pace, and the night burnt on and on, until—at last—the stair ended abruptly in its deadly shear, and there were no more steps to climb.

The giantess Nea awaited us, still holding Mom, who was trussed up like a baby and singing quietly to herself. The song was crass and folksy, *very* Onabroszia Q'Aleth: a drinking song about Nirwen the Forsaker. How she'd wandered into Bellisaar and got herself fucked by every cactus, coyote, snake, vulture, scorpion, and wild dog of the desert. And at long last, limping but still horny, the Fifteenth Angel slept with the moon herself—who gave her ten children in quick succession, all giants. Nine were perfect beings—heroic colossi: gorgeous, honorable, intelligent. One was a villain named Zilch, doomed to die young, and Nirwen loved that one best.

"Yes," Nea hushed her quietly, her low voice drifting back to us. "I know that one. Gently now, Doma—we are approaching the Hellhole. The crevice is full of echoes, and it's only a hundred meters from here to the rampart. We don't want to be overhead."

Nephilim, I presumed, were masters of understatement. They had to be; everything else about them was so over the top.

I stretched my neck back to gaze at Tyr Hozriss rearing above us. The silent tower overwatched the whorled dunes of southern Bellisaar. A bitter black wind blew down over the serac and whipped my short hair straight up from my head. It smelled of mesquite and creosote, of sage and of sand. Not a hint of petrichor this time of year; the rains came later, if at all.

I looked up because I did not want to look ahead, and down—to the place where the salt steps crumbled away into ice, and the fissure opened up like a scream.

So close to the Hellhole, the ice was no longer smooth and blue but chipped and mottled, cobweb-white. Another black breath blew up from the depths below, this one smelling only of ice, ten thousand years of ice. I listened and it sighed again, as if something inside the serac slept uneasily. The wind chilled the sweat on my brow—which made me realize I was sweating.

Nea was unclipping a coil of rope from her jangling belt. "You are here. Very good. Your turn then, Domi Jen," she said to Dad, approaching him. "Time to harness up. Quickly now."

She glanced at the ramparts, and I could read the tension in the dim silhouette she cast against the sky. But the southern watchtower and its environs remained dark and quiet. Most of the patrols were concentrated between Tyr Valeeki, the west-point watchtower, and the area around QHI's dump-lifts in Hirrahune's district, halfway down the southwestern serac. Cherubtown.

Tyr Hozriss was no more than perfunctorily patrolled. Bellisaar was at the bottom of the continent; not much lay to the south of us but more Waste and, eventually—so our contraband maps informed me—the sea.

Dad stood ready to follow Nea's instructions as she knelt to weave her ropes around him, explaining everything in her under-hush. When she fell silent, she sat all the way down on the ground so that he could peer in at Mom, face to face. To our surprise, she was sleeping.

"Broszia must feel safe," Dad remarked.

"And do *you* feel safe, Domi Jen?"

Nea actually seemed to want to know—as if it mattered to her, as if she would stop at any time, and carry both him and Mom back down the steps, and leave Gelethel without us if he asked her to. He didn't.

"How about just Jen?" Dad's wheezing laugh was jovial, if thin. He white-knuckled the straps of his harness under each armpit. "And safe is never the way to feel on an adventure. I'll be fine."

"All right, then—Jen." Nea smiled down at him. "I promise you, you'll soon have your fill of ice. Henceforth, you will hold the rocks, and take your whisky neat."

"You bet." His face mostly in shadow, Dad glanced over and waved a pinkie finger at me. "See you on the other side, Ishtu."

Nea took me by the elbow and backed us both up as far as we could get from the Hellhole without falling off the stair. There, setting her stance like a tree taking root, she planted her left foot forward, her left hand holding the rope knotted to Dad. The rest of the rope was wrapped almost all the way across her waist, gripped by her right hand. On her command, Dad plonked himself down on the sloping steps, scooted forward on his buttocks to where the salt met the white-cracked ice, and dangled his legs over the edge of the Hellhole.

I stood beside Nea, watching her pay out the line of rope as Dad slid closer and closer to nothing but space.

And then, he went over.

Nea blew her breath out slowly. She fed out the rope even more slowly. The only sound in the world was the fibers of the rope scraping against her gloved hand as she controlled the friction. Controlled his descent.

I realized I wasn't breathing. Hadn't breathed since I don't know when. My thoughts were so cold they had begun to crystalize. They ran down Nea's patient line like fire along a fuse, racing toward my father, following him down and down and . . .

Without looking at me, Nea said, "The ice is not infinite. It only feels that way."

I turned away from the Hellhole before I blacked out. Then I scrabbled down five, six, seven steps until my shaking grew so convulsive I couldn't move another inch. My arms and legs were numb. I put my face between my knees. Everything was pressing in, squeezing in. Was this how Betony felt as the angels had drowned her? My heart . . .

"There, Doma Q'Aleth." Nea's whisper carried down to me. She was talking to Mom, but I knew it was for my benefit. "He's made it down. See? That's his signal, that tug. Easy, no? Your turn now."

Which meant I had to return, to drag myself back up the steps and watch as Nea carried Mom right to the edge of the Hellhole and laid her there in her canvas cradle, laid her where the salt sloped into the dropping dark.

She was kneeling beside Mom, feeding two ropes through the clip on the cradle harness. When she was done, Nea placed a hand on Mom's white hair, like an angel blessing benison wine.

Watching this nephilim was exactly as strange as encountering with my saint's eyes a new Invisible Wonder. Even describing her to myself felt like raving with sun-sickness. Behold the giantess: talons of ice, teeth of ice, helmed and gauntleted in pure black shadow. Behold the spell-tech button on her collar that glows like a single blue eye. Behold how her colossal body burgeons, on this cold-crackling night, with a dozen ropey tentacles, each an umbilicus into the void below.

Standing swiftly, Nea tossed the second rope—the tag-line— into the Hellhole, and then leaned out over it.

I shut my eyes, shut out the sight of her, but heard her call something into the darkness. Her voice echoed; I couldn't hear the words, or the answer that came back to her. If one did.

But when I opened my eyes again, she was nodding to herself, and turning and walking away from the Hellhole, satisfied.

"Jen has the line. I must stand back farther now and be Doma Q'Aleth's anchor. Come with me, Domenna," she commanded me.

Dizzily, I came to my feet, my mouth full of bad water.

This time, though, I didn't watch the rope, or Nea's face, or my mother—Onabroszia Q'Aleth, the once-great, now ruined, Garbage Queen of Gelethel—sliding into the Hellhole. I craned my head to the sky instead, and prayed.

Alizar the Eleven-Eyed was waiting there to welcome me.

He was there, in the firmament, in the clusters of star-like eyes and the spaces between them. He was also all around me, sitting in my bones: jewel-flame flower bells, feathering ferns, the fluttering of membranous wings, a warm and golden thing, like a lamp filled with fireflies.

Pure poetry, Q'Aleth, Betony told me admiringly, from the inside of my mind. *You know, you gonna be a poet, you gotta get yourself some ink. In the real world, real poets are head-to-toe tattoos. 'War flowers,' we used to call 'em, in Rok Moris.*

"You're here!" I was so delighted to hear her voice again, I almost looked around for her.

In the Seventh Anchorhold, actually. But I'm rootin' for you. Or—yeah, yeah, Bug, I know—prayin'.

I closed my eyes to see her more clearly. Against the white walls of her anchorhold, Betony's heavy hair was loose, black at the roots, red at the tips. She was sitting cross-legged on her bed of pink rock salt, which was covered in silks and furs. Her dark face was pinched with concern and concentration. Her eyes were like lamps filled with fireflies.

My panicked breathing slowed. My lungs were not my own; my friends were breathing for me, angel and saint together. I inhaled, and drew in not the shallow gasps that brought only a be-graying numbness, but deep, easy breaths. My racing heart calmed. The roaring in my ears settled. All was quiet.

Nea's own breathing was tranquil somewhere behind me.

"And . . . Doma Q'Aleth is down," the nephilim whispered.

"Thank you," I said and sighed, and opened my eyes.

"Your turn ne—"

A noise interrupted her.

We both froze and glanced toward it—not at the ramparts above, but at the gate below—far below, at the bottom of the steps. The cage rattled. Someone was testing the lock. Voices. Sonorous, confident. A bark of command. A ready assent.

It could be no one but the Holy Host.

Nea's eyes were very, very wide. "Into your harness," she said, whipping me toward her. "Now."

"No. Take this."

I shucked off our packs, shoved them at her. She clipped them all on so quickly to various loops on her webbing that her hands blurred.

"Are you ready to rappel down right now?"

"Domenna—"

"I can't get my parents to Sanis Al alone. You can. You *must*," I hissed. "Nea, please. Don't leave them down there with the ghosts."

She did not argue—there was no time—just placed an enormous hand on top of my head. Even through her gloves, I could feel her body heat, like a wildfire.

"I will see them safe," she swore.

The cage rattled again. This time, I heard the scrape as the gate was pushed open, chafing against broken paving stones and salt pan. Nea was moving swiftly to the edge of the Hellhole. She plucked one of the ice axes from her belt, dropped to her belly, and slid over the edge backward, feet first. I crept as close as I dared to watch her, but had to drop to my hands and knees to get even as far as two meters from the hole.

There was her anchor, just below the rotten white ice. Two clean holes, drilled into the perfect, deep blue. She climbed right down to it—*kick, pick-pick, kick, pick-pick*—and grasped the two ropes she had placed before she met us. One rope ran through the top hole of the anchor and was threaded through the bottom. A second rope was tied to the bottom of the first. Nea grasped both ropes together, let them fall between her legs, wrapped them up and around her right hip, over her stomach and chest, and over her left shoulder. She grasped them, leaned back, her legs perpendicular to the wall, appearing almost as if she were sitting, and gave me a little nod. Then she moved her chin toward the lapel of her jacket, tapping the blue button there—and the ghostly little light winked out.

Slowly, trembling again, I backed away from the Hellhole. My palms were cut in a dozen small places, stinging with salt. My fingers were shaking, freezing cold. My knees, scraped from such rough usage, bled through the rips in my coveralls. Back, I scrambled. Back and down. Down the steps, hugging them, head down, eyes on the solid bricks beneath me.

Safely back, safely down.

Down a few more steps. Away from that drop. Away from that icy emptiness. Away from escape, from my parents, from . . .

I backed into something hard. Into hands that reached down and plucked me into the air. For a moment, my spine connected with a scaled surface. The smell of leather and bronze enveloped me, the smell of ozone and fresh-welling blood and dirty feathers. Hard hands turned me around in the air, set me on my feet again, held me until I could stand on my own, and then released me.

"Niece," said Hosseril of the Holy Host, second in command to the Captain of the Hundred-Stair Tier. "What are you doing here?"

I stared up at him. Several angels stared back from my good uncle's face. Turgid galls shaped like pouting baby faces pushed out from his forehead. White enfouldred foam frothed at the corners of his mouth. A hawk's head jutted from his left ear. A spray of long fingers and even longer fingernails spiked up from his shoulder.

The angels were there—four of the fourteen. Watching me. They would know if I lied. Zerat Like the Lightning himself had been inside Host Razoleth when he commanded me to stay away from the serac. *Me*, specifically. Just yesterday.

Other warriors from Host Hosseril's cohort were spreading out behind him on the steps, rank on rank, heads upturned, eyes shining white. The Holy Host, as the angels had promised, were trebling their guard, as on the ramparts above, so below on the streets.

Talking to them would not help. Weaseling and waffling and negotiating were useless. All the tricks my bad uncles had taught me in the back alleys of Gelethel would not avail me now.

I had one goal: to lure Host Hosseril and the squad he commanded away from the Hellhole. I must give them no excuse to put ears to the ground or torches to the dark. No spears or arrows must fly from the lip of cracked serac into the icy black below, where my father and mother and the nephilim who rescued them might even now be waiting at the bottom like trapped fish.

And then, clarity.

I didn't have to outwit them. All I had to do was lead them *away*. All I had to do was get the Holy Host to chase me down the steps.

Thankfully, angels liked it when people ran.

Deep Focus: To Sit Below the Salt

B ENEATH THE DESERT, BENEATH THE SALT PAN, BENEATH THE
domes of the Celestial Corridor and the shell-like anchorholds
of the Celestial Cenoby, there was darkness.

And in this darkness, the angels kept their prisoners.

Not for long. It was only a matter of time before they tried and
sentenced their prisoners, singing themselves to a consensus regarding some properly histrionic finale. I could hear them even now,
thrumming from the possessed body of Host Hosseril. Mouth-slits
opening all over my good uncle's skin.

Count the angels covering him like paper cuts, like seeping sores:

Zerat Like the Lightning. Wurra Who Roars. Tanzanu the Hawk-
Headed. Rathanana of Beasts. Kirtirin: Right Hand of the Enemy
Twins. Impossible Beriu. Childlike Hirrahune. Thathia Whose Arms
Are Eels.

Count the angels absent from the Host:

Shuushaari of the Sea. Olthar of Excesses. Murra Who Whispers.
Kalikani: Left Hand of the Enemy Twins. Imperishable Dinyatha.

And, of course, Alizar the Eleven-Eyed.

Absent were all the weaker angels: those who, while not friendly to
Alizar, and while falling in line with Zerat and his ilk, had not actively
attacked or harassed the Seventh Angel since Nirwen's departure. Did
they fear him now that he had paraded the powers of the godhead
before the Celestial Corridor? Were they hiding behind their saints,
watching to see how his power play would play out? Or were they busy
on the ramparts, raining fire and salt onto the cherubs?

Wherever they were, they were not here in the saltcellars, crowding Host Hosseril's fleshly chariot, chittering in seven-part harmony,
seven separate red-hot knitting needles going right through my eyeballs.

What to do? How to handle her? How to punish the apostate?

Being caught with a key I ought not to have had, on the southern steps where I ought not to have been, close by the only egress
from Gelethel—and that, a secret kept by the angels and the Holy
Host—meant my execution, of course.

The question was . . . how?

Drown me in the Sacrificing Pool? But that would not be very
satisfying, would it? The pool was for pilgrims, after all—to cleanse

their filth, make their deaths fit for the angels—and I was a Q'Aleth, a citizen of Gelethel!

Dash me down into Cherubtown from the heights of the serac? Fitting, since I apparently wanted to flee fabulous Gelethel to live there in squalor. Why not drop me right at the dumpsite—where a fine fat Gelthic body like mine might feed a fortnight of desperate pilgrims?

Or, better yet! Consign me to a lonelier fate still—one of no use to those god-rotted scavengers. Walk me back to the Hellhole where they found me. Yes! Toss me unceremoniously into that lonesome and perpetual night, with none to see me, none to mourn my name.

Or . . . well . . . but it had been *such* a while since their last auto-da-fé! How grand a good blaze could be, such a sight to behold! The angels stopped burning criminals at the stake years ago, when a few of the early saints too loudly and too often lamented the stink. But what were the plaints of long-dead saints in the face of angelic desires? Did I not merit a punishment equal to my crime?

For—and this could not be denied—I was a special occasion. I, Ishtu Q'Aleth, only child of a favored family. An apostate. A forsaker. A follower of the Fifteenth Angel. A traitor.

Where is your father? sang all the angels, and before me in the saltcellars Host Hosseril demanded, "Where is the immigrant your father?"

I was hanging from my feet. I was bound to a wheel. I was pinned to the wall. I was tied to a chair. I was flung backward into a water barrel. I was, I was . . .

"Gone, good uncle," I said, again and again—but sometimes only in my mind.

Gone, screamed the angels, like a migraine aura. *Gone?* And Host Hosseril's flesh crawled and rippled with their revulsion as they sang their hymn of displeasure, like guts wrenched fresh from a carcass, stretched into strings.

How could he be gone? And where could he go? Why did he dare? What was he when he came to them? A dirty hunted Dogman of Koss Var! What had they made him? Their chosen one. Chosen! By the fourteen! To be a citizen of the Angelic City! This pilgrim, this *criminal*, this Jen LuPyn—how did he dare? He was asked to do *one thing* and *one thing only*: to run his movie palace for the glory of the angels. He was treated like a prince, like a very native babe of Gelethel—he even married the beautiful Onabroszia. They gave him *everything*! And he was *gone*?

"Gone?" roared Wurra, through Host Hosseril's too-stretched mouth.

"Gone, good uncle."

They knew I spoke the truth. The angels could not sense Dad anywhere within the serac. They! Who could, if they so chose, extend their radiant essences from ice wall to ice wall, overlapping the diamond and invading everything and everyone within it—like a city-wide stench, like music howling from the paving stones—they! *They* could not sense him. Jen LuPyn was outside their purview.

Gone, or dead.

Dead! the angels sang. *Heart-withered, blue-stuck, frost-limned.*

Deciding this, they dismissed my father, and turned their attention to Onabroszia Q'Aleth.

Where is your mother? they howled. And Host Hosseril, leaning over me, pulled seven ways, metastasized by angels, demanded, "Where is my sister, your mother?"

"Gone, good uncle."

So he asked me again.

And asked me, and asked. Again, and again.

Never did his eyes lose their white shine. Never did his tone vary from amiable curiosity. This was not my bad Uncle Eril, who still wept at all the old movies we played at the Quick, even the corny ones. Not our beloved Eril—who would have followed his sister, the Moon Princess, the Garbage Queen of Gelethel, into fire.

Uncle Eril knew exactly where my mother was, and he wasn't telling Host Hosseril. And neither was I.

He understood—we both did—that Onabroszia Q'Aleth had gone long ago, to a place neither her brothers nor her daughter could follow. She had wandered into her own inward desert, vaster than Bellisaar, and from those wastes where she had strayed no one could retrieve her.

No one but the angels, who might at any time have cured her. *Now* they regretted her? *Now* they keened?

O Onabroszia! wailed the angels. *Fairest daughter of our city! She whom we sponsored from a child! The highest we have ever raised any Gelthic maid short of sainthood! Where has she gone and why did she go?*

They asked this through Hosseril their Host—through his fists, his whip, through the angelic attributes that burst from his appendages. But no matter how many times they asked, I gave them the same answer.

I told them "gone" until they took my tongue.

Was it pliers? A knife? Nothing so mundane. It was Tanzanu's curving beak. It was Zerat's cauterizing flash.

And then I too was gone.

Like my mother, I wandered all the way inside myself, into the very flame at my heart's core, there embraced by Alizar the Eleven-Eyed and Betony, my sister-saint.

I felt nothing but their breathing all around me. Heard nothing but the faint flutter of wings, and Betony whispering:

"That angel Wurra's a real wink in the tusher, ain't he? I'd like to pike him where he pisses."

Or:

"You know which angel I could live without? All of 'em. No, not you, Bug. You're not an *angel* anymore, remember? Gotta think like a *godhead* now. Oh, Bug, on that note, got a query: are the hells real? Which one's worst? Gonna send my bratty brother there. Ha—just kiddin', Q'Aleth. Know you got a soft spot for the kid. And he worships you. Gave him a sweeper of his own, didn't you? Never knew a kid could love vacuum cleaners so much—but swear to Bug, it's all he ever asked for his last five birthdays. Not that I could swing it, war and all. Glad you worked that out for him. Really gets to you, don't he? Shitty little hairshirt."

But she said the last almost fondly.

Or:

"Hey, Q'Aleth. Ishtu Q'Aleth. Ish, my beloved. My sister. All done now. Your uncle—is he really two people? Whenever you think of him, my vision goes all prism-y—anyway, he's gone. Him and all his creepy angel augs. Saltcellar's clear of the Holy Host. I'm comin' down. Wake up."

Wake up.

I opened my eyes, which were already open—which were peeled open, pinned open, stapled to themselves, staring.

Betony was grinning down at me where I lay on the floor of the saltcellar, and her grin was a thin mirage over her horror. But I felt it in her gentleness, how she spoke so gruff and glib, how her tears fell on my opened ribcage.

"Got you good, didn't they?" she commented. "Bug says the angels flashed mad when they couldn't enter you. Like to work a body from the *inside*, he says. But they couldn't get inside *you*. 'Cause you're his saint. But they don't know that. Drove them waxy."

Her grin went grimace. Just for a second. Then it curled back in place. She was a natural bad uncle, cheeky in the face of terror. I'd have to tell her that, once my tongue grew back.

"You be jammy now, spar. Jam cake. Jelly roll. Sweet 'n' easy. Bug's workin' on puttin' you back together—from the inside, Q'Aleth. New parts, new heart. Growin' you just like a garden."

This body, which no other angel could invade, was altogether occupied by my angel. My godhead. I was more Alizar than myself, so much of me had Host Hosseril stripped away.

But Alizar was changing all of that.

My bones receded back into my flesh like shipwrecks into the waves. My blood-blooms furled down to bud again, smoothed themselves to unmarked skin. New fingernails pushed right out from the snipped, burnt, stumped bits left, and new toenails, too. And new teeth. A new tongue.

And then I screamed.

Betony was right there, plopped next to me on the floor. She was sitting against the wall, braced, so that when I slumped out of my rigid levitation, she could catch me and lower me down. She held me, as my leaking blood dried up and blew away like dust, as my scalp re-sutured itself, as my hair came unmatted and stuck up in all directions, as my skin-flaps folded back in and rejoined the rest of me. And when I could manage it, I turned the unexposed part of my jaw to her, and I showed her that I could still, after everything, smile.

"Want some water?"

"Please."

The word wheezed out like air through a broken bellows. Apparently Alizar was still rebuilding one of my lungs. He blew it up like a balloon; I could feel it glowing in my breast like a tribute to the dead before it was sent into the sky. I tried to wet my lips—I had lips again—and found that I was too parched to succeed.

Betony opened her hands.

"Bug?" she said, and her palms filled up and spilled over with pure sweet water. I bent my head and drank, and drank. And when there was water enough in my body again, I wept. I leaned against her shoulder, and wept.

That was how the boy, Ali, found us.

"Bet!" he yelped, and we both snapped upright.

Alizar Luzarius was staring at us from beyond the bars of my prison cell. Betony let out a noise that was mostly growl.

"Come to gawp, lizard dick?"

"What are you doing here?" her half-brother demanded, haughty and offended.

"Tendin' the sick and dyin'," she told him. "That's arrant saintly of me, ain't it?" Her chin jerked up, and I saw all too well where Ali had learned his death-before-shame face. "What're *you* doin' here? And," she added more curiously, "what the hells you wearin'?"

Ali's skinny shoulders straightened under Dad's old black and gold Quicksilver Cinema livery. "My uniform," he said, very stiff and grand, but now with more pride than arrogance.

"He's my manager," I whispered. The wheeze was less but my voice was still not strong.

Ali's gaze flew to my face. I must not have looked too bad by this point because his pinched features relaxed in relief.

"They said, they said . . ." he stumbled to repeat what "they" had said, words which had obviously sent him scurrying to find me. "The Holy Host came to the movie palace. They wanted to search the place everywhere. They took some of your things," he added. "I couldn't stop them. I—I'm sorry. I, I hid your library card. But . . . but he said you'd be here, in the saltcellars, and that I could find you if I was brave enough to come."

"Who said?" I croaked. Croaking was good. An improvement.

"Um," Ali's large brow screwed up in concentration. "Host Ira-zhul Q'Aleth," he pronounced. "He came with the others. There were so many of them, and—" he scowled— "and they turned the Quick upside-down. But they didn't harm anything. Said Quicksil-ver Cinema was blessed by the angels. And Host Irazhul, he said that you were his sister's daughter . . ."

He glanced at me reproachfully, as if hurt that I'd never men-tioned once in the whole two days we'd been acquainted that I had relatives in the Holy Host.

". . . and that you were going to be executed for treason. And he asked me what I was doing at the movie palace."

"What did you tell him?" I was now well enough to sit up against the wall, with Betony's help.

"I told him you'd hired me to be your manager." At that flash of pride, that shoulder-wiggle, that straightening of his spine, I could not help but smile.

I felt Betony struggling with her own response: smile, scowl, smile, scowl—a series of micro-expressions skittering by on the in-side of my mind. None of it showed on her face. She did, however, loose a snort so soft that if Ali hadn't flared his nostrils at her, I wouldn't have known she'd made an actual noise. I cleared my throat, nudged her to quiescence.

"And what did Host Irazhul say to that?"

The real question was, I thought, was it *Irazhul* at the Quick today—or was it Uncle Zulli *pretending* to be Irazhul? I'd been to see him and Madriq just before going to Mom and Dad's house . . . how long ago was that now?

Ali cleared his throat importantly. "He told me that it was very well, me being the manager, and to carry on. He called me 'Mister Ali'! He said I was doing the Angelic City a great service by keeping the doors of the Quick open. He said, to reward a job well-done, he would return later with papers, and claim me as a foundling for the Q'Aleths. He can do that," Ali informed me ea-gerly, "because ghosts are unwanted scraps, and therefore legally fall under the province of the garbage industry. But if Q'Aleth Hauling Industries claim me as salvage, he said, I won't be a ghost anymore!"

Oh, Zulli! I thought, reaching out across time and space to fling my arms around him one last time. *You big softy.*

Ali went on, "He also said that, with you . . . out of the way . . . I'd soon be owner of Quicksilver Cinema. Me! But then, I—I thought . . . I didn't want that. You, out of the way. So I came here, to ask the angels to maybe, maybe spare you."

Betony stiffened. "What did you offer them? They don't just give out favors, sebum. Angels always want somethin'—just like everyone else, everywhere else we been."

Ali turned to her, his tar-colored eyes glowing with the death-fires of martyrs. "I offered myself as sacrifice."

Betony's mouth swung open. "You little—"

I felt it then, yawning inside her like that icy black rift at the bottom of Hell: her despair. That she, Betony, who would have given her life to spare his (and had!)—must forever be consigned to watching her brother offer it up to every passionate cause.

Ali interrupted, "—they refused!" His voice broke. "The angels refused me, Bet. They said I don't count—because *you* are a saint, and saint-kin are sacred, exempt from sacrifice. You are a saint, so *I* don't count!" he repeated, his eyes flooding with such aggressive tears that she had to turn her face away from him.

After some quick, shallow breathing, Ali wiped his face and turned to me. "So I wanted, Doma Q'Aleth, I don't know, I wanted . . ."

But he couldn't seem to say what he wanted. He wanted, I thought, to say "goodbye."

Wearily, I patted Betony on the arm, crawled over to the bars of my cell, and beckoned him down to my level. Immediately, Ali sank to a crouch, his expression earnest, his eyes still pooling with tears.

"Isn't there anything I can do for you, Doma?"

I had my reply ready, and hoped he'd listen. "You do whatever Host Irazhul asks you to do. And you go to the library, like I told you. Read books. Every book that interests you. When you've read enough books to understand yourself a little better, ask your sister for forgiveness. Watch movies. Eat whatever the angel Olthar puts in front of you, and trade for better. Be kind to pilgrims: don't forget where you come from. For the rest," I shrugged, "live. Live a long life in Gelethel, and for the godhead's sake—" Ali flinched; he already had the Gelthic god-flinch down pat— "be *happy*. You bought your happiness dearly enough."

I slipped my hand through the bars to set it on his shoulder like Mom used to do. "Now—go. With my blessing."

Ali, ever obedient, rose to leave.

At which point, his namesake, Alizar the Eleven-Eyed, decided to make his appearance. Apparently, he was feeling more than a mite mischievous after all the miracles he had wrought in me, his saint. He was feeling, in a word, zoomy.

And so, Alizar the Eleven-Eyed splashed out from the tips of my fingers in an arc of green-gold fireflies. Seven times seven this swirling flame zipped around Ali's head, before hurtling back into my cell, and then out again—darting and weaving between the prison bars until the Seventh Angel—the godhead—was all tangled up in them like a quick-growing vine.

He swelled, he greened, he ramified: each twining tendril of him growing and lengthening, sweating sap, until, like a forest reclaiming lost desert, Alizar's thewy vines prized those iron bars apart.

Of course, this was not showy enough for him; Alizar was, at heart, a clown. He wanted a rumble, a rooting, a verdurous upheaval. He wanted to turn all the ruins into flowers.

So he did.

Alizar pulled Bower from the saltcellar stones, and made it bloom.

Chunks of compressed halite and iron and stone fell. Falling, they turned into the glowing bell-like flowers that Alizar favored for his personal appearance—blowzy, drowsy angel trumpets the size of chalices—which clumped at Ali's feet like he was the statue at their chosen shrine.

I knew that Ali could not see angels. He never could and never would—though, like Mom, the longing for Invisible Wonders had all but bent him inhuman. And so I had no idea, at first, how he was tracking all of the angel Alizar's activities so closely.

"Not an angel." Betony took my hand in hers and squeezed it. "Bug's a god now, spar. Anyone can see gods, if the gods want seein'." She examined Alizar with a critical eye as he disported himself about the saltcellars. "Never knew a godhead so vain as our Bug. But then," she shrugged, "I never knew a godhead before Bug."

Each of Alizar's attributes danced before Ali's astounded vision— arcs of fiery light, green-staining vines, enormous flowers—until, overwhelmed, Ali crashed to his knees. He pulled his attention from Alizar and gazed up me instead, with an expression I'd only seen before on those who worship the angels.

"You're a saint!" He was weeping from the miracle. He had gathered up as many of Alizar's flowers as he could hold to his thin chest and was busy burying his whole face in them. Betony shook her head and sighed, but said nothing. "You're a *saint!*"

"Shh," I said, letting my sister-saint help me to my feet. "Don't tell anyone."

Extreme
Long Shot:
Floodwaters

I N THE END, MY DEATH WAS AN AUTO-DA-FÉ AFTER ALL. BUT DON'T let that stop you from watching.

♦ ♦ ♦

F IRST, WE SENT ALI HOME. *HIS* HOME NOW: THE QUICK.
"You'll be alright," I reassured him. "Lock the doors till evening. Stay inside—*stay away from the ramparts.* Open tonight as usual. That's your job now." I wasn't at all sure it would still be his job come nightfall, or if Gelethel as we knew it would even still be standing, but it would give him something to think about.

"Yes, Saint Ish! At once!" Ali beamed at me, his arms spilling over with flowers, and he ran—ran!—where yesterday, he could only crawl.

Betony stared after him.

"He'll be alright," I said again, trying to convince both of us.

"Yeah, I dunno." Betony shook herself from the head down. "He's such a fuck. He's such a little kid."

Alizar breezed between us, chiming crystalline wings and urgent eyeballs, spurring us on, through this corridor and that, the rat-paths of the saltcellars, and on and on, and into a small hall with some stairs leading up.

To the barracks, as it turned out. Which were emptied of the Holy Host.

Or—almost.

Uncle Eril was hanging by the neck from one of the light fixtures in the ceiling. It was a monstrous appliance, the handiwork of some fanatic designer, with brass coils and long glass tubes blown into the stylized spirals iconically associated with Zerat Like The Lightning.

My bad uncle was not dead. Yet. Eril had been a Host too long to die so easily. It might take him hours to suffocate. Perhaps he'd thought he had hours, with the other warriors of the Holy Host away at the ramparts, and the angels occupied with Cherubtown. In his present state, not activated by any angel, he would indeed choke to death, and soon, if we did not pull him down.

"Alizar!" I cried out, just as Betony bawled, "Bug!" at the top of her lungs.

But Alizar was one step ahead of us. My feet were already lifting right up off the ground, and I flew to the ceiling as if launched. Too fast, too fast! I grabbed one of those gleaming brass coils to stop myself, swinging around to face my uncle. His tongue was protruding from his mouth; his face was flecked with strange spots. I forced myself not to look too closely for fear it would freeze me, and grasped the rope my Uncle Eril hung by right at its seventh knot.

The knot frayed apart at my touch. Then each successive knot exploded, until the choking loop itself burst from my uncle's neck as if repelled by his flesh. He would have fallen, but I caught him by the collar and lifted him away from that abominable light.

He had shed his kidney-pink armor, his helm and gauntlets, and was dressed in a simple shift, like a penitent, or a child who has readied himself for bed.

I began to lower us. It was as if we were floating in water—in one of Shuushaari's public fountains, where Uncle Eril had taught me how to swim—only now it was he who was lying on his back, trusting the hands beneath his shoulders to keep him afloat. Locked together like this, in trust, we drifted lightly to the ground.

He was not conscious. His face was riddled with scarlet petechiae. The bottom of his clean-shaven neck was branded with an inverted V from the rope.

I stroked the side of his cheek.

My gentlest of uncles. My beloved Uncle Eril, whose favorite movie was *Balais of Entayle*: a swoony courtly romance, full of outlaw ladies lying in ambush on the God-King's Highway, ready to pluck rubies off the brows of pretty young noblewomen, and rebel poets locked away in towers needing rescue, and the God-King of Koss Var: a shadowy menace at the center of it all. He was always talked of, never seen—or, at most, a hint of profile as he bent to whisper in the ear of one of his advisers. Even his throne was always shot from behind. He was terrifying, like the angels of Gelethel. Of course, the poets and the outlaws won against him in the end. That's what they did, in movies. Maybe the only place they ever did.

And that's why we need movies, Uncle Eril had once told me. *That's why it was such a great good thing—the day your father came to Gelethel.*

Betony knelt on Eril's other side, resting a tender hand upon his chest. "Which way?" she asked, and I knew what she meant: which way did I want us to push him?

A terrible choice.

Uncle Eril had always been sorrowful—persistently, unceasingly sad—for as long as I knew him. This was his chance to escape all of that, to go back to the salt, and I could help him. The three of us, together, could help him.

But it was I who had pushed him to this, today—I, and the angels—for they had ridden him hard and forced his hand against me, his niece, whom he had left for dead in the saltcellars. And then they had abandoned his flesh, left him sick and sore and wild with regret, all of his memories still cruelly intact, as they themselves flocked to the ramparts to teach Cherubtown the lesson of the ages. They would be occupied now, the other angels, and would not turn their attention back to the Host they had used up for some while.

"We call him back," I decided. "Alizar, Betony—we have to breathe for him."

Betony nodded. Alizar was already sinking tendril-first into the V-shaped mark on Eril's throat. He did it so delicately, with such woebegone diligence, that Uncle Eril's chest began to move almost at once. Betony kept her hand on his heart, I kept mine on Eril's head. The entire time, Alizar was pouring images into us, translating Eril's afflictions from the inside, sharing them out so we might experience them all.

A chalice pierced through with holes, leaking wine.

A chariot upturned in combat, crushed under the wheels of other war machines.

A dead tree, strangled by vines.

This last one startled me, for I associated vines and green growing things with Alizar—and this was a vision of Alizar as parasite, Eril as host.

The image burnt to ash as I opened my eyes. Alizar was angry—as much with himself as with the other thirteen angels—but he just as delicately lifted himself back out of Eril and returned to his place hovering above us.

Regrets and remonstrations continued to course out of him, into us:

He should have acted sooner, done better, been braver; he should have gone for the godhead without waiting a hundred years for Nirwen to rescue him. He should have . . . .

Uncle Eril moaned.

I recognized that parched sound. I'd made it recently myself, down in the saltcellars. Imitating Betony, I cupped my hands to his lips. Water spilled out of my palms before I'd even prayed for it: more than water—benison water—shining like moonlight and alive with healing.

Uncle Eril sipped, semi-conscious, until he was awake enough to spit it out again, horrified. He opened red-speckled eyes and stared desolately around. He would have screamed, I thought—as I had screamed—except his throat was still too damaged.

"No, no, no," he rasped. "Why . . . why didn't you leave me?"

I leaned over him, stroking his heavy hair back from his brow. "O my uncle! I could not. You would not have asked me to. Nor would you have done so, had you been in my shoes. Please forgive me. Please understand."

Finally, he saw me. His eyes focused. His mouth formed my name, but he couldn't speak it. He thought I was a ghost, perhaps, or that he had joined me in death.

"I'm here," I said. "I'm alive. You didn't . . . Host Hosseril didn't kill me, Uncle Eril."

And he started to sob.

That was what one did, I supposed, when one was pulled back from the dead.

◆   ◆   ◆

"I CAN'T GO BACK, I CAN'T," ERIL KEPT REPEATING LATER, WHEN Betony and I had helped him to clean up and dress. "I can't be taken again, Ish, I can't. I should have waited. We have our quarantine phrases, now—" Betony and I stiffened to attention at that, and even Alizar's chiming stilled, but Eril went on, distressed— "I should have waited till I could take one of them out with me. We all agreed to it. Now that Broszia's gone. And you—you were supposed to be gone too. We were never supposed to find you; I don't know how they heard about your assignation at Tyr Hozriss, but I . . ."

"It's all right, it's all right, Uncle Eril," I tried to soothe him. "I'm whole, see? It's as if they never touched me."

He pinched a bit of my torn and bloody coveralls between his fingers. I covered his hand with mine.

"I will tell you everything, Uncle Eril, if—if there is time." I glanced at Betony, who nodded. "If there isn't, come see Saint Betony here, any time day or night, and she will be able to explain it all. But for now, Uncle Eril—before we make any more decisions—I have to ask you," I dipped my head, trying to catch his eye, "what did you mean by 'quarantine phrase?' What did all my bad uncles agree to?"

Eril seemed to stop breathing. He touched his throat, where the V-shaped mark now glittered golden-green. The small flecks on his face and in his eyes were no longer red but shining like chips of mica. Alizar's marks were upon him, but he did not yet know it. Uncle Eril hated mirrors.

"We're done," Eril said flatly. "My brothers and I decided, as soon as you and Jen and Broszia were safely out of here, that we were through. You can't resign from the Holy Host—you can only die in service. But we *will not* wait another sixty years for that relief. We have spent years imagining and planning our final exit; at times, the thought of it was the only way I could get myself out of bed in the morning. Today, Razoleth led us in our morning meditations. He assigned us a quarantine phrase: two words we could speak to ourselves, or to each other, the very next time we feel the angels taking hold. It will allow us—for a short time—to seal off our minds from angelic incursion. Though the angels possess our bodies, our brains should, briefly, remain our own. We thought that if we . . ." he glanced uneasily between Betony and me, "if we took our own lives while the angels were still inside us, we might kill them too. Or at least, damage them."

"Is that canon?" Betony asked me in an undertone.

I shrugged. I'd never been to the Hagiological Archives; I didn't know all the teachings of the saints but what the Seventh Angel—the godhead—had told me.

It is . . . unprecedented. Risky, Alizar admitted. *It might work?*

Eril was starting to stutter, "But I . . . after . . . after the saltcellars, I couldn't wait . . . couldn't bear the thought of them, of them entering me a-again." He was shredding at the edges, his words boiling off into the threat of unstoppable sobbing.

"No, no, of course not, of course not, it's all right," I said, crowding in to hug him. "You did the only thing you could, Uncle. I would have done the same."

He began to grow calmer, even as I despaired. Poor Uncle Eril! Raz! Poor Wuki! Poor Zulli—what would Madriq do without him? What would young Ali do? And how could I go on—wherever I went in this world—knowing that back in Gelethel, my uncles were nothing but bones in the salt?

Above me, hovering near the ceiling, Alizar chimed and whistled, winked and tinkled. All I had to do was reach up to him; he would give me anything I asked for. Anything.

And I knew what I had to do.

"I can protect you from the angels," I told Uncle Eril. "You won't ever have to use your quarantine phrase, because the angels will never enter you again. I promise. Uncle Eril, you don't have to leave this world until you are ready—not a second sooner."

He brought the heels of his hands from his eyes, and his face was wet, amazed as a babe woken from a bad dream.

"You can't, Ishi," he said. "No one can."

"Uncle." I took his hand. "Haven't you guessed by now? My secret? You may as well know it—now that Mom's gone."

Now that all of Gelethel might be gone before the day is out, I thought but did not say.

Eril was silent, his eyes downcast, gaze fixed on the blood-stained hem of my trouser leg. He looked exhausted, dejected. Everything in me, like it always did, longed to comfort him. Alizar was a-whir with the same desire, and beside me, Betony looked so frighteningly, fiercely ready to slay whole demon armies for him—and she didn't even know him, except that he was mine. But we all stayed very still, waiting. Until he spoke. Until he *recognized* me.

"You"—and Eril finally looked up at me, smiling with just the corners of his eyes—"are the daughter of Onabroszia's desire. You are the truest saint of Gelethel. The saint who walks free."

But then his smile flickered. Misery flooded him again. His dark hair fell into his eyes as he began shaking his head.

"But *all* the angels have saints, Ishi! You cannot fight them, not with only Alizar to protect you. They will rip you apart—and him as well! You cannot keep me safe. And I would die, *I would die*, to keep you safe. To prevent myself from, from . . ."

"Uncle Eril!" I joggled his arm until he focused all his wild fear into this present moment. "I *used* to be a saint of the Seventh Angel. I'm not anymore." I leaned my forehead against his and whispered, "Eril Q'Aleth, *there is no Seventh Angel*. There is only Alizar, the new god of Gelethel. And we"—here I stood, pulling him with me—"will make it so that no angel ever, *ever* possesses you again. Saint Betony?"

Betony rose up behind him. We locked our wrists together, enclosing Eril in the circle of our arms. Glancing at the scintillant sphere of godhead above us, she asked, "Hey, Bug. How's this goin' down?"

Alizar was too excited for translatable words. He was shedding feathers and petals and image after flashing image of

{*revelation*} {*ritual*} {*now*}

"With honey and beeswax, we seal him," I interpreted for Eril's sake. "With pollen and drupe—"

"—with rich loam and cool stone, we seal him," Betony and I said together. "By the bounty of Bower, Eril Q'Aleth, we seal your sovereign soul against all angels."

Heavy golden light dripped down.

◆ ◆ ◆

AFTERWARDS, WHILE ERIL RESTED, BETONY AND I STOOD A little aside, and argued.

"He can't stay here," I cast a revolted glare up at the horrible spiral light above us, where a bit of rope still clung, "and he shouldn't be alone. He's still very fragile. I have to get to the ramparts before my uncles trigger their quarantine phrases and do what cannot be undone. They have to know there's another way—that I can seal them off from the angels—that they don't have to die to be free."

"Well, yeah, and I'll trot along and help," Betony insisted. "Got two legs and a godhead, don't I? Could fly the fuck up those stairs as good as any other saint—right at your side. Where," she added vehemently, "I *belong*."

She did belong with me, always, cradled in my skull, hand in hand, back to back, saint with saint. I hated to leave her behind in this city, with people who did not love her as I did.

"Yes," I said. "You could, my sister. But I'm asking you to take Eril to Bower. He needs you more than I do."

Betony folded her arms tightly across her chest, and I could see her wishing, just for a second, that I were her brother Ali's size, so she could sit on me and subdue me until my temper tantrum passed.

"Q'Aleth," she said through gritted teeth. "I met three of your family now, yeah? One killed me. One killed you. Now you're off to get yourself killed savin' three more of 'em. What's with the death wish? I don't get it!" She stepped close to me, right under my chin. I was of average height for a Gelthic citizen. Though Mom's people were tall, my Dad wasn't, really. Betony, I realized, was tiny. And she was also immense. "I seen enough death!" she spat. "I ain't sendin' you to yours without backup, spar. Got me?"

"Betony," I began.

But then I had a better idea than arguing with her. Just as she had smiled with my lips, and flashed her thumbs up with my hands, now Betony opened her mouth and said exactly what I was thinking, word for word, in my cadence and with my Gelthic patterns, so different from her own:

"You know what is going to happen up there! Alizar and Nirwen are ascending to the godhead. They have spent a hundred years amassing power enough to overthrow the angels and rule Gelethel: Nirwen, by perfecting her nephilim in some secret lair in the heart of Bellisaar; Alizar, by lying low and making Bower bloom. They need both of us. One to remain. One to cross over. You and I are at the heart of their plans."

Before I could make her say anything more, Betony clenched her teeth and ground her jaw, so I continued with my own mouth.

"I have to go. I have to go alone."

"To the ramparts," she hissed resentfully, involuntarily.

"To the top of the serac," we said together, and clasped hands.

But Betony was also shaking her head. "I don't care. I should be there. I *will* be there."

O my saint, Alizar the Eleven-Eyed told her mournfully. *I need you here with me—in Bower. And everywhere else in Gelethel, come the time.*

"But Q'Aleth . . ." Betony's lambent eyes sparked with prophecies that the godhead was pouring into us both. Fire and salt. Ice and floodwater. Almost gray with terror, she gasped, "I can take it! You know I can. I . . . I already did it once. You saw me. Ain't right you should bear that too, nobody should have to. . . ."

"No one should have to bear it *twice*, Betony," I said gently. "It's my turn now."

♦ ♦ ♦

*Y*OU SCARED? MY SISTER-SAINT ASKED ME FROM ACROSS THE CITY, from the heart of Bower. She sat cross-legged beside my sleeping Uncle Eril, where he lay in the soft green tiles of Alizar's mossery, both of them shaded by a flowering chilopsis.

"Nah," I said aloud. "I've seen this movie. Remember—*Life on the Sun?*"

Spar, that film was old when I was sperm. I grew up with talkies.

"It's so great. No, really," I insisted when she chuckled tiredly.

The sinking sun was of course right in my eyes—still high enough that the serac did not block it, but low enough to be obnoxious, and to tell me that the summer hour was growing late. Strange to think that in King's Capital, Koss Var, where Dad was from, it was the middle of winter. I shaded my face, and jabbered on—out loud, since it served the double purpose of reassuring me and scaring everyone away from the blood-stained, ragged woman talking to herself.

"So, the movie's all about how Sanis Al got its current god, Kantu. Well, that's what it's about *philosophically* anyway. It's a war movie at heart. But there's all this setup: years of drought, famine, civil unrest, dissent at the Shiprock, child sacrifice to stave off the worst. But of course, that *was* the worst. Things got so bad, our hero Kantu had to come along and become their god and take back control. Bring the rain. She had to make *herself* the sacrifice. That's how it worked in Sanis Al."

Don't see how all 'em angel sacrifices hereabouts yielded you gethels any great godsdamned result, Betony mumbled.

"Well, first of all, ritual sacrifice of a scapegoat isn't the same as *self*-sacrifice. Any saint can tell you that. Second of all, what do you mean no great result? We got *you* out of it, didn't we?"

Dungballs, Q'Aleth. But Betony sounded flattered.

The northwest and southwest walls of the serac were narrowing on either side of me as they shot toward the bottleneck of Tyr Valeeki, the western watchtower. It grew colder as I approached the dark blue ice, and soon, I was walking out of the sunlight and into the west-pointing shadow. Tyr Valeeki, fang-like, rose above me.

So, you ain't scared. But . . . are you ready?

I looked up. The white steps zigzagging their way to the ramparts, and the ramparts themselves—running from Tyr Valeeki all the way to the QHI dumpsite ten kilometers to the south—were packed with warriors of the Holy Host. All of them were radiant with angels: their attention, for the moment, directed outward.

"Shit," I breathed.

We have you, Betony told me sternly. *We're holdin' you between us.*

We will not let you go, my saint, said Alizar.

I swallowed at the sight of all those stairs. My knees creaked and shrieked. "Um . . . Bug?"

Betony laughed in surprise at my use of the nickname. Somewhere inside me, the god Alizar grew a plumy, sparkly, rainbow-and-rose-petal tail, and began wagging it like an overgrown dragon-pup at his first sight of a doughty maiden fair.

Yes, my saint? Yes? What can I do for you?

"Can you . . . give me a boost?"

It was quite something, not having to take the stairs.

◆ ◆ ◆

I FOUND UNCLE ZULLI FIRST, PARTLY BECAUSE HE WAS STATIONED right there at Tyr Valeeki, and partly because Alizar dropped me right smack on top of him. I didn't even wait to catch my breath before I looked straight into his cold white eyes, and spoke the quarantine phrase:

"Bad Uncle."

The angel rays vanished from his eyes as though snuffed. The half of his face encrusted in Shuushaari's barnacles began to shimmer. I watched as the First Angel reared up and rose out of him, frightened as an oyster suddenly shucked of her shell. I stared at her next, who thought herself invisible to me, and let her know that she was seen.

"The godheads are coming," I told her. "I wouldn't stay anywhere near this serac if I were you."

Shuushaari whipped herself into nothingness—but I could not tell where she decided to go, or whom she would warn before she went.

I bent down to the astonished Zulli and hauled him to his feet. "Ish. *What?*"

"By honey and beeswax, I seal you," I began, and didn't end until my bad uncle was safe from all angels.

Zulli began patting himself down almost immediately, as if searching for some stowaway angelic attribute in his back pocket: an eel, a pearl, the head of a hawk. There was nothing.

"Uncle Zulli," I said urgently, "Zulli, listen to me. I need to find Wuki and Raz."

"They aren't . . .."

He looked around, gathered me up under his arm and drew me into a sheltered doorway where the other warriors of the Holy Host—and their angels—would have trouble seeing us.

He whispered, "I mean, they're all *Hosts* right now, Ishi—not for fakes, but—" he glanced at me, and then threw up helpless hands at whatever expression he encountered there. "What are you even doin' here, girl? I thought we got you safe out of this rot!"

"I'm not a girl, I'm a saint—and even if I weren't, I'm thirty-eight years old! Now," I said briskly, before he had a chance to recover, "I have just retired you from the Holy Host, Zulli Q'Aleth.

Congratulations. Go home to your husband. Make sure that boy Ali at the Quick grows up to be a good man. No matter if it means him eating half your share of Madriq's cakes, and you telling him your worst jokes! Right now you're the only Q'Aleth in Gelethel who knows his name. Can I trust you to leave now—fetch Madriq, fetch Ali, fetch anyone who will listen to you, and bring them to Bower—or as close to the center of the city as you can get?"

Uncle Zulli peeled the bronze helmet from his head. He contemplated it for a moment, then turned, wound back his arm, and hurled it over the crenellated parapet. It arced, glinting, into the burning desert beyond.

Released, his black hair porcupined straight up, just like mine, and he ruffled a bemused hand through it.

"I don't know what in Nirwen's Hell is going on," he said. "But you're givin' me that Broszia look, so I know my answer. I'm outta here. And, Ishi . . ."

He touched his face again, where the angel Shuushaari no longer rode his flesh like her chariot. "Thanks. My niece. My saint."

◆ ◆ ◆

WUKI WAS HARDER TO FIND, NOT LEAST BECAUSE THE ANGELS had diverted part of their Holy Host to apprehend me.

Those white-eyed warriors, however, weren't much more than a distraction—no matter how many attributes they bristled, or what mighty swords they brandished. Alizar was only too happy to lob me high into the air and out of their reach. Between us, Betony and I made a game of foiling the spears and arrows that came flying at me, transforming them into increasingly harmless and ridiculous things, things to make our god giggle: balloons, confetti, silly string, paper flowers, real flowers, stuffed toys, and once, when two Hosts launched a small rocket my way, a circus tent—the big top—which dropped down like a mushroom cap over a considerable length of the ramparts, bringing red-and-white-striped darkness and confusion to the warriors milling beneath it.

A circus! cried Alizar. *There has never been a circus in Gelethel! Tell me of the circuses you have seen, my saint!*

Later, Bug, Betony promised. *Bedtime stories all around.*

When I came to a section of the ramparts empty of the Holy Host, Alizar eased me lightly onto the parapet. I leapt from merlon to merlon, balancing like a dancer, my knees the knees of a twelve year old . . .

My knees?

"Alizar! Are you fucking with my anatomy—*against our agreement*?"

Oh, Ishtu, just this once? he wheedled.

"Oh—!"

. . . and because I knew that this was probably going to be the last gift my Alizar would ever give me, and because I knew that the end, my end, was rushing toward me like a flood of blood rain from the west . . .

"—I accept," I said. And then added, "Thanks."

You're welcome! Alizar shouted joyously, and all the youthful elasticity and buoyant energy and dazzling speed that he could put at my command pounded into my body. I ran across the crenellations like they were god's own teeth—south, toward my Uncle Wuki.

Confetti and big tops were, well, wonderful, but I wished I could expel the angels from the bodies of all the Holy Host. Warriors who were not my uncles, however, hadn't trained their minds with trick mazes and with quarantine phrases. They had no special code to separate out one spare bit of themselves, keep it sacred, keep it for their sovereign own. Most of them had worked all of their lives to be seats of the angels. It was their vocation. They consented, enthusiastically, to be so used, and it was in this consent that the angels had truly taken root, branching out from that utter faithfulness like hyphal networks and spreading through their Host's entire foundation, body and soul. There was no space left to dig out the angels without scooping out most of the Host along with them.

So I spared the warriors my exorcisms. But as I ran along, I tried to make Alizar promise that one day, all of Gelethel would be safe from infestation by angels—or by gods.

Gods? Even me?

Betony took our brewing debate into her own hands with a firm, *We'll talk later, Bug.*

And so my sister-saint assured me that she would carry on this conversation after I was gone. I let it go for now.

"Where is he?" I wondered aloud, and my words were whisked away by the high wind. "Where's Wuki?"

Further south.

Further south, it turned out, was where greasy black smoke was rising from Cherubtown.

Apparently, the Holy Host had been busy setting fire to the Gelthic dumpsite all afternoon. From there, the fires had spread through the whole of the dried-up shantytown—and the way-station—and the ancient little shrine that had stood outside the serac for almost as long as Gelethel had been the Angelic City.

Cherubtown was in flames.

But—and this was odd—it was a Cherubtown curiously empty of cherubs. I stopped running to take it all in. Barefoot and balancing on the parapets, I turned to scan the desert for any sign of life.

My eyesight sharpened (Alizar again, ever eager to help), and all at once I could focus in on them clearly, as if staring through a telescope: several kilometers out, a hasty smudge of refugees stretched quite a ways across the dunes.

Surrounding them was a semi-circle of giants, all of whom were straddling enormous, gleaming viperbikes. Some sat casually, some were upright and alert, as if awaiting a signal.

"Zilch?" I whispered. And then, ashamed at forgetting the first lesson Nea had taught me, self-corrected, "Sorry. Nephilim?"

Nirwen sent them, Alizar explained. *They are to protect her cherubs from all enemies—from Gelthic angels, from their siblings gone Zilch, and other terrors of the desert.*

Betony chimed in: *Terrors? What, like those demon armies you was rappin' about, Bug?*

Alizar shuddered, her words instantly conjuring for him the slinkycold/quickburrowing/twicetongued/insideout/mildewsmog-withteeth demonic things that had pursued the god Gelethel and her angels across Bellisaar ten thousand years ago. His memory of that time was so visceral, so venomous, and still so immediate that I almost puked it out of me right there, his fear and disgust in my mouth.

But Betony, half a city away from me, flung out her hand—and so, therefore, did I—and I caught myself before I puked myself into a belly flop right over the serac.

That was close, Q'Aleth.

"Too close."

I huddled down, clinging to the merlon beneath me with both arms, and turned my head to spit the taste of mold out of my mouth.

Sorry, Ishtu, Alizar said penitently. But any remonstrations I might have returned to him were cut off at tongue's root as I perceived, from my new vantage, what I had originally missed:

Not all cherubs were hanging back in the Bellisaar dunes as the fires of the Holy Host consumed the last hope of home they had.

Some were swarming the serac.

Forgetting my nausea, I scooted sideways and leaned as far over the parapet as I could, peering at that section of serac that ran along the dumpsite to the smoky south. A line of furious, determined, possibly demented refugees from Cherubtown seemed to be climbing the ice with their bare hands.

The leaders were already more than halfway up the wall. More followed. Not many—a few dozen, maybe, all told. No match for the numbers of the Holy Host above.

But no matter what the Host flung down at them (chunks of salt, torches, rocks, spears, other saboteurs) some invisible force—dome-shaped, like a gigantic parasol—deflected the missiles and scattered them harmlessly into the smoldering middens below.

She may have allowed Cherubtown to be consigned to flame, but Nirwen the Forsaker was brooking no harm to befall a single lock of hair on her cherubs' heads. Not now that her powers were ascendant. Not anymore.

"But *how* are they scaling it?" I muttered, flattening my body until it was practically horizontal, and leaning almost all the way through one of the crenels, trying to make it out.

Alizar obligingly augmented my eyesight. Again.

I saw, and shared what I saw with my sister-saint, that what had appeared at first glance to be bare blue serac that the cherubs were shinning up was in fact a long ladder. It was wide enough for five people at least to climb abreast, and carved out of the ice itself.

Only the god of Cherubtown could have made such a thing. Only she had the tools to carve the serac like that. Nirwen the Artificer.

This wasn't part of the plan, Alizar murmured. *They were all supposed to stay well back—safe! In the dunes, with the others! The ladder was for* her. *Not* them.

"I think," I surmised slowly, backing myself up, palms flat, belly down, and slipping off the parapets to walk the solid salt-bricks of the ramparts once more, "that when they saw that ice ladder, some of the cherubs disregarded any instructions Nirwen left them and started climbing. I think they're . . . angry."

Anger ain't the word, Q'Aleth, Betony said, in a tone of voice I hoped to never to hear again.

"Whatever they are, they're moving really fast."

Nirwen must have spiked the food and drink at Cherubtown's surprise Feast of Saint Betony yesterday. She probably stuffed her chosen people with more benisons in a few hours than all the Invisible Wonders together managed to manifest in a given fortnight. The cherubs on the ice ladder were moving so rapidly that even I—I, who'd learned how to fly that day, how to prance across the parapets like some kind of teenaged gazelle-girl—was astonished. Though their bodies were small and lean, they all looked strong, not stunted and skeletal like the other pilgrims I'd seen on petition days. After years of paucity, the god of Cherubtown had not stinted on the gifts she bestowed.

I was so busy looking ahead that I did not see what was before me: Host Wurrakai, charging forward, a war axe in his hands.

"Bad Uncle!" I shouted, but Host Wurrakai did not stop, could not hear me.

Flaps of flayed flesh had grown up over his ears. Clusters of baby faces sprouted from his forehead and cheeks to sing to him in shrieking voices. Wurra Who Roars had opened a second maw on the underside of his jaw, and was howling along.

I froze, watching the axe fall. I looked up at its edge, my eyes crossing as they focused on my own razor-thin reflection bearing down.

The blade cut the first layer of skin on the bridge of my nose.

It cut no further.

Alizar, terrified and enraged, knocked the axe ajar, sending it fly-ing. And then he scooped me up in a hook of serac-cold air and flung me high over Host Wurrakai's head. Alizar tumbled me through space like a pilot operating his toy aeroplane remotely, with radio transmitter and joystick, and landed me squarely on my good uncle's back, jarring my everything.

Host Wurrakai stumbled but did not fall, and I was too dizzy to do anything but cling to him with all my shaking limbs, and re-member, remember, in too-fast flickering monochrome, how Uncle Wuki used to take me up on his shoulders when I was a kid, and run around Mom and Dad's backyard pretending he was my Zilch giant whom I'd tamed to my hand, calling me "Moon Princess, Queen of Smugglers," as we enjoyed a thousand adventures together.

And then, and then, I was taking the gory flaps of flesh over Host Wurrakai's ears—Rathanana's attributes—in my fists, though the blood of them slicked my fingers. And I was ripping them out of his very scalp, leaving bald patches where hair would never grow again. And I was stuffing the torn flesh rags between the doughy little lips of Hirrahune's attributes, snuffing their meeps and squeaks. And *then* I shoved my whole fist down Wurra's gaping mouth where it howled under Wurrakai's jaw, and silenced his roaring.

"Bad Uncle!" I screamed again into Host Wurrakai's open, bleed-ing ears.

And Uncle Wuki's shoulders stiffened beneath my hands.

"Ishi?" His mind was his own again—for the moment—and he was terrified. His voice was as high and fearful as a child's.

This time, instead of fleeing like Shuushaari had fled Zulli, the angels in Uncle Wuki fought me. They rippled through his body, multiplying their attributes. Rathanana tried to unseat me by push-ing great swollen lumps of matter—bulbous proto-beasts without limb or face—right out of Wuki's back.

But this time, Uncle Wuki was also fighting them. When the angel Wurra's roaring mouths began opening up all along both of Wuki's arms—every one of those mouths ringed with rows of bar-racuda teeth—in order that Wurra might use my uncle's arms to tear me off of his shoulders, and then simply to tear me, Uncle Wuki clenched his great fists. Grunting with the effort, he folded himself down to a fetal position, crushing his arms between his knees and his chest.

Wuki's muffled shrieks, and the small, vicious, chewing sounds of Wurra feeding on Wuki's flesh, frenzied me with worry. I seized one of Hirrahune's vapid little baby faces where it bloated the back of Wuki's skull at the occiput, and squeezed its chubby cheeks between my fingers, growling, "I will rip you out of him, Ninth Angel, and give you to Alizar to eat! How do you think turnabout will taste—god-eater?"

The angel Hirrahune's attribute whimpered, blinked cowardly wet eyes at me—once, twice—and then fled, vanishing from between my fingers.

Sensing the desertion of his fellow angel, Rathanana's great bestial lumps—until that moment writhing and rising beneath my knees—suddenly stilled. I turned all my attention to them.

"Rathanana," I greeted him, laying both hands deliberately over one of those trembling lumps. "You were with Saint Betony in the Sacrificing Pool. You devoured her death. I should lay you at her feet. What would an angel like you look like, mounted like a trophy on the wall of the Seventh Anchorhold?"

The lumps on Uncle Wuki's back deflated so abruptly that I slid off of him and tumbled to the brick walkway in a way that would have wrenched my old knees—had Alizar not recently given me new ones.

"Uncle Wuki," I said, crawling over to him, "let me see your arms."

"No, Ishi—I—"

"Please. Please, I have no time."

His arms were fountaining blood from shoulders to wrists, still trying to devour themselves. So I did the only thing I could think of: I started sealing off Uncle Wuki from the angels—with Wurra Who Roars *still inside.*

"With honey and beeswax, I seal you—

"With pollen and drupe—"

How the Sixth Angel clamored and yelled, how dozens more mouths opened on Wuki's face, on his chest, his legs, his back, how the very bricks beneath us began to shatter at the sound of Wurra's celestial rage.

"With rich loam and cool stone, I seal you—"

How he gnashed his ten million tiny teeth, and grew ten million more, teeth within teeth within teeth.

"By the bounty of Bower, Wuki Q'Aleth—"

But all the angel mouths in the world could not stop Alizar the Eleven-Eyed, godhead of Gelethel, from un-Hosting this Host.

"I seal your sovereign soul against all—"

The angel Wurra fled.

H OST RAZOLETH, CAPTAIN OF THE HUNDRED-STAIR TIER, straddled the parapets, legs wide, each foot planted on a separate merlon. He was staring down at what was left of Cherubtown. He held in his left hand a spear that was no spear at all, but a dazzling arc of never-ending lightning, emanating from the palm of his hand.

He awaited the arrival of the first cherubs who dared climb the serac. The minute they breached the parapets, he would drive Zerat's lightning right down through their skulls, piercing their throats, their lungs, their viscera, their loins, purifying them with heavenly fire from the inside out.

In his right hand, Host Razoleth held nothing, for he had no right hand anymore, and no arm either. His shoulder simply extruded a writhe of moray eels, bright green against the flayed-salmon sunset, oral jaws and pharyngeal jaws agape, waiting for their first taste of cherub flesh.

I slowly approached the eldest and strongest of my good uncles, keeping to the ramparts below. Above me, boosted by the parapets as by a pair of great stone shoes, Host Razoleth towered taller than I had ever seen him. He seemed a second Tyr Valeeki, a tower built of angels. I advanced, and was allowed to advance. Host Razoleth had issued orders that he be the one to deal with me.

The closer I came to him, I saw why.

One by one, the greatest and most powerful of the Invisible Wonders who ruled Gelethel were sucking back their angelic presences from the Holy Host at large, and flocking instead to Host Razoleth, engorging him, engulfing him, reenforcing their seats in his body. This was to be my punishment, then, or the start of it: to witness my uncle crammed beyond all endurance with angels. To watch them as they corkscrewed, not just a single thread of themselves, but the whole entirety of their magnificent manifestations, down into his flesh. Making him eight thrones in one.

Yes, eight I counted. Eight I named. The same eight who'd been present in Host Hosseril in the saltcellars—only more so. Zerat. Thathia. Wurra, whose wide mouth had again taken up residence, as it had in Host Wurrakai, just beneath Razoleth's chin. Tanzanu, whose black talons and sharply curving beaks jutted up out of my uncle's own vertebrae like the spikes and spines of the prehistoric monsters who'd once roamed Bellisaar. Rathanana, who had transformed my uncle's right leg into a wolf, his left into a bear. Kirtirin: Right Hand of the Enemy Twins, whose elegant twelve-fingered hand was pushing itself out from Razoleth's stomach, while from its palm, another twelve-fingered hand was already growing. Impossible Beriu, who was a color I could not describe, a sound I should not have been able to hear, a taste in my mouth that did not match the odor in my nose—and all of it poisonous, poisonous. And lastly, Childlike Hirrahune, who vied for her place somewhere on Host Razoleth's body and found it at last: covering his face with a half dozen faces of her own.

My good uncle had no face left. His eyes were two Hirrahunes. His nose was Hirrahune. Each of his ears and his mouth were a Hirrahune. All of those tiny, bow-lipped, defiant, flaccid faces, watching me as I approached.

Approached, and counted all the angels absent from this Host:

Shuushaari, who'd fled Uncle Zulli at Tyr Valeeki. Olthar of Excesses, whom I wished well and far from here, pouring himself into popcorn and beer at the Quick. Murra Who Whispers, who made Gelethel a place of cleanliness and quiet contemplation once a fortnight. Kalikani: Left Hand of the Enemy Twins, who probably considered me a friend, since her brother was my foe. Imperishable Dinyatha, who loved the movies.

And, of course, Alizar the Eleven-Eyed, who flamed in me.

And, of course, Nirwen, whom I'd never met, but who'd chosen Betony, and who for this would have my gratitude forever. Or for the next five minutes.

Host Razoleth, and the angels who all dwelled inside of him, turned to regard me as I paced toward him. And because they were facing me, they did not see the first cherub—the one leading the charge—make it to the top of the serac.

She was tall—as tall as a nephilim—and clothed in the tatters of a refugee. Her face was burnt away—whether by acid or fire, I did not know—but her eyes remained, whole and unscarred: the cold, deep blue of the serac itself. No pupil or sclera. Just endless blue. Two of Alizar's most central eyes were that very color. I now recognized that he must have manifested them in her honor.

Her hands shot through the crenels to grasp the inner edge of the parapets. She heaved herself onto the ramparts behind Host Razoleth. Reaching beneath her dirty outer robe, she removed two spikes of pure blue ice from the immaculate black webbing she wore beneath. And she plunged the spikes into the faces of Childlike Hirrahune where my uncle used to have ears.

The rest of the angel faces shrieked.

Staring over his shoulder at me, the cherub gave me one shockingly short nod.

Hey! That's my pal Scratch! My boon spar! Betony cried out in astonishment. *She with the rebel cherubs?*

She is their mother, Alizar replied, satisfied.

Mother Scratch. Father Bloom. Nea the Nephilim's passphrase flashed through my mind. But there was no time to sink into saintly revelations, for Nirwen, god of Cherubtown, was turning away from Host Razoleth as if he were of no consequence. As she bent over the parapets to help another cherub over the ramparts, I leapt at my uncle. His left leg, Rathanana's bear, swiped a swatch of flesh from my flank. His right leg, the wolf, snapped at my thigh. I swung up Kirtirin's forest of branching hands, climbing out of range of the lower beast-limbs. Twelve times twelve times twelve times twelve fingers grasped at me, seeking to pull me apart. Thathia's eels darted at my face, tangled all around me, sent their aspic to slicken my path. And Zerat, Zerat, in his form of a blue-white spear of fire, burned so brightly it was like climbing into the heart of a star who wanted to kill me.

But I reached my good uncle's shoulders, at last, balancing upon the disparate parts of him like a monkey on a treacherous tree. I felt I had scaled the serac itself. The ramparts were far below me, and the ground was much further away than that. Letting me cling, he spun on eight paws, so that he faced the serac, and my back was to the empty air.

He was preparing to hurl me down. All the way down.

I looked into his eyes that were not eyes, and I grabbed onto the two icicle spikes jutting from the angel-swollen sides of his head, and I yanked them out.

"Bad Uncle!"

I could not see my uncle smile, for the angel Hirrahune was his mouth. My uncle could not embrace me one last time, for his arms were not his own. His legs would not move in the direction he bade them; there were too many legs, and the angel in them was too strong. Nothing of him was his own except his mind.

But the Razman had always been so very, very strong-minded.

The quarantine phrase—the one he'd invented, and planted in each of my uncles, and in himself—took hold, took root, and he wasted no time.

Raising his arm, he swung Zerat's lightning bolt at me—which was exactly what Zerat wanted him to do—and blasted me off his body. Not, however, off the serac and into the ruins below as the angel had planned—but torquing his body at the last moment, hurled me back behind him, onto the ramparts.

Two hundred million volts passed through my body at one third the speed of light. Had I not been a saint with a god in me, I would have remembered nothing from that moment to the next. But I was, and he was, and I remembered everything. I flew out of myself and far above myself, but I saw everything.

I saw how Uncle Raz threw himself backward, over the serac, and fell two hundred meters to the bottom, his fall unbroken even by a single smoldering midden heap.

I saw him take all eight angels he carried with him, and watched them, from my bird's eye view, as they tried to flee his body in the six point three nine seconds between his fall and the impact.

I saw Scratch—Nirwen—the scar-faced giantess—leap up to take his place on the parapet, robes billowing, and call out to the angels below in a song stronger than any I'd ever heard in the Celestial Corridor, even when all the Invisible Wonders were singing in harmony.

Alizar was not the only god who could seal off a sovereign body, it seemed. I had used his incantation to keep the angels *out* of my uncles. Now, Nirwen was using hers to keep them *in*.

I saw myself screaming.

I screamed and I screamed, and I tore myself down from my bird's eye view and back into my body, and lifted myself right off the ground as if I myself were a second lightning bolt passing through me. And I tried to follow Uncle Raz down—to fly down to him as Alizar had taught me, to swoop beneath him, break his fall, snatch him in my arms, lift him up—just as I'd lifted Uncle Eril earlier, just like that—breathing for him, *bringing him back!*

But Nirwen caught me before I went over. She pulled me back. Held me close. Her arms were pilgrim arms, wiry prisons, and I hung between them, enervated, my throat scraped raw.

He's gone, Ish, the god of Cherubtown whispered. *He took eight angels with him. It's done. And now you have one last thing to do, Saint Ishtu.*

All around us, more cherubs were swarming over the serac. They launched themselves from the top rung of the ice ladder onto the parapets, and then down to the ramparts, and then at any of the Holy Host who still stood by.

But many of the Hosts, finding themselves deactivated of angels, had started fleeing towards Tyr Valeeki, or leaping onto the dump-lifts, or taking the nearest emergency ladders back down into Gelethel. Wild-faced cherubs followed them close behind, some screaming for blood, others just bent on finally—finally!—entering the Angelic City, the paradise so long denied to them.

End this, Saint Ishtu, Nirwen told me. *You must end this . . .*

Alizar—heretofore a voice, an icy and invisible wind over the ramparts—manifested fully before us. He unfolded wings upon wings—some of feathers, some of delicate chitin, some of thin but tough patagium—and I fell into them, and was enfolded.

"Raz!" I cried to him. "Raz is gone—he's gone—he went over!"

I know. I know. He was so brave, so ready. He knew what he had to do.

And so did I.

I wanted to ask if it would hurt.

I wanted to ask if it would be slow or fast. Slower than six point three nine seconds. Faster than a lightning strike. Would it hurt like Host Hosseril had hurt me, so profoundly that I felt nothing until I began to heal? Or would it hurt like it hurt now—much, much worse than anything I'd endured in the saltcellars, or anything before or since. This all-over grief that was like drowning in air.

Well. One way to put an end to *that*, anyway.

Untucking myself from his wings, I let Alizar lead me to the place where I should stand: the exact center of the ramparts, at the halfway point between the edge of the serac closest to Cherubtown, and the edge of the serac closest to Gelethel, with a god standing behind me and before me.

Before me, the godhead Nirwen reached her arm over her head, and drew from a sheath at her back a great spear of ice. Raising this high above her head, she drove it down into the ramparts between her body and mine. It pierced the salt brick and cracked the serac beneath it, splitting the ice deeply, and sliding in until it was wedged solid. A slender blue pillar.

My pyre.

I stepped forward and wrapped myself around it, a twining vine trained to grow up a trellis. A flower about to bloom. I leaned my sweating forehead against the freezing ice, and allowed myself to fuse with the material. No separating us now.

Behind me, the godhead Alizar gathered himself into a hurricane of wings. I felt the wind of him at my back. I felt the heat. The light. I smelled him, green with growing things.

And then I felt him everywhere, and he was no longer separate from me, for he was blowing himself right through me: a solar wind, a stellar nursery. I was his fatwood, his tap root, his heart knot, and Alizar released into me all those billion billion billion pinpoints of gold-green light that he contained within his lantern self, and each one of those points was the seed of a star.

Every molecule of me burst into flame.
Wing. Light. Wind. Ice. The heart of a star. The heart of a saint.
And I am become kindling.
And I am become bonfire.
And I am become detonation.
The heat that melts the serac.
The floodwaters rising up.
The river that flows in four directions, and drowns me.

ELLIPSIS

THE FIRST THING I SAW AFTER I DIED WAS THE FACELESSNESS OF god.

All the pictures and carvings and statues I'd ever seen of Nirwen the Forsaker depicted her with her face gashed out. And that was how she appeared to me now, after the end of everything: a giantess as big as the sky, with an empty black oval where her face should be.

At the bottom of that black—maybe—stars.

Her rags had fallen away. She wore coveralls, like me. Sensible boots. Her wide belt bristled with all kinds of tools, devices, automata, other things for which I had no name. Her hands were massive, gentle, ridged with callouses. When I saw them, their shape, I thought at once of the nephilim Nea. Nea, I now realized, had her mother's hands.

I rolled over on my side, and vomited up what felt like a whole saltwater river.

"Saint Ishtu," said the erstwhile god of Cherubtown.

Erstwhile, because there wasn't any Cherubtown, was there? Not any longer. I didn't think there was even still a Gelethel. Not like the Gelethel I'd known, anyway. That was what we had wanted, wasn't it? And yet, and yet . . . had anything of the Angelic City survived? Or of the six angels who had refused, at the last, to stand against Alizar?

I tried to see beyond Nirwen, but she was everything, everywhere. Nirwen, whose face was the night sky.

But then she tilted her head, and the night shifted. I could see beyond her, further off from that faceless face. There was another sky, this one of dawn, and it haloed her in its frame.

It was a desert dawn: parched white with a hint of peach, remorseless, cloudless, perfect, without scrub or shadow.

"The serac has fallen," Nirwen told me softly, sinking down in the sand beside me.

Too softly: my ears were still logy with water. Water leaked out of me, out of my hair, my nose, my clothes, my crevices. All of it was immediately absorbed into the thirsty sand I was lying upon. My whole head felt grainy. My mouth tasted like a hundred years of salt.

"Do you wish to see?" Nirwen asked.

I must have moved my head in a way that indicated willingness. Or perhaps Nirwen merely decided it was time I stopped lolling about the dunes of Bellisaar. Either way, she lifted me up high in both her arms and, cradling me, turned me around so that I could behold what we had wrought, she and Alizar and Betony and I.

We were standing on a tall dune about a kilometer or so outside of Gelethel. I'd never seen my city from this vantage, nor ever could have imagined it—the serac, with its uncanny cliffs of glittering blue ice, must always have impeded my mind's eye view. But now the serac was gone. And I saw (for here in the desert the dunes ran high, much higher than the Angelic City, which sat below sea level) the white domes of Gelethel, the white arches and white streets, all gleaming out across a shining expanse of river.

"The river surrounds the city on all sides," Nirwen told me, satisfied. "The diamond of Bellisaar now runs as meltwater. It flows in four directions at once, has no source and no mouth, and the brine of it has been purified by the death of a self-martyred saint. It is a hallowed wet. Once unpotable, now it flows clean and clear, sweeter than any water in the world. Anyone may drink from it. The sick shall come to it and be cured, the weary find rest, and gardens shall spring forth from its banks—from *both* sides of its riverbanks. Trees will grow there, vines and shrubs, sedges and grasses and mosses. My cherubs will settle near its floodplains, and more people will come. They will dig canals to water their crops, and wells and reservoirs for their families and their flocks, and all the Lands of Nir surrounding these four rivers will grow fertile and be farmed, and all the people in it, prosperous and favored."

She told this to herself like a story she already knew. I wondered if the god Gelethel had also told herself such a story, as she pulled her palace out of the salt. The palace she had died in. It was the story of a beginning—but not even Nirwen could know how it would end. Not even Alizar.

Still.

It was a good story.

"The Land of Nir." I worked my brine-dried lips around the words. My mouth seemed to be functioning, but it wasn't emitting much in the way of volume yet.

Nirwen set me gently down. I was unsteady but found I could at least stand. My coveralls were mostly dry now, damp at the crotch and under the armpits. What I could have used was a long drink of real water and an even longer piss.

And possibly some time alone, out from under the all-seeing eye of a god, so that I could start processing some of what had just happened.

So I could think about what it meant to go supernova and melt the serac, yet still remain me enough to subsequently drown in its meltwaters, and then be resurrected again.

So I could think about Alizar and Betony, on the other side of those meltwaters where I could no longer dwell. And my uncles—if they lived—who remained there. And my parents, somewhere beyond those western dunes, in the company of a nephilim whose mother had just resurrected me from death.

So I could think about Uncle Raz.

Tears stung my eyes. And, as if that triggered a wellspring inside me, my mouth began filling with cool water. It flowed over my tongue as if I had just drunk from a fountain, and washed down my throat, sluicing the salt away. I was refreshed throughout my body, distracted from my grief. When I tried to speak again, I found that my voice was stronger.

"Nirwen," I asked the god, "will you build a bridge from the Land of Nir across the waters to Gelethel?"

"We will build a hundred," Nirwen replied, "Alizar and I."

I smiled. Or tried to. I really had to pee.

"Then I wish you both luck, Artificer. And a host of saintly architects."

And some privacy for me, while I'm at it, I silently added.

But of course, there was no such thing as privacy among gods. Nirwen touched the back of her huge hand to my cheek. She smiled down at me with such a glint in her all-blue eyes that I understood she knew perfectly well the reason I was hopping from foot to foot like my Uncle Zulli after too much apple tea, squirmingly waiting for her to leave me alone so I could drop my coveralls and cop a squat.

"To you, Saint Ishtu, I wish luck, and good health, and adventure—" Nirwen gestured to the dawn horizon, "and that the roads to the world will open before you in welcome."

"Thanks. Sure thing. So long, Nir—"

"And," Nirwen added, "if you would: please bear my love to my daughter when next you meet her in Sanis Al. You saved her life on the serac. She would have sent you through the Hellhole before her. Yet you let yourself be taken in her place. Nea would not have survived the angels or their tortures; she is nephilim, not saint."

"No problem."

I didn't know if Nirwen knew for certain that I would meet Nea in Sanis Al, or if she was merely prognosticating a likelihood, godlike. But I found the thought encouraging. The world as I'd known it was ended. But it was an end I'd worked towards; it was what I'd wanted.

And now I had another task. I knew my next destination. I knew whom I had to find. All three of them.

Just. Needed. To. Make. A. Pitstop. First.

"Oh, all right, Ish," said Nirwen the Artificer, Nirwen of the Land of Nir, Mother Scratch, god of Cherubtown, formerly the Fifteenth Angel. "Enjoy your piss in peace."

And she was gone.

Shucking my coveralls, I immediately loosed a river to rival the one surrounding Gelethel. And when I was done, I stood up and buttoned up.

The horizon unfastened before me: sand and sky—infinite fathoms of each—both, in this odd morning's gloaming, the same peculiar shimmering sea-foam blue. I stretched out my arms as far as they could go, opening myself to that blue, and let out a yawn that nearly cracked my jaw. Then, I pulled back from all that vastness, and looked to the place where Nirwen had just been standing.

Parked on the sand in that very spot was a brand new viperbike. Not a Zilch-sized one either. A me-sized one. Chrome and leather, with a sizable tailpack strapped to the pillion behind the rider's seat and stuffed full of something I hoped was clothes and food.

I went to it, my hands flying out before me eagerly, as if possessed of angels, to unzip the top of the pack. A few sheets of paper spilled out, each one drifting in a different direction.

I picked one up at random and read aloud, "*The Moon Princess.* By J.L.P. Dedicated to my daughter, Ishtu."

It was a screenplay. Dad's screenplay. *The tailpack was stuffed with Dad's screenplays!* No food or water or fuel or supplies or anything practical—and all I wanted to do was jump up and down and dance. I couldn't care less what I lacked. I had Dad's *screenplays!*

Falling to my knees, I scrambled around, picking up every single one of the fallen papers before they could blow away.

And then, still kneeling, clutching the papers close, I spun to face east. To face Gelethel. Fabulous fucking Gelethel.

"Alizar!" I called to him, and oh, the city seemed so far away—and its new god and his good Saint Betony with it. But that was a lamentation for later. For now, I had only one thing to say.

"Thank you!"

No answer. Just the wind, stirring the top layer of sand around my feet.

"All right," I said aloud. "No point hanging around here any longer. Guess I'll have to try this baby viperbike out. At least, I presume it's mine. If it isn't, well . . ." I shrugged, and put on my best Onabroszia voice for exactly nobody but myself. "Well, then, Q'Aleth Hauling Industries is within its rights to claim this junk as salvage."

I started looking around the viperbike for compartments, saddlebags, rings, attachments. But though I found plenty of detachable pieces and secret storage, I did not find any keys. Neither was there an ignition to put them in. (In the movies, there was always an ignition.) Even the dashboard was blank: no fuel gauge, no odometer or thermometer.

Disappointment, panic, and the deep grief I was fighting to keep at bay seized me. I sank onto the seat, and leaned forward onto the handlebars, resting my head on my forearms.

"Maybe it's Nirwen's idea of a joke," I murmured. "Or a toy. I mean, who abandons a viperbike in the middle of the desert?"

On the center of the dashboard, right below where my face hung between the two handlebars, a great golden eye, large and lashless, opened up against the blank readout screen. It glowed. It flashed. It stared soulfully right into my face, and then—slowly—it winked. Or blinked. Whatever it is a single eye can do.

I bolted upright. "Alizar?"

The eye rolled to the left, glanced back at me, and rolled to the left again.

Taking the hint, I grabbed the helmet hanging from the left side of the handlebars, and jammed it onto my head.

Surprise! shouted Alizar. His voice rang clearly through my skull, as though amplified by the helmet.

Happy feast day, Saint Ish! Betony added. *Fuck, wow, that bike is hot! Hear it purrin' all the way over here. Nirwen says it's powered by your touch and thought. Practically unstealable, she said. 'Course, in my experience, some people like a challenge . . .*

She sounded wistful.

"Don't touch my viperbike, Saint Betony."

Ain't very saint-like of you, Betony sniffed. *Shouldn't you be palmin' it over for free without me askin'?*

"Nah," I teased her, then immediately felt guilty about it. "Why? You really want it? I could see if I could get one of the cherubs to ship it across the river to you. Once they get some boats. Or build some bridges. Or something . . ."

Nah, I'm stable, spar. Rode enough bikes in my life. Rode enough everything. Glad to walk a spell. Besides, you need it—journey you'll be goin' on. Eh?

"I'm going to Sanis Al," I said—and really believed it, for the first time since announcing my plans to Uncle Zulli at Mom and Dad's house all those lifetimes ago.

Of course you are, Ish! said Alizar, as if there had never been any doubt of it. Silly god-Bug. *And we will be checking in as often as you want us. Our connection will become much more tenuous the further you roam from Gelethel, but Nirwen said that wearing her helmet should help you to hear us.*

Betony added, *Hope that thing's comfy, Q'Aleth, 'cause you and it are gonna be real boon from now on. From now till . . .* She paused as if to make some calculation. *Say, Bug, when was it you finally gonna let us die? Twice seven times eleven years, you said? And*—Betony was starting to sound very smug and saint-like indeed—*Bug says he's startin' the countdown from* now, *not from when we was born, so you and I can bang out together for all our days.*

Twice seven times eleven years wasn't what Alizar and I'd agreed to, way back—when I'd insisted he let me live out a normal lifespan. But maybe a longer life wouldn't be so bad. Now that I had better knees, and a viperbike, and Dad's screenplays, and Betony. Now that I could—when the occasion merited it, and with Alizar's remote help—kind of fly a little. Or at least bounce really high.

After all, I was living for two now. Uncle Raz would never look out over the dunes of Bellisaar from the other side of a melted wall. He had chosen free fall so that we could all walk free.

"I miss you so much already," I said. To the Razman. To Betony. To my own dear godhead, who'd loved me as his own for most of my life. "But I have more than I'd ever hoped for . . . and I am so grateful."

Alizar made a hum of disappointment that was like radio static playing directly in both of my ears.

But, Ishtu, your gratitude comes betimes . . . you have not found your other present yet!

Bug! Betony yelled at him. *We pacted on this, collect? You were s'pposed to let her come happenstance to it!*

Oh, bells.

On the dashboard, the god of Gelethel's golden owl eye pouted. But only for a moment. The next moment, it had grown a thicket of lashes three centimeters long—which it batted with unbearable wistfulness up at me.

Won't you have a little look-see around, my Ish?

I reached out a finger and stroked those curly lashes until his eyeball began to purr.

"You're too good to me, Bug. I promise I'll do a nose dive into those packs of yours in a bit—before I take off the helmet. But first tell me—how's the city?"

Betony answered for him: *Fuckin' busy, spar! We made a hale mess. Your Uncle Wuki's in charge of the burials. Zulli and Madriq set up an outdoor kitchen in Bower, feedin' everyone. Everything's upheavin'. Half the angels dead, the other half hidin' in the Celestial Corridor. No one knows when, or if, the next benisons'll come. So they're all lookin' to Alizar—who's workin' his garden overtime. Eril's there too. Set up a hospital tent with the help of a few pilgrims who know what's what, herb- and plant-wise. Lotta people hurt when the serac came down. Some gethels washed to the far shore. Some cherubs washed in—some of 'em climbed in—no tellin' who's who, so everyone's keen* to accept whoever as an accident of the gods. The saints have all come outta the Anchorholds. They're mostly pretty okay. I think. No stew, spar. It'll all be—

"Jammy?" I guessed.

Betony cackled, and so did I, and it was good—so, so good!—not to be alone.

"I wish I could be there," I told them both, leaning my head against the dashboard, right next to Alizar's eyeball. "I wish I could help too."

You are helping, my saint, Alizar assured me. *You are outside the loci of my genius, traveling abroad to give me wider notions of the world. If I ever knew its many ways and wonders, I have forgotten them these ten thousand years in Gelethel. It is not good, Ishtu—it is never good—for gods or angels or human-kin to forget the world beyond their walls. I need you, my saint—my first and most secret saint—to move through this world for me, and teach me all you learn.*

I swallowed, and nodded, and wiped away my tears before they splashed onto Alizar's eyeball. "I can do that," I whispered. "I can do that for you, Alizar."

There's a whole lotta sand to explore out there, Betony observed. *And it's a war-torn world, Q'Aleth—landmines and all. What's a saint to do?*

Kicking up my legs, I swung around on the seat until I was facing the back, and the large pack on the pillion.

"This saint," I told them, "is going west to find her Mom and Dad. I need to know Mom's settled, and help with that if I can. Also, I owe my dad a tap-dancing psi-ship movie musical at the best nickelodeon in the Red Crescent. And *also*," I added, bending over to check out the back of the viperbike: fender, tail lights, rear paddle tire and all, "I have a message for a nephilim—from the god, her mother. Can't neglect that. And after *that . . .*"

I trailed off, seeing for the first time, a second bag, much smaller than the first, lashed securely to the tailpack by thick velcro straps. The last time I'd seen this particular bag, it had been going down the Hellhole clipped to a loop on Nea's webbing. It was mine. It contained the gift my bad uncles smuggled into Gelethel on my thirtieth birthday. The day the Razman, whose rarely flaunted hobby had been stage prestidigitation, had pulled the gift—bag and all—out of his hat at my surprise party in Mom and Dad's backyard.

Alizar and Betony said nothing as I unzipped the bag. But the silence in my helmet buzzed with their bated breath.

Inside the bag was my Super 8 camera.

The kind made for home movies. The kind that recorded sound. The one I'd never yet used.

My heart broke like the serac, and the floodwaters poured through me once again.

O my uncles! My worst of all possible, best, and most beloved uncles!

O Razman! Who'd kept all his secrets so close for so many years, then doled them out to me one by one until he had none left.

O Onabroszia! Who destroyed her own brothers to spite the angels—those brothers who, in the end, helped to defeat those angels.

O Dad! Who'd given up everything to come to Gelethel, then given up everything again to leave it.

But I would make it up to him, starting now. I would learn to use my uncles' gift to me; I would move through the wide world as they could not. And I would record it all, what I experienced and what I remembered, so that our stories would live on, long after my own memory, like Mom's, failed me.

"After *that*," I whispered to those in Gelethel who could still hear me, "I think I'll make a movie."

Acknowledgments

I dedicated this story to Gene and Rosemary Wolfe, who once named me their "honorary granddaughter." Rosemary passed in December 2013, Gene in April 2019. I wrote much of this in fall and winter of 2019, while in mourning.

It was certainly the fastest I've ever written three drafts of a novel, and the tight deadline made me more than usually nervous of my prose. Happily, I had married an award-winning writer two years prior to that. By sheer virtue of his genius, and the attention he lavishes on my drafts, he shaves multiple drafts and countless years off my writing process. So thank you for that, Carlos Hernandez: beloved.

Years ago, when I first attempted something like this story, I knew it would eventually have something to do with early cinema. Magill Foote's invaluable insights on the subject were an enormous inspiration. Much later, while researching the current book, I asked Facebook (in despair) if anyone knew anything about alpine rescue. Robert Peterson, whom I've never met outside the virtual world, just happened to know an angelic ton. He lent me his ice-climbing expertise and some fabulous online resources; I am endlessly grateful. All mistakes are my own.

As usual, love to the Infernal Harpies: Caitlyn Paxson, Tiffany Trent, Ysabeau Wilce, Nicole Kornher-Stace, Jessica P. Wick, Patty Templeton, and Amal El-Mohtar. Gratitude to my RAMP writing group: Joel Derfner, Liz Duffy Adams, Delia Sherman, Ellen Kushner, and Carlos for cheerleading the early draft. A holy thank you to my mother Sita, unfailingly enthusiastic about all my literary endeavors. I remember the Erewhon Salon fondly: a beautiful gathering place which we lost, like so many other things, to Covid. It was there I debuted the first chapter and learned that I might be writing something termed "body horror." Who knew?

Finally: thank you to Mike Allen, Jessica P. Wick, and Amanda J. McGee, for your brilliant novellas in *A Sinister Quartet*, where this novel also appeared originally. What a banquet to sit at that table (of contents) with you! I loved all the goofy online events we did in the heart of the pandemic, trying to shed some light on the darker side of fantasy.

—C. S. E. Cooney, November 2022

C. S. E. Cooney (she/her) is a World Fantasy Award-winning author. Her books include *Saint Death's Daughter*, *Dark Breakers*, *Desdemona and the Deep*, and *Bone Swans: Stories*, as well as the poetry collection *How to Flirt in Faerieland and Other Wild Rhymes*, which includes her Rhysling Award-winning poem "The Sea King's Second Bride." In her guise as a voice actor, Cooney has narrated over 120 audiobooks, as well as short fiction for podcasts such as *Uncanny Magazine*, *Beneath Ceaseless Skies*, and *Podcastle*. As the singer/songwriter Brimstone

Photo by Marie O'Mahony Photography

Rhine, she crowdfunded for two EPs: *Alecto! Alecto!* and *The Headless Bride*, and produced one album, *Corbeau Blanc, Corbeau Noir*. Her plays have been performed in several countries, and her short fiction and poetry can be found in many speculative fiction magazines and anthologies, most recently: "A Minnow or Perhaps a Colossal Squid," in Paula Guran's *Year's Best Fantasy Volume 1*, "Snowed In," in *Bridge To Elsewhere*, and "Megaton Comics Proudly Presents: Cap and Mia, Episode One: "Captain Comeback Saves the Day!" in *The Sunday Morning Transport*—all in collaboration with her husband, writer and game-designer Carlos Hernandez. Forthcoming soon from Outland Entertainment is a table-top roleplaying game co-designed by Cooney and Hernandez called *Negocios Infernales*. Find her at csecooney.com.

Lightning Source UK Ltd.
Milton Keynes UK
UKHW011032070223
416609UK00008B/2269